THE VISITORS' BOOK

By the same author

Novels
Mothers
Confessions of a Prodigal Daughter
The Awkward Girl
Has Anyone Seen Heather?
Emigrant Dreams
The Last Summer

Biography
Kitty O'Shea: A Life of Katharine Parnell

MARY ROSE CALLAGHAN

THE VISITORS' BOOK

BRANDON

A Brandon Original Paperback

First published in 2001 by
Brandon
an imprint of Mount Eagle Publications
Dingle, Co. Kerry, Ireland

10 9 8 7 6 5 4 3 2 1

Copyright © Mary Rose Callaghan 2001

The author has asserted her moral rights.

ISBN 0 86322 287 0

Design: id communications, Tralee
www.idcommunications.ie
Photography: Giles Norman Photography, Kenmare
www.gilesnorman.com
Typesetting by Red Barn Publishing, Skeagh, Skibbereen
Printed by The Guernsey Press, Channel Islands

In loving memory

Joe McKenzie, 1975–1998
Robert Hogan, 1930–1999

JANUARY

Thursday 1st:
Something's happened.

It's the mid hour of night now, and I'm writing this in bed on the laptop – I've decided to keep a diary about our return to Ireland. Charlie's asleep beside me. If I drink, can't sleep at all, but he shows no signs of waking up – the B & B absolutely resonates with his snoring. I'm seriously afraid he'll wake the whole house. Well, to get back to what happened – we didn't get the keys to our new house yet, although promised, and the prospect of these lodgings over New Year didn't help our mood yesterday. So to cheer ourselves up, we went to the pub for a New Year's Eve drink.

It was crowded and smoky – which I hate as it gets to my chest. But we were enjoying ourselves until an American girl came over and asked Charlie if he was Seamus Heaney?

Idiotic.

He was ordering second drinks. She was a sexy, tight-jeaned redhead of about twenty with killer eyelashes – ominous.

He was delighted. "Now, why'd you think that?"

She giggled. "'Cos you look like a poet."

I don't like to call a girl a trollop – it generally goes against my principles to call women names – but she was pressing her inflated bosoms right into Charlie's face. Brazenly. And she must be a bit thick, too, and that's putting it mildly. Hasn't she noticed our most famous poet's white haired and Irish? Charlie's dark haired and American and must be fifteen years younger.

Then she sat on our bench – just cooly asked was it free? Me about to say no, but Charlie thrilled – nauseating.

Of course, they got on first name terms immediately. She's Erin something, and gradually moved up the pub bench beside Charlie, batting her spikes.

Then she went on about Heaney again.

I couldn't believe my ears. The resemblance is non-existent. If anything, Charlie's ruddy complexion and frizzy hair give him a look of Robin Williams – who's nothing at all like Seamus Heaney. I suppose horn rims give him an intellectual air, but she's an idiot.

"It's your hair," she giggled again. "And sweater."

Charlie touched his wiry black hair. He fingered his black polo-neck and got even ruddier. "Well, I've edited poetry. I worked for Random House, in New York."

"Wow, Random House!" She inched closer to him.

He nervously made space on the bench. "Uh – it's a conglom-erate now. The writer's disappeared from the scene." He cleared his throat importantly. "Now it's the cult of personality."

She wriggled eagerly. "I can sleep my way to the top?"

He frowned. "Uh – something like that. Or else be Whoopie Goldberg, then hire a writer to ghost your memoirs."

Erin giggled again.

Apparently she's a poet. A poet? My God. This couldn't be worse, as Charlie loves poetry, considers himself an expert on all that modern bilge. And to make things worse, Erin invited us to a reading in a week or so. Hell. But Charlie thrilled. Went on and on about publishing. How they're all too big for comfort, blah, blah, blah. How he hated the way things were going, and that was why we came back to Ireland.

I'd heard it all before.

Couldn't take my eyes off Erin. Why is it, when you hit fifty, everyone looks young and beautiful. Charlie was terribly flattered by her attentions and ended up buying her a gin and tonic – several. I sipped Guinness – Charlie always said I was a cheap date, and it hasn't done me one bit of good either. I don't like it – not Guinness, *Erin*.

Why on earth did I suggest the pub? Afterwards we ate at a Chinese restaurant – I had sizzling prawns and Charlie his crispy roast duck. At midnight the bells of Christ Church rang in the New Year. They could be heard clearly in our B & B, bringing back my childhood. So we got up and went outside to the street. Dublin's not such a bad old place. People came out of the house next door and shook hands, wishing us a happy and prosperous New Year. Everyone kissing and hugging and toasting the future. By now Charlie his old self again, which he hadn't been all day. Kissed me. Then toasted the dark with a nightcap. "Here's to us, Peggy."

I held up my glass. "To us."

Friday 2nd:

We're in our new house. Got keys today and moved from the B & B with two suitcases, laptop on my knee, toaster and electric kettle in taxi boot, Charlie up front with the driver.

Hallelujah!

It's been a long haul.

Have to admit my heart missed a beat as the taxi stopped outside our house. It's trendy Dublin 6, but the street's run down. There's even rude graffiti on the walls: "Up the IRA!" and "Fuck the British!" – and other stuff like that. Charlie has no tolerance for squalor, but he didn't seem to notice and got out and proudly unlocked the hall door. Then froze.

Me behind with laptop. "What's wrong?"

"Spider!" he croaked.

I'm used to coping with his phobias.

"Kill it, Peggy!"

Put it safely on to the pavement. No time to argue about a spider's right to life.

Charlie took off his baseball cap and looked around critically. His nose was red from the cold. Inside was drab, dark, dirty, with a broken landing window and damp spots mottling dreary wallpaper. I couldn't help thinking there's so much to do. It's a small artisan in Rathmines. A two-up and two-down. Not new at all really – about a hundred years old. The street's blind, a row of smoky Victorian cottages huddled in an enclave behind the town hall. Our yellow-brick terrace of three at one end, called Khyber Place, just off Khyber cottages.

The driver helped with our stuff. When he'd dumped the cases on the living room floor, Charlie paid him. I felt like someone off the *Mayflower* – except we've come the other way. Life has boiled down to a few possessions – liberating in a way. All my New York clutter disappeared into the Goodwill shop. *Had* to give things away, so did. Amazing what you can do if you have to.

As taxi roared off, hung my coat behind hall door, remarking that at least they'd left hooks.

Charlie flicked a light. "But taken all the bulbs."

He inspected the downstairs gloomily. Then we went up the narrow stairs. "I didn't notice that before," he said, pointing nervously to the stained bedroom ceiling.

I was behind him. "What?"

"Roof's leaking."

I peered up. "It's only a loose slate."

He paced the tiny landing. "What if we need a new roof?"

Didn't want to contemplate that possibility. The roof's OK, but kept my patience. Felt sorry for Charlie – men are less able for things. He's very stressed. After all, we've spent the last six weeks living on top of each other, and that's not any good for a marriage. Before that, all the usual stuff – flying over here from New York, finding the house, getting surveys, more surveys, arranging the mortgage, and, finally, beggaring ourselves for the rest of our lives. Dublin houses have rocketed in value. I'm pale at the thought of what we paid for such a dog box – all for a stake in the "ould sod". But didn't express this to Charlie. He's forgotten how ecstatic we were to have actually *found* a house – and for this price in Dublin's booming market. Gradually his illusions about Ireland are shattering. It started when they served instant coffee in the B & B. He's typically American – but doesn't know it.

Followed him downstairs. At the bottom, he froze again, hands over his eyes. Another spider. Did the necessary again.

Charlie's spider phobia's almost as bad as his snake phobia. But no snakes in Ireland, thanks to St Patrick – that's one myth that appears to be a fact. That is, none except for the human variety – I've a strong suspicion our estate agent was one. Definitely slithery. He advertised the house after we sent back the contract – tried to gazump us. A new thing in Ireland, now that everyone wants to come and live here – returned emigrants like me, Americans like Charlie, EU citizens, and all the new-age travellers, refugees, aliens, asylum seekers and what-have-yous. How'd we get so fashionable?

Our street's named after Khyber Pass – apt, because the area's a pedestrian pass to Rathmines through a corporation yard with dump trucks. We're mid terrace. The house's like something from a Lowry painting, narrow with the hall door opening on to the street. All it needs is a factory chimney stack in the background – but there's plenty of smokeless smoke from the cottages. It was

built in the days of coal ranges, and there's a generous shed at the
back. Told Charlie yesterday we could turn this into an office –
eventually. He was definitely untaken with the idea. Just stared at
the cobwebs. Sometimes think he's no imagination. And sometimes, he seems to hate the house.

It's to be expected. His cleanliness phobia won't let him wear
shoes indoors, or anyone else, so he's bound to be upset by such an
old and dilapidated place. But it isn't fair to be carrying on. He did
sign a contract, as well as me. The truth is, he's having a damn mid-
life crisis – and this is the reason we're here permanently, instead of
just for holidays. Anyway, it's wearing me out. But back to yesterday – I said things would look better when we threw out the carpets. Lifted a corner of one, but dropped it immediately –
creepy-crawlies underneath.

Charlie looked resigned. "This'll take more than throwing out a
few carpets!"

It will. You pay for everything in life.

I was looking forward to our house. I've never owned one before
– or had a mortgage. We rented in New York, like everyone else. I
mean, it was Charlie's brilliant idea to downshift in the first place.
He wanted to retire to *Tír na nÓg*, the land of youth, and all that.
I was happy in old New York with cockroaches and all mod cons.
But again, said nothing.

"There's a helluva lot to do, Peggy!"

I agreed.

While he humphed and groaned, I walked around, taking men-
tal stock of what to throw out. Carpets and curtains are always
included in house sales here – don't know why. Ours are fit for the
skip, which will cost more money to hire. Everything's a terrible
mess – wallpaper hanging off, doors hanging off kitchen presses,
another broken window in the kitchen. Cobwebs everywhere.

And no garden. The kitchen's built in the backyard, and the bath-room's outside. It's scary, and hard to know how the housing boom will end. And all thanks to us returniks, grabbing up prop-erty and pushing up prices, according to our estate agent the first time he showed us round. And all the wealthy yuppies working in computers, he added, nodding in my direction. (*Moi?*) Told agent we were well past the yuppie stage and could buy a house in Tus-cany for half of what we paid here. New York would be cheaper still. But he kept up the hard sell, saying the house was reeking with potential.

"Reeking with damp. And plenty of fresh air, too," Charlie snapped, pointing to the outside bathroom.

Agent's hands were deep in the pockets of an offensive camel coat. He muttered that we could connect it up "eventually" – an apt word, as right now we're broke. He also said, as it's near town, we won't need a car. Lucky, because we can't afford one. The vari-ous fees and taxes have digested all our money.

Finally unpacked our suitcases – amazingly, there's a built-in wardrobe in the bedroom. A place to put things. But this didn't cheer up Charlie, who didn't speak all afternoon. I think he misses our cats. But this neighbourhood isn't suitable for replacements – grey pavements and not a tasty bird in sight. Only flocks of portly pigeons which look too much for any cat. Our New York cats were indoors. This house's too small. But what's a home without a cat. Maybe we'll get one.

Well, we both worked all afternoon. I cleaned the century's grease in the kitchen, while Charlie pulled off the ancient wallpa-per in the front room – there're layers and layers of newspapers underneath. There's no heat at all, only an open fireplace. Ordered coal which didn't appear. So Charlie carried a bag on his back from Rathmines – nearly killed him. He panted and sweated so much, I feared a heart attack. But he wouldn't accept any help. Felt guilty about carrying light bulbs.

Our new bed didn't come either.

It was promised for the "afternoon", but we waited and waited. Charlie grumbled again. So, about 4p.m., I went in search of a phone – ours still unconnected. Both public ones vandalised. Finally got through in Rathmines post office and asked about our "Beautiful Dreamer" mattress. Told to hold for the bedding department.

Cut off.

Rang back – line engaged.

Got through again – told to hold again.

After wasting £2, was told their van *had* come – at a minute past noon. I said that wasn't the "afternoon". They said it was. Technically they're right, but don't believe they called. No note, and this is Ireland where everyone's late. After some arm-twisting, they promised to bring it back tomorrow. We're dreamers to come back to this country.

I've decided to give in and get a mobile – maybe I won't get a brain tumour.

Later:

Tonight Charlie wanted to go back to the same pub. Me suspicious that he wanted to see Erin again. But no sign of her – thank God. Had a lovely time and met a pleasant couple. Later we lit a fire and curled up on the floor under our new duck duvet. We're the happiest people in the world. I'm silly to worry about red-headed poets. A new year. A new life. A new house.

Saturday 3rd:

Bed came – very comfortable. Glad we got the firm mattress.

Phone connected, too.

Also, had my first hot flush. Menopause? *Moi?* It couldn't be. Felt I was glowing, but don't think Charlie noticed – too busy worrying about the house. When I tell him I'm menopausal, he says, "You're too young for that!"

Then, "What age are you, Peggy?"

Grrrr! Older than you, baby, but said nothing. No one ever believes I'm four years older. Nearly five actually, but Charlie doesn't know, as I've never shown him my passport. It's silly, to have such an age complex, but can't help it.

This evening I walked up to Rathmines. All human life's on the street. There are big families, single mothers, old people and oddities – lots of oddities. And pigeons. It's like stepping back in time to the world of O'Casey. Well, Paul Smith, the famous novelist, whose people lived here, according to Mrs Murphy, the local shopkeeper, who's full of information about the area. Her story-book corner sweetshop has a discreet hand-painted sign – *M MURPHY*.

She knocked on our door with a potted plant this afternoon – a busy Lizzie. She's a kind, plump woman in a floral apron. With crow's-foot eye wrinkles from smiling too much. "Happy New Year, and I hope yez'll be happy here."

I was touched.

Invited her in for coffee, but she wouldn't come. Charlie delighted with the plant and said we must buy everything we can from her. Fine with me. I hate supermarkets, so would far prefer to shop locally. Mrs Murphy has most basics. Everything from turf to toothpaste – tea, sugar, flour, potatoes. And shelves and shelves of baked beans. The shop has an old-fashioned spicy smell. She sells sweets by weight from big jars and puts them in brown paper bags. Also fizz bags and toffee bars which make me wish I were ten again.

Think we'll be friends.

Her husband sits in the back room and never appears in the shop. Looking at him, I'd say he's never heard of the mid-life crisis. That hasn't hit Ireland yet. They're both so happy and placid. Her chat's great, too. She loves Gay Byrne and *The Late Late Show*. This afternoon she was leaning on the counter, reading a tabloid story about Bishop Eamon Casey, who's been converting the South Americans since being exposed as an unmarried father here. A scandal a few years back, but now he wants to come home.

I said they should let bygones be bygones.

Mrs Murphy shook her double chins crossly. "I never believed a word of it!"

I told her it made the New York papers.

"It's a calmation!" she said.

Defamation? Calumny? Anyway, a nice word.

She pointed angrily to the newspaper photo of Annie Murphy. "That woman invented the whole story. Lies, all lies!"

"But Peter, the son, resembled the bishop."

She snorted in disbelief.

I pointed out that Annie was the responsible parent.

She humphed. "The bishop sent money."

I smiled. "Robbed from Paul to pay Peter."

I was proud of my joke, but she didn't get it. People never get my jokes – Charlie says they're so awful.

"The Jezebel threw herself at him!" she insisted. "Men are weaker than us."

Weaker in the head, definitely. But this is still Ireland. Despite the Celtic Tiger, it's hard for people to accept change. Bishops are only meant to slap children at confirmation, not father them. Still, times are changing.

Sunday 4th:

Read the papers. Worked all day on the house. Chest bad from steaming wallpaper and terrible smell of paint.

Monday 5th:

House cramped, but we're getting to like it in a nervous sort of way. Or I do. Charlie's either in hilarious form or the depths of depression. I worry about these mood swings. Looked in the health shop for some soothing herb tea. Found camomile, but he wouldn't take it. Accused me of trying to poison him. He's the same about vitamins.

We've finally steamed off all the wallpaper in the sitting room. Charlie wants everything perfect immediately. He's incurably romantic. At first he had hankerings for the country – some cottage in the west. His family emigrated before the American revolution, but he's convinced he has roots in Connemara – somewhere near Clifden.

"If we lived in a thatched cottage, we could flog a book to a US publisher," he sighed over dinner last night.

Glad I refused to do a Michael Viney. I offered to write a book about resettling in Dublin.

Charlie looked sad. "You're not reflective, Peggy."

Reflective? That's unfair, when I've tried to educate myself. I read books all the time, mainly American fiction. Irish fiction is too depressing. But maybe that's a polite way of saying no one's interested in an old bag. You have to be thirty-something, not an anon fifty-something to be marketable nowadays. Older women are for the sexual skip. Dial M for menopause – it happens at fifty-one, which gives me twelve months more. 360 days to be exact. But surely my life's as interesting as anyone else's? But Charlie says I'd be wasting my time – James Joyce said it all. Wrote the only novel

worth reading. And no one's interested in our street. But I was
born and bred in this grime. After school, did a commercial course
in nearby Stephen's Green, so I'm home in more ways than one.
And the Celtic Tiger's roaring, but to deaf ears around here. The
cottages sell for unmentionable sums, though most locals are poor.
But there's a wealth of material here. Stevie Smith wrote *Novel on
Yellow Paper*. Why not *Novel on WordPerfect 5.1?* With Windows
all over the place now, it's almost as ancient as yellow paper. After
all, Jane Austen wrote about her society. I can use mine. What did
she say? One or two families in a village are an excellent thing to
work on – something like that. This street is like a village, brim-
ming with ordinary life. That's so much more interesting than historical romance or anything like that.

One rather odd woman, called Mona, obsessively sweeps the
lane leading to Rathmines. She wears a headscarf like a Second
World War wife and has a fag hanging out of the side of her
mouth. Her horrible little yapper, Sweetie, lies deceitfully asleep in
the street, then makes a piranha-fish dive for the ankles of passing
pedestrians – particularly Charlie's, whom he/she especially hates.

I passed Mona today, saying cheerfully, "Lovely day."

The weather's an endless topic of conversation – don't know
why, as it rains three hundred and sixty-five days a year.

She went on sweeping furtively.

The dog snapped at my ankles.

Mona ignored it, as I tore up the lane. Got home, ankles intact,
and later asked Mrs Murphy about her.

"A bad case of nerves," she sighed. "Mona can't stand dirt. She'd
sweep up all of Dublin if they let her."

Mrs Murphy also told me Mona's husband has heart trouble.
He's in and out of hospital, and she herself regularly goes "in" for
a rest – to a psychiatric hospital. But they love having her because

she cleans the place from top to bottom. Wish she'd sweep round the corner to our street. The kids throw litter everywhere, and the wind drives it into a heap outside our house. And her horrible dog does his business right at our hall door. Drives Charlie insane. He says it's some sort of canine territorial thing. The dog's asserting itself. Apparently dogs, like men, desire to dominate. But Sweetie looks too senile to be thinking of things like this. Why can't he/she/ assert her/himself elsewhere? We can do without the irritation. I've sprinkled pepper outside our door, but it does no good.

Tuesday 6th:
Philomena knocked today — the single woman in her thirties who lives next door. (A mother and middle-aged son are on the other side.) Philomena's a pigeon-chested countrywoman who works in the civil service. She wore ironed jeans — odd. And her hair was very neatly coiffed in an old-fashioned Jackie Kennedy way. Glasses hung on the end of her nose. Teeth squirrelish.

"The kettle's on," she said chirpily. "Time for a coffee?"

I had.

Her house was conventionally furnished and tidy.

"I'm off work with a nervous breakdown," she said cheerfully first thing.

She looked OK to me, but over several cups of coffee she told me the story of her life. Her breakdown's caused by living on the street, hating her job and breaking up with her boyfriend. She's on tablets because he went to Saudi Arabia without her. I said she was better off not going there — considering how they treat women. Women have to wear veils, hadn't she heard? She hadn't thought of this, but it seemed to cheer her up.

Then she proceeded to tell me all about a local Peeping Tom, a boy called Packy, who intimidates her. He looks in the window when she's undressing, and stalks her when she goes to the shops, so she's afraid to go out alone. Said I'd do her shopping. As I left she asked to borrow our Hoover. So dragged it from the glory hole under our stairs and took it next door.

When Philomena returned the Hoover, Charlie was annoyed. "Now we'll have to breathe in all her dust."

Said I'd change the bag – you'd think it was radioactive. But Charlie can't help his phobias.

He says I'm mad to do her shopping. Should've told her to draw the curtains – then the Peeping Tom couldn't peep. Maybe he has a point, but have to be neighbourly. Also, I think we'll be friends. I need some badly. What with working at home, I'm feeling lonely. But I've written to Alice Amethyst, reminding her she promised to come. I hope so. I can't live without friends. Bobbye Ann Gross has promised to come, too.

Wednesday 7th:
Extremely worried.

That awful girl, Erin, rang and invited us to her poetry reading – it's in *The Brazen Head* pub off the quays. Charlie much too delighted and eager to go. When we got there, some young people were already reading. Erin among them – still all spikey eyelashes, bosoms and tight-jeaned buttocks. But, I have to say it, pretty in a pubescent way with that glorious thick red hair. She read a poem about menstruation – only remember a few lines:

> My blood is good, my mark of Eve,
> It pours and heals and, like the earth,
> Makes room for seed. . .

God, anything goes nowadays. Will someone please tell me, is this bilge really poetry? I'll be glad to pack in my mark of Eve. That prospect's the one good thing about the Big M. Always thought "the curse" a great description of women's bodily functions.

Charlie entranced by Erin reading.

Typical.

Her red hair hung to her shoulders and bounced to the rhythm of her reading – fascinating, really; her confidence. Hell, is Charlie going to cash me in for a newer model? Maybe I'm paranoid, but divorce is all over the place and we won't necessarily escape. I could never believe my luck in marrying Charlie. Lately, I've been thinking of the day we met. It was all fate. I worked for a company who printed his company's books. He came into the office and it was love at first sight. I was over thirty-five then and thought myself past the use-by date and too old for him. "Take not an elder to thyself," Shakespeare warned. But Charlie ignored this advice. It was a case of where's the nearest bed. Ah, sweet youth.

It's not fair. Charlie still seems young enough for acne, while I look fifty. My hair's greyer and skin older. Oh, I can dye my hair and rub cream on my skin, but I have to wear glasses all the time now. Blast it. Why is there always an Erin waiting in the wings? Makes me even sorrier for Hillary Clinton.

We were chucked out of the pub at closing time.

"I like Erin's poetry," Charlie said on the way home.

Knew he was going to say that. I often wonder if this happens to other marrieds – you have a thought and your partner answers it? But I grunted something in reply, pretending she didn't register with me.

"Lively, wasn't she?" he insisted.

"If you like the 'curse' school of literature," I said.

Just then a car roared past, so didn't get his reply. But don't understand modern poetry. Let it all hang out and don't bother about rhyme or reason. Or metre or matter. Charlie writes the

same stuff himself. Why couldn't he be a writer in New York? My
hope is he'll get sick of Ireland and we can go back. I'll give him a
year.

We walked on home through Dublin's burgerland and Tigerish
traffic. Imagine falling for someone because they said you looked
like Seamus Heaney?

"Dublin's different, isn't it?" I changed the subject, as we risked
crossing the Rathmines Road.

"Yeah, but people don't rummage through garbage for food."

"Kids beg here." I pointed to a depressed-looking youth
wrapped in a blanket. "They're all over the city."

Charlie dropped some coins into his cup. He has the biggest
heart and never passes anyone. I have to give him that.

After a bit, he said, "I'm glad we left New York. We'd become
plastic people."

I laughed. "Only half plastic."

"I was sick of McDonald's."

I said they were everywhere – even India.

"Well, I was sick of that MacApple thing."

"It's an Apple Mac."

"Whatever Mac it was, it did me in," he said, as we passed the
Swan Shopping Centre. "My sight went."

"Age," I said meanly.

At McDonald's window, I looked in. "What've you got against
Big Macs? Everyone looks happy."

Charlie humphed.

I make our living on a computer, but he's dense about them. He
thinks they've some sort of inner life, which will zap him if he even
sleeps with a switched-off one in the room. He won't have a mobile
either. And if an appliance doesn't work, he'll throw it out rather
than check the plug.

Later:

It's the middle of the night and Charlie's asleep. I've insomnia again, from too much drink, and am sitting in our Dickensian kitchen, tip-tapping on laptop. Can't help thinking of the past. How Dublin has changed. In the old days, it closed down for the weekend. Grafton Street was sober and sedate. Ladies in awful hats imbibed tea in the stifling claustrophobia of Brown Thomas' Social and Personal Café. The nice thing was the intoxicating smell of coffee roasting in Bewley's window. That's gone now, but the café's still there and still crammed. The city's almost as crowded as New York. You see brown faces all over the place, cleaning car windscreens and selling *The Big Issue*. The street buzzes with carnival life. There are performance artists and pavement artists. Weekend visitors clog the pubs, so you can't even get a drink. It's a place my parents wouldn't recognise. People get mugged and pickpocketed. In my lazy-hazy youth, the main crime was bus fare evasion. I was once put off a bus for trying to save tuppence. Imagine being that poor? You forget so much. Maybe it's just as well.

But have to admit to midwinter blues. Honestly, there are only a few hours of daylight in an Irish winter day. We should've come home in the summer. I miss New York – the tall buildings, the delis, the buzz, specially the *New York Times*. My friends, too. None here. It was wonderful to awake to the honk of cabs. I thought I'd burned my boats when I married, but now I'm back at Go. Why couldn't things stay as they were? I had a credit card and a job in America. I escaped my hang-ups. All that Catholic brainwashing.

But I didn't reckon on the menopause – not mine, Charlie's. It ain't true that men don't have it. They don't get hot flushes but itchy feet. And itchy somewhere else, too. He's definitely taken with Erin. He's been dreamy since her reading.

Another thing: Charlie's always saying there's something

"missing" in our life. What? Gourmet cooking? Or kids? I'm not a bad cook, but never got pregnant. But Charlie already had a daughter and didn't want more. So I'm the one who should be missing kids. People often say they're sorry for my kidless state. But I'm sorry for them. Honestly, when I saw how my New York friends' kids behaved, I thanked God for my four cats. They never answered back or mixed with the wrong crowd.

But we're here now, dear diary, and have to make the best of it. It was right to come home. New York was too much for Charlie. OK, he lost his Madison Avenue publishing job in a rationalisation plan, but that wasn't the real reason for leaving. No, he was a book editor, and as long as people still read, he'd probably have gotten another job – eventually. But the end came with the murder.

Charlie was in the 42nd Street subway station. An old Hispanic man was looking up the track the way you do, to encourage the train, when a hooded black youth tipped him over and fled.

A train screamed to a stop – too late.

There was no motive. Racial tension, maybe, the police officer just shrugged casually. Or it could be drug related – someone hearing voices. No one knew the old man. And no one seemed to care. Violence is part of New York. Every day. But it plunged Charlie into black depression. He walked around in a daze. He was inconsolable about the old man. It seemed an affront to his manhood that he couldn't have helped him. Shortly afterwards he discovered one testicle was bigger. I thought it was worn out from too much sex. But no – it was cancer. But they got it in time. Thank God, it was curable. They've made breakthroughs on other types, too. I read the other day that some tumours have been cured by the cells of a young woman from Baltimore called Henrietta Lacks. She died years ago, but her cells are still living and have worked as antibodies. So the outlook's good, but Charlie's illness will always be with me. He was so

ing – said his testicle

"We're going to Irela

Then he gave away a

another job. Charlie consi

York, but his father was sout.

him. It hovers at his shoulder

Leonard's *Da*.

Our American friends warned   26   oubles,

bombed by the IRA. We nodded,   ng rid of our

Upper West Side apartment and m   r things. We found

homes for our cats, then cashed in Charlie's pension and came east.

Like most Americans, Charlie's in search of happiness. Dublin was

the inspiration of his hero, James Joyce. And Ireland's a little bit of

heaven fallen from out of the sky one day. He wanted a bohemian

life. He even wanted to start a commune of poets – put my foot on

that. He's an ageing baby boomer.

But he begged me to say yes to the move. We'd breath fresh air

at last.

The fresh air bit's dubious. There's a smog problem in Rath-

mines. And a drug problem all over. Violence is a daily event.

Tried to console him about the murder. His depression would

pass. He had to shake it off, otherwise he'd get sick again. There's

good and bad everywhere. Thirty years ago, when I was a new

immigrant, New Yorkers got off trains to show me the way. And

once in the Grand Central subway station, I'd had the opposite to

Charlie's experience. A toddler slipped through the gap on to the

track while boarding the train. Everyone stared in horror, includ-

ing me, but a big black man leapt for the door and held it open till

the child was rescued. Then disappeared, unthanked, into the

crowd. There are all sorts.

finish his book. He's writing on the
on T. S. Idiot. My joke and not bad – but
compare an evening to an etherised patient.
really writing on Eliot's American influences. He
modern poetry, especially T. S. Thank God, he's abandoned
the commune idea and instead is planning to start his own publishing company here – for Irish poetry. He has five thousand dollars left out of his redundancy money. He's not a business man, so
I fear the worst. He's too young for Social Security, so I'm the
breadwinner. Hope we make it.

Thursday 8th:
I now understand why people pay decorators. The kitchen looks as
if a flock of pigeons have got loose there. Charlie grumpy and saying I should leave it to him. Hate when he criticises me. But things
are looking better. With our new bed and a few sticks of old pine
furniture, we're reconstructed Victorians.

Saturday 10th:
Poopdeck Pappy, a local character, came into Mrs Murphy's while
I was chatting today. (Feel guilty for not going in for a few days.)
He's a ragged alcoholic with chubby red cheeks and a rope tied
around his overcoat. He usually sings cowboy songs outside the
Rathmines post office, but was crying today – it went to my heart.
Mrs Murphy gave him £1 – she has an emergency fund from his
relatives. Still, good of her. She told me the latest gossip about the
neighbourhood.

Apparently, Packy, the boy who pesters Philomena, is the
scourge of the street. His parents won't do anything about it. They
just blame the woman. Now there's a big row because she went to
the police and the boy was questioned.

Then Mrs Murphy asked about the house.

Told her it was damp.

She shrugged. "When the summer comes, it'll dry out."

Logical, I suppose.

Sunday 11th:

Still raining.

Charlie's never been unfaithful, but now he's reading poetry all day. He got a letter from HER this morning which he didn't show me. Tempted to look for it in his pocket, but didn't descend to such depths. Blast Erin. If I'm to be cashed in, how'll I cope? Everything's so different from my youth. I'm from the navy gabardine era. The Ireland of long Latin masses and cold wet St Patrick's Day parades with endlessly dreary floats. School was always cold, and no one had heard of the Beatles or Mary Quant. Ireland equalled Catholicism to me. Dev, John Charles and Pope Pius XII actually gelled in my imagination into one thin grey male in glasses. It seemed to be Lent all the time. That's why I was afraid to come home – ghosts would jump out of the grave, like in *The Night of the Living Dead*.

Charlie had a completely different upbringing. His adolescence was full of sunshine and root beer. He went for hamburgers after movies and danced endless nights away with endless girls like Erin. Or they necked to the small hours in parked cars. Is that why he says something's missing now? You fall apart when you get older. But in many ways, life's better. You don't have so many tangled briars to get through. At least, that's what I thought, pre-Erin.

Monday 12th:

Ireland having a hit of bad weather, but yesterday Charlie went to his first Irish class in Rathmines. He's learning the language.

He came home full of enthusiasm and shouting, "*Masha deli*, Peggy!"

Didn't know what he was saying. It sounded like Indian.

"*Masha deli*, Peggy!"

"*Masha* what?"

He threw down the book. "You Irish lost your language through laziness!"

A typical simplification, and he's talking rot – the language was lost in the last century through economic necessity. No one in Boston or New York spoke it. The Irish wanted their children to make their way as servants in the new world. But I didn't argue the point. Went peacefully to bed. Lying there, I thought: was Charlie trying to say "please" – *Más é do thoil é?*

They say happiness can never be experienced, only remembered. Maybe that's true. My heart still misses when I see Charlie unexpectedly. And I'm happy to be doing anything with him, even steaming the century's worth of wallpaper off the house walls. It's quite a job, as every time the previous occupants decorated, they put on another layer of wallpaper, over an underlayer of newspapers. We've nearly finished the upstairs now. One of the papers was dated 1904. Charlie said it was a symbol. "Of what," I asked? "Joyce," he answered. How could I forget? It was the year the Maestro met his true love, Nora Barnacle. There you are, you learn something new every day. Sometimes feel stupid compared to Charlie.

Tuesday 13th:

I wanted quarry tiles on the ground floor, but Charlie wanted cork tiles. Cork won.

A marathon task, which I expect to be fruitless as floor is damp.

In between decorating, I plug in the computer and set about bringing in the bread, while Charlie contemplates T. S. Idiot and

Irish poetry. Feeling better about things. Maybe Ireland won't be so bad. And Charlie'll forget about Erin. I noticed a few friendly cats in the neighbourhood. And even if McDonald's has spread eastward, time has made other improvements. There's a toll bridge and a motorway, for God's sake. You can buy real coffee now, and nobody goes to mass. Condoms are displayed discreetly in the chemists. Women have more to do than sip tea. They're in the Dáil; there are even women boxers. Luckily, my job's portable, thanks to the computer. Today Mrs Murphy asked if I wrote fiction. Said I'm a hack writer of instruction manuals. Also I squeeze lives and works into CD ROMs. In the multi-media microcosm, only need a phone and modem. I can work from Dublin, Dubrovnik, Darjeeling, Delhi, anywhere.

Friday 16th:
Charlie fussing about no trees in the street, so we bought a silver birch and put it in a barrel on the pavement outside our house. It blocks cars and things, but, so far, no objections.

Sunday 18th:
It's happened.

Erin McGrath rang Charlie to ask if she could leave her poetry around to the house.

An hour later the bell went. I opened the door a couple of inches.

She smirked – much too cheerfully. "Hi, Peggy!"

"Hi. . .!"

She was wearing a long red dress, a Levi jacket and Nike runners. Her red hair was shorter, her green eyes greener, lashes spikier. Her freckled skin glowed wonderfully. She handed me a big brown envelope. "This's for Charlie."

I grabbed it from behind the door.

She peered through the slit. "Time fo' coffee?"

I'd had enough coffee for the day and was about to shut the door in her face when Charlie came into the hall. "It's Erin – fuckoffey," I said – couldn't help it.

He looked puzzled.

She waved past me on tiptoes. "Hi, Charlie!"

He lit up. "Erin. Come on in!"

Had to let her past.

"Take off your shoes!" he ordered – he does this to everyone who comes into our mosque: workmen, the chimney sweep, the coal-man. It's embarrassingly eccentric.

"Peggy's fussy!" he joked.

Fuckoffey smiled coyly. "Older people usually are."

Older people? *Moi?* Jesus. Wanted to pull her hair out. But instead just watched, as she obediently kicked off her new Air Nikes and padded up the hall in stocking feet. The name Fuck-offey has a Russian ring to it, *n'est pas*? Naturally, she stayed for dinner, then after-dinner coffee, then after-coffee drinks, then after-drinks drinks. We had spaghetti, which she gobbled up like a starving urchin. Doesn't she get enough to eat? Not that I care. But honestly, doesn't she feed herself?

"Are you in college?" I asked, for something to say.

She batted the spikes. "Yes, Trinity."

We nattered on in an awkward way, while she made eyes at Charlie. Wanted to say, STOP MAKING EYES AT MY HUSBAND, but instead politely asked all about her family. They're from Done-gal originally, but her parents emigrated to New Jersey in the six-ties. Her father made it big in construction, so sent her to Wesleyan College in Connecticut and then back to Trinity, where she's doing a post-graduate diploma in Anglo-Irish studies.

Fuckoffey didn't leave till after eleven. Charlie insisted on a taxi – acted like she'd be assaulted, battered and raped, walking home. But she had no money with her, so he gave her £10.

Afterwards I said, "Pushy, isn't she?"

He frowned over the manuscript. "She's a good writer."

Why are men such saps?

"With a sense of humour," he added.

What did that mean?

"A 'bloody' sense of humour?" I suggested.

He sighed. "Don't be an idiot, Peggy."

"I was thinking the same about you!"

He scowled and lit a cigarette.

There's a basic difference in the way men and women relate, I've read. Women want intimacy, but men crave independence – not talking's their way of asserting it. Dread being alone. Like working alone, reading alone, but not living alone. What would I do if Charlie wasn't here to cook dinner for?

"Heard melodies are sweet, but those unheard are sweeter."

Who wrote that? Can't remember.

Monday 19th:

Charlie's Irish class night. This time he came home saying, "*Lead hull,* Peggy?"

Lead hull?

"What about *masha deli?*" I said. "Did you find out what that meant?"

"*Lead hull,* Peggy."

"What?"

"*Lead hull's* short for *masha deli.*"

Figured it out in bed – *le do thoil* – also means "please" in Irish.

Tuesday 20th:

My mother's anniversary. She's dead for thirty-two years today. Daddy's gone for forty. Can't believe it. Time fugits OK. Walked round to Fitzwilliam Square where my mother slaved as a house-keeper for a rich doctor. She did everything for me. I was to make it into the middle classes via office work. There was no question of college. I was only a girl. In summer I played tennis in the square with the rich kids, although I didn't own a racquet. The house is a PR company now. Peered into the basement where I did my home-work every night, terrified of getting slapped the next day. In my convent school the nuns wore big leather belts around their waists, but they had a special short one for girls who didn't know their spellings. It leaves a mark on you, that sort of thing. But hate all the modern whining.

Thursday 29th:

Charlie's tree doing well – a good omen.

And Mona sweeps around the corner now, all the way to our door. Lovely. But Sweetie still picks the same spot to deposit his/her goods – why our doorstep? I said that wasn't very sweet of her, but Charlie didn't laugh. He never laughs at my jokes. Things going better between us. I could've been up the wrong tree about Fuckoffey – after all, Clinton's denied sexual relations with "that woman" – AKA Miss Monica Lewinsky.

This morning went into Mrs Murphy's for milk – always buy that from her. She told me some of our "neighbours" were threat-ening to burn Philomena out – as an informer. Me shocked. But she shrugged and said it would probably blow over. Hope no flames blow in our direction.

As I left she pointed to her newspaper photo. "Look at that fel-low, Haughey."

I peered at the big nose. "Politicians are a mixed bag, something like bishops."

She ignored this. "Have you ever seen Haughey?"

I shook my head. "Only on TV."

We both lamented that the other half lived it up, while the rest of us struggled to pay our taxes. Politician bashing's the latest Irish spectator sport.

"Well, he never denied his roots," Mrs Murphy protested finally. "He never forgot the people of Donnycarney."

"But did he invite them to Kinsealy?"

She pondered this, flicking through the paper. "Maybe he didn't, but what're you Americans doing to Clinton?" This an accusation.

Told her I wasn't American. (Everyone around here thinks I am.) Told her the Paula Jones accusation was being investigated. And others were coming out of the woodwork – Monica Lewinsky for one. She sounds like another Erin – an oversexed adolescent preying on older men. Maybe I should write to Hillary?

"But what's oral sex?" Mrs Murphy looked at me with innocent blue eyes. "Do they sit around talking or what?"

Took a deep breath. "I think – he exposed himself."

She leaned forward, whispering. "Back or front?"

"Front."

"I love Clinton!" she shrieked. "Look what he's doing for the people of Northern Ireland! They should leave him alone. Would you put him out of your bed?"

I said the problem would never come up.

She shook her chins regretfully. "I wouldn't. And look at poor Jack Kennedy! They won't leave him rest in peace either." She paused, looking puzzled. "*Where* do American men get the energy?"

"Fresh fruit?" I suggested.

"No, it's something in the water! We'll have to get it for our men!" Promised to get her American water.

Friday 30th:

Raining cats and dogs – but at least the days are getting brighter.

Lately we seem to have a new member of the family – Fuckoffey. I think she's obsessed with Charlie – he got a five page letter yesterday and another the day before. All about poetry.

Had a nightmare last night. Dreamt Charlie and I were in our old Volkswagen. He was driving, but suddenly slumped over, saying, "Peggy, I've had a heart attack." I tried to reach the brakes, but couldn't. The car sped forwards out of control. Woke up sweating. What's it mean? Is the Volks our marriage, speeding out of control because of his foolish heart? Bad news is that Charlie sent back Erin Fuckoffey's poetry, suggesting some rewrites. He wants to meet her again. He's infatuated, I know it. It's a truth universally acknowledged, that a married man in possession of a good wife must be in want of a mistress.

FEBRUARY

Monday 2nd:
Henry and Rose are coming.

Their letter was on the hall tiles this morning. Recognised Rose's writing immediately – relieved it wasn't Erin's.

Told Charlie at breakfast. He sat across the table, fully dressed and buried in his newspaper, pretending not to hear. I suppose we're typical marrieds – for the moment. He'd finished his Danish while I still struggled with my gruel – Charlie makes no concession to modern fads and hates anything low-fat. It worries me – as he's been so seriously ill – but then his heart is OK.

I scanned Rose's letter again, deciphering the scrawl. "*Henry's studying at an Academy of Life Long Learning,*" and he'd "*read some dumb book about the Irish saving civilization and wants to see some castles. But the fool won't believe me that there's only thatched roofs in Ireland.*" She'd seen all the postcards.

Are there any thatched cottages left here? And February's the bleakest month of the year for travelling. They're *his* stepparents, yet they write to me. Why on earth did Charlie invite them? "They're coming next week."

Charlie read on – he's a morning person, while I need gallons of coffee to wake up.

I pulled my gown around me. Our new heater was on, but my breath still hung in the air – wind whistles through gaps where the kitchen windows are supposed to meet the walls. But Rose's letter concentrated the mind. "Rose got a charter from Kennedy – a bargain."

Charlie looked up. "That figures. Why're they coming?"

Why were they coming? He was in denial. Or had forgotten. Or was preoccupied with Fuckoffey? Men forget when things don't suit them, I've noticed. Despite our problems with the house, Charlie's so proud of our new life that he called his stepfather last month: "We gotta place, Henry! Come on over."

He probably didn't expect to be taken at his word.

11a.m.:

Need to write here when in stress. It's a month since we moved in and met Fuckoffey. Actually she's called around a few more times on the pretext of borrowing books, which Charlie gladly gives. He's *difficile* about lending his books to anyone else. He goes out to the library every day. Is he meeting her there? Daren't follow him to find out. My nerves are wound up. Imagine they're something like the inside of a clock, ticking at breakneck speed, especially now that Henry and Rose are coming.

Also, worried about money.

And impending menopause – mine. What'll happen? A pause from menstruation? Or a pause from men? – an American friend told me Margaret Attwood called it that. Will I turn into an old bag? My hair fall out? Grow on my face? My toenails wither? My breasts sag? Nowadays oestrogen deficiency is treated like some sort of disease. How come our mothers never mentioned it? Is it some conspiracy by doctors and drug companies?

Also, the more I try, the less gets done.

And everything's so dear here – especially booze. Our first month's been a struggle. Despite Mrs Murphy's prediction that the house would dry out, we discovered mushrooms growing out of the sitting room walls – a non-edible variety which had to be gotten rid of. It was expensive and awful having workers in the house – muck everywhere. We try to economise, but Charlie can't do without buying books. *I Married a Bibliophile* wouldn't be a bad title for my novel, except people might think it something nasty, like a paedophile. Of course, a bibliophile's an addict too. He buys signed, limited editions and can spend his last penny on a book – Charlie does this all the time. Also we need a bottle of wine now and then – nightly actually. Recently things are bad – Charlie's reduced to Guinness and *moi* to water: tap.

Now that we're having our first visitors, I feel like that saint who prayed for chastity, but not yet. Know I shouldn't even think it, but I'm not up to Charlie's stepparents. Oh, I know we're not absolutely broke, but Charlie's five thousand dollars is earmarked for publishing idiots like Erin. And there's the outgoings on this house. And we'll end up spending more than we can afford on Henry and Rose. On top of that, they're fractious – VERY.

OK, the house's in some shape. It's nearly all painted, except for our bedroom, and there are new curtains. Also, I got the small storage heaters on the electricity bill, but we've no spare bedroom, an outside bathroom and no fridge, 'cos Charlie stubbornly refuses to put anything more on our ESB bill. (It's OK to buy champagne, but the never-never is a no-no.) Henry and Rose won't like that – no fridge.

And they won't understand area's character either. Discovered the enclave of neighbouring cottages was built for Victorian firemen, and our terrace was once the orchard of a Belgrave Square house. The square originally housed British army officers, who spent most of their lives in India – hence our name, Khyber Place. There's an Oxford and a Rugby Road near by. There's a Chelmsford,

Cheltenham and Charleston, all reminders of our colonial past. But all this'll be lost on Henry and Rose. They won't appreciate the street characters either. Or have heard of the famous crime lord who was shot down the road.

Later:

After lunch today I watered the plants in our "yard" – about as big as a large coffin – four by eight, but big enough for greenery. I'm planning a mediterranean patio – lots of climbing geraniums. Only trouble – not much sun. But I'm trying. Plants are therapeutic. I can talk to them. Can't say the same for Charlie, who, as usual, read the paper in the kitchen.

His *Irish Times* indicated a lack of interest in Henry and Rose's visit. He's still pretending he didn't invite them. I worry about Charlie. Is this another assertion of independence? Or is he going senile? Said we'd sleep Henry and Rose in the sitting room, as our small bedroom's used for work – mine. Charlie said it'd be crowded, and why were they coming? I said they must need a change.

Change is a fact of life. It's all round you. It happens whether you need it or not. After all, it's tipped us into this poor Dublin street. But we're getting to know the neighbours – slowly. There's a family of children opposite – the O'Reillys. Mostly, except for Mrs Murphy, the others keep their distance. After all, we're rich Americans.

Tuesday 3rd:

Charlie's publishing Fuckoffey's poetry – Damn!

And he plays her bloody *Oasis* record over and over. Little cow called round yesterday evening when we were putting photographs into our album – they were all spread out on the kitchen table. Her boobs almost touched it as she picked up a snap of our wedding

day. Charlie hirsute in collar, tie and business suit. Me blissfully
happy, in white lacy blouse and blue velvet skirt. Both wore red
roses. We were in the Plaza Hotel for lunch with our two witnesses
and had ordered *Plat du jour.*

"Ooh," she cooed over the snap. Then blurted, "You look like
mother and son."

Me the mother of the groom? On the happiest day of my life?

Didn't the poor girl realise what she'd said? Obviously not, 'cos
she smiled tenderly at the wedding snap.

Then Charlie breezed in.

"Like your beard, Charlie," she simpered.

He rubbed his bare face regretfully. "You do?"

Result – Charlie's regrowing his beard. He lost the first one with
the chemotherapy and didn't grow it back. I prefer him clean-
shaven. Now he has a shadowy stubble. It's awful, but consoling
myself by keeping busy, getting ready for Rose, who's another
cleanliness freak. Got detergents in Mrs Murphy's. Most families
on the street get things there on tick, and we do, too. It's handy to
pay on Saturday. Also, it supports the small shops against the giant
supermarkets. A bit like King Canute holding back the tide, I
know – it won't do any good in the end. But, for the moment, it
helps Mrs Murphy.

She's given up talking about Bishop Casey. Today she leaned
cosily over the counter as I packed the six different detergents into
my bag. Told her about Charlie's stepparents coming. She was surprised by him not having "ordinary" parents, but this is still Ireland. So didn't explain that many Americans get divorced once,
and sometimes twice. Or that Charlie was a grandfather and had
been since his early thirties – the American family's alive and well.

Ordered extra milk.

She jotted this down. "Yes, Missus."

She always calls me "Missus", although I've kept my own name, Peggy O'Hara. But love being a "Missus". And Charlie's not the worst. He's helping prepare for the visitors – promising to clean the bathroom, etc. The only thing: he can never find the cleaning things. Doesn't know where things are in his own house.

Suggested Henry and Rose sleep in our bed to get them out of the way. We can make do with couch cushions on the floor. But Charlie won't hear of it. So I bought a second-hand mattress in good condition from the Vincent de Paul, which is now standing up in the hall.

Saturday 7th:
7.30a.m.: a car braked in the street.

Our bell shrieked madly.

Charlie in the bathroom, so I answered it, feeling idiotic in my dressing gown. It was Henry and Rose's bullied-looking taxi driver – an hour earlier than expected. He rubbed his ear nervously. They were in the back of the cab. Rose's head was down, while Henry peered through the window, waving with relief at me. "Peggy!"

It was like he'd seen life on Mars or something. I waved back. "Henry!"

Then called nervously to Charlie, while Henry hauled huge bags from the boot. He's a dark swarthy man and wore a touristy white Aran cable-knit tam-o-shanter, with a matching sweater bulging under his raincoat. Although in his late seventies, he's vigorous. A retired second-hand car dealer from Brooklyn, lately a golf fanatic.

Charlie came to the door. "Good to see you, Henry."

Henry dumped a suitcase on the kerb and hugged him. "How's the health, old pal?"

Charlie rolled his eyes upward. "Great! This is good cancer country!"

Henry laughed nervously. Although Charlie's "cured", mention
of the disease makes most people uneasy. To be honest, it's a definite conversation stopper. No one wants to talk about cancer. So
I'm forbidden to tell anyone. It's hard to talk about my fears, but I
can write about them here. Henry and Rose are family, and among
the few who know. They were very supportive at the time.
Although when Charlie was growing up, he clashed a lot with
Henry. It was the usual thing – Henry wanted Charlie to go to
business college, but he won a scholarship to university where he
ended up with a Ph.D. But wars of yesteryear, Charlie says. Actually they aren't blood relatives at all, but extended family. An American scenario – Henry married Charlie's mother, a widow with a
small son – Charlie. Then Henry raised Charlie; and after his
mother died and Charlie was grown up, Henry married Rose, his
second wife. What'll they think of Dublin?

Charlie asked about the flight as he helped Rose out.

"Fine – but yeh didn't write us any directions," Henry
grumbled.

"You don't need directions – just take a cab."

"HE drove around in circles!" Rose screeched, pointing at the
driver, who grappled breathlessly with a case.

Her voice is high and scratchy. She looks years older than Henry,
and teetered now in killer heels. She's a retired dental secretary,
small, with tatty, badly dyed brown hair and bad feet. Her lined
face is pinched, and she always wears too much red lipstick. It
looked odder now, as she, too, was decked out in a white Aran hat
and shawl. The high heels were a ridiculous contrast and dangerous on the slick pavements.

"I said yeh guys couldn't live in a slum!" she yelled, looking
gloomily up the drab street as Henry paid the driver. Our
geranium-filled window boxes were the only splash of colour.

They're keeping Charlie's tree company – it has buds already. But the taxi roared off, nearly killing it.

"Be careful!" Charlie waved a fist at the fleeing car.

I hugged Rose awkwardly. "You must be tired."

"Sure as hell am!"

Complaining's her main hobby, and she indulged it now, click-clicking inside. "The plane was torture – no damn smoking."

While the men hauled the huge suitcases into our dark and narrow hall, she plonked on to the sitting room couch, throwing off her shoes. "And that sonuvabitch wouldn't –"

"Yeh smoke too much!" Henry bellowed. "An' don't call me that, Rose!"

"What?"

"Sonuvabitch!"

"But yeh are!"

As he frowned furiously, she waved a dismissive hand, turning to me. "No smoking in the plane. Then Dublin airport. Then the taxi. Is this America, or what?" She sighed moodily. "There's no smoking anywhere in America, Peggy."

"Yeh shoulda stayed there!" Henry bawled.

"Aw, listen to that jerk!"

"You can smoke here, Rose," I said shakily.

She lit up eagerly. "Too many damn kids on that damn plane. Wouldn't let me sleep either."

"Next time, stay home!" Henry roared again.

"Woke me up for salmonella chicken!" Rose made a vomiting noise.

"Rose!"

"Aw, shut up, Henry!"

I felt weak. Honestly, Henry and Rose were hardly in the door, but already tearing each other apart. Rose offered Charlie a cigarette, but he declined and took out his own. Henry slumped into the far end of the couch, neurotically batting the smoke. "You still smokin', Charlie?"

Then Rose screamed, "Leave 'im alone, you jerk!"

I sat between them, a buffer state, pitying all the people in Rose's life who'd broken dental appointments. They looked critically round our artisan gloom. The sitting room's small and dark, but cosy. Definitely cosy. We're cultivating the cottage look – white walls and cork tiles on the floor. The furniture's old stripped pine. Charlie's made shelves for our books, which are out of their postal sacks. All we need now are our cats. They were such gentle, civilised, undemanding creatures, now gone for ever – still miss them terribly. More so now. Henry and Rose do that to me.

Charlie broke the silence, beaming proudly. "Well. Whatcha think?"

Older people definitely unimpressed.

"It's cosy when the fire's lit and the curtains are drawn," I blurted.

Devastating silence.

Henry glanced at the cast-iron mantelpiece. "That fireplace work? Or is it decoration?"

"Sure, it works." Charlie patted the black surface. "That's craftmanship. They knew how to do things then."

The mantelpiece makes the room. It's inset with lovely antique orange tiles. We found it in Francis Street, and it was put in at a knock-down price by a neighbouring tombstone cutter. But it was a culture shock for Henry and Rose. Or maybe the house itself was. Americans expect too much of Ireland – no rain and wall-to-wall carpeting for their wall-to-wall souls. They want everything – donkeys at the airport and their own bathroom.

The fireplace seemed to fascinate Rose, who stared at it as she shivered in her shawl. "Butcha burn coal? Yeh got no real heat?"

"Coal's real heat," Charlie reasoned.

"But modern heat?"

"We have storage heaters for back-up," I said quickly. "And a small two-bar electric. Plug it in, Charlie – they're cold."

As he jumped up, I put a match to the fire.

"Hmm, that looks smoky," Rose whined again, as the fire-lighters took off. She turned confidentially to me. "Yeh wouldn't prefer the West Side, hon?"

"In Dublin, it's north and south," I explained. "This is the South Side, Rose, south of the Liffey."

Her eyes widened with curiosity. "But I mean Noo Yawk, hon. Yeh prefer . . . this?"

As I nodded, Henry and Rose sniffed. They think the world ends at Kennedy Airport. New Jersey's outer space. I offered break-fast, but they weren't hungry. Actually Rose made another vomit-ing noise, saying they got stale muffins on the plane. She wanted a drink.

We were dry, so I looked pointedly at Henry's duty-free bag. "That for us, Henry?"

It was – vodka for me and bourbon for Charlie.

No orange juice for the vodka, so ran around to Mrs Murphy's shop. Next shock – no ice.

Rose freaked again. "Yeh mean there's no ice box?"

I was embarrassed. "We're getting one. . ."

She shook her head disapprovingly. "Jesus!"

Charlie irked. "It isn't as hot here, Rose!"

She pulled her shawl around her. "It sure ain't!"

Henry looked shocked. "Don't the health people object?"

I caught Charlie's eye. We were both thinking the same thing: how'll we stand this visit? But our spirits lifted temporarily, as we breakfasted on bourbon and screwdrivers. I pointed to the kitchen corner. "I'm putting the fridge there. Though it'll spoil the Victorian look."

"The Victorian look?" Rose was tipsy now. "Yeh have delusions of grandeur, hon. This place's. . ." Her voice tailed off under Henry's stare. She belched, then blurted, "A hovel!"

How could she? After all our efforts? Charlie looked hurt, but I tried to take it on the chin. Henry and Rose are from a different culture. Despite its generous coal shed, our house is tiny — although generations of big families were reared here, with no bathroom and only a cold tap in the yard. But the house reeks of history. Ghosts come out of the walls, as well as mushrooms. But no point in explaining to Henry and Rose. They sat there drinking and acting insulted that we'd invited them. How dared we? To them it's a week in Sing-Sing.

"'To be, or to be, that's the question,'" Henry muttered.

"Aw, shut up, Henry!" Rose slapped him.

"'To be, or *not* to be,'" Charlie corrected.

Finally suggested they nap in our bed, explaining they'd be on the mattress tonight. But when she saw it in the hall, Rose screamed, "I can't sleep on that!"

I was alarmed. "What's wrong with it!'

"Someone's died on it!"

Henry yelled and they got into another squall. What did Rose mean? How can Henry stand her? But why didn't I buy a mattress cover? OK, the mattress had some small signs of wear — but no serious stains.

"OK, you two sleep in our room!" I avoided Charlie's eyes.

"We can't put yeh guys outta your bed," Henry muttered hypocritically.

But Rose elbowed him. "They're younger!"

After they went groggily upstairs, we sat in the kitchen, looking at each other despairingly, afraid to speak in case we'd be overheard. Then there were funny thumping noises. Then grunts and groans. The house shook with the noise of lovemaking.

Charlie looked tiredly upward. "Heroic."

Wonder if we'll be doing it at their age? Lately, Charlie doesn't feel like it, and I don't push him. Our love life's on ice for the moment. That's why I'm so scared of Erin. I've suggested wearing black stockings with old-fashioned suspenders, but Charlie won't hear of it. He says it's childish. That, "People in love don't need things like that." My heart turned over. Does this mean Fuckoffey? Or me? Which of us is he in love with?

And how'll we survive Henry and Rose's visit? Last Christmas ended in tears all round. Rose freaked because her darling, Charlie, had to iron his own shirt. A man ironing? His OWN shirt? "Jesus, Peggy," she screamed, as if I were a torturer of little children, "what kind of a wife are you?" I said I didn't iron, and we were cultivating the wrinkled look.

And Rose criticised us eating out so much. And me buying frozen food. And cutting the crusts off Charlie's sandwiches. I suppose they're typical in-laws.

Sunday 8th:
Visitors sleeping in our bed, and we're downstairs on the mattress – permanently. Charlie blames me. It isn't fair, considering, 1) they're *his* stepparents, and 2) he invited them.

Visitors jet-lagged, so hung around all day yesterday. House desperately crowded. Had to talk to one sane person, so escaped into Mrs Murphy's. But when I asked for a tin of tomatoes, she shook her chins crossly and said she wouldn't have many customers for that. Are tinned tomatoes so exotic? Got fresh tomatoes and changed the subject, telling her my visitors were staying for another week. She said that'd be nice for me, but I told her my premonitions of disaster. She told me not to worry. Soon they'd be gone. Then I got the latest gossip about the neighbours. Packy our Peeping Tom's been in bad trouble before. He was sent away for stealing two pounds from an old age pensioner and breaking her finger while he was at it. His trouble with Philomena has made for bad feeling between the blow-ins and the natives. Although Irish, Philomena's a blow-in like us.

Monday 9th:

Awoke with bites this morning. Charlie had some, too. Fleas? Is Rose right about the mattress? Vacuumed it thoroughly.

Otherwise things OK – sort of.

This afternoon we introduced Henry and Rose to the sights of Dublin. Charlie brought them on the grand tour – St Patrick's Cathedral, the Bank of Ireland, Trinity with its Book of Kells, which all seemed to bore Rose. Then we went to the National Gallery, where I spend hours most Sundays. Rose's interested in art, but nothing there grabbed her either. Not even Francis Danby's *Opening of the Sixth Seal.* I'm always awed by its wonderful contrasts of light and dark, thinking it says something about man's fate – how we're all so helpless and in the dark. But Rose tip-tapped on, shaking her head in disapproval – she does this all the time. Even our famous Caravaggio – *The Taking of Christ* – didn't impress her. And neither did Jack B. Yeats' paintings.

"Crap," she muttered, as we queued for a bus home. "A muddy palette. What's his name, Keats?"

Charlie gritted his teeth. "Yeats! Jack B. Yeats! He's the poet's brother. One of Ireland's greatest painters."

Rose snorted. "Oh, yeah?"

The bus ran into gridlock. Typical Dublin. We'd have walked it in twenty minutes but for Rose's damn heels. And who'd we run into in Rathmines? Erin Fuckoffey, of course – coming out of Super Valu as we were going in. She batted the lashes. "Hi, Charlie!"

"Hi!" he said matter-of-factly. I looked for signs of embarrassment or confusion, but saw none. "I want you to meet my stepparents," he said.

"Gee, you have parents?" She batted again, as if puzzled by something very unusual. "Hi, everybody."

As they stood chatting in a circle, I walked on to the meat counter. Where's she from, the Moon? Everyone has parents or stepparents at some time or other. They don't come down with the stork. Watched Charlie surreptitiously in the mirror, but he didn't tarry with her. He was too busy with Henry and Rose, who, of course, looked around the shop critically, comparing it unfavourably to their market back home. NOTHING in Ireland compares favourably to ANYTHING back home. But Henry seems to like this quaintness.

"Bye, Peggy!" Erin called cheerfully to the delicatessen at the back of the shop.

I waved. What else could I do?

On Castlewood Avenue, Charlie told me she'd moved to Rathmines – alarm bells rang immediately. Why can't she move to the west of Ireland? Or, better still, Siberia? At home we poured drinks and I felt better. Later, the men watched one of Charlie's cowboy videos, while Rose and I drank and cooked in the kitchen. I made chilli for dinner, à la Julia Child, while Rose kneaded bread at the kitchen table – it had proved while we were out. She's a wonderful cook and really into good food; she says bought bread's poison. Charlie says she gets up early and bakes before breakfast at home. He thinks I should, too – bake it on an open fire, preferably, lit with a couple of rubbed-together sticks, like a Girl Guide.

Rose plaited strips of dough into a loaf, and sprinkled it with brown sugar and cinnamon. While it baked, the house filled with delicious aromas. I asked if she still baked daily at home.

She dragged on her cigarette. "Naw, cookin's dumb."

This was odd – to her, ANYTHING in a packet's poison. She's a gourmet and almost on arrival went through my cupboards, throwing out my malt vinegar and buying me an expensive balsamic variety – she says there're thirty-two types of vinegar. Are there? You learn something every day.

She stared angrily into her drink. "Henry's got a bimbo."

This was odd, too, considering the tell-tale sounds of love making we'd heard earlier. Tried to be reassuring. "Oh, I don't believe that."

She raked her tatty hair. "But he's writin' poetry."

"Poetry?"

"Yeah, love poetry. He's in love."

"Maybe he's writing about you."

She banged her glass on the table. "Aw, don't be nuts. He expects me to live like a fuckin' nun while he communes with his muses."

Muses? What was she saying? She doesn't live like a nun. We'd heard them earlier. The earth shook, the house at least. But now she was crying.

I touched her shoulder gently. "Henry's getting older."

"He's a bastard."

"But men get tired. Even younger men."

"They're all bastards," she sobbed.

I poured her another vodka.

"I got it, Peggy!" Her speech was slurred and she grabbed my hand conspiratorially. "Charlie has someone on the side."

I was startled. "Another woman?"

She nodded vehemently.

"Oh . . . I don't think so." I'm jealous of Fuckoffey but feel nothing's happened between her and Charlie. Not yet. She just writes or phones all the time about her blasted poetry. And he's too nice to brush her off.

Rose downed her drink. "You sure he hasn't another wife? Besides the first – I don't count that klutz."

I shook my head. "No."

That "klutz" was Lisa, the girl Charlie got pregnant in high school. Their shotgun marriage only lasted a month, then they went their separate ways. But they've always remained in touch – because they're good people and for their daughter Molly's sake. One summer we all went on holidays to New Hampshire. It was fine. I got to know Molly and her precocious son, Jacob, who was an odd little boy then. Molly got pregnant as a teenager, too, and is in her late twenties now. Jacob must be about fourteen now. He's said to be a genius.

Rose grabbed the vodka bottle and slopped some into her glass. "He has someone tucked away."

My heart squeezed. What was she saying? Rose has an awful knack of being right. But she couldn't know about Erin. "There's a girl he's keen on," I said nervously.

She banged the table. "Knew it!"

"But it hasn't gone anywhere – it's one of those infatuations between a young girl and an older man. We met her in the super-market."

Rose made a face. "He's infatuated with *her*?"

"No, *she* is – with him."

"All men are bastards!"

Then an awkward silence, which I broke, "Why'd you say there was someone else?" Does Rose know anything about Charlie that I don't – something Henry knows? My mind raced.

She banged the table again. "'Cos yeh guys are so fuckin' poor! He must have some bimbo!"

I was relieved. "Houses cost a lot, Rose. You've forgotten."

She humphed. "This place *cost*?"

I wanted to say "shut-up", but didn't. "There were all sorts of fees."

She snorted in disgust. "But Charlie was earnin' good money in Noo Yawk."

I didn't say he was made redundant. Or about the murder he'd witnessed. How much it had upset him, perhaps caused his illness. That he was now having a mid-life crisis and only had five thousand dollars left – which he was shortly planning to throw away on publishing idiots like Erin.

"Charlie's a dreamer," I said. "He loves Ireland."

She was still puzzled. "Didn't yeh guys save some?"

New York's spend city. The more we made, the less we seemed to have. It's the same since we came to Dublin. Henry and Rose are notorious scrooges. Despite being comfortably off, they're staying with us in this tiny house. But they're invited, so I can't complain even if they are mean. At home, they make gourmet soup out of scraps. I don't mind boiling a leftover roast chicken carcass for soup, but draw the line at gnawed drumsticks.

My chilli turned out OK. Rose showed me how to turn the leftovers into tamale pie. Also gave me her recipe for Hallah bread.

Tuesday 10th:

Rose has a tummy upset. She says my chilli's poisoned her. Crazily, she thinks it's been affected by having no fridge. Doesn't she realise the whole country's a fridge? Especially this time of year.

Charlie still grumpy about sleeping on the mattress. And I'm being eaten alive by something – covered all over in itchy bites. But still no evidence of fleas – no red spots on the sheets. Charlie had bites today and acted like they were skin-cancer growths. After lights-out last night there were more grunts, groans and thumping from upstairs. Me envious. Both of us curled up in foetal position, too tired and nervous of making noise for sex.

Charlie stared at the ceiling. "Jesus, will you listen to that."

"Rose says Henry's in love," I whispered.

"Seems to be!"

"No. He has a bimbo."

"Another woman?"

I nodded.

"Balzac!"

The thumping continued.

Plaster fell off right on top of us.

I choked, laughing.

Charlie jumped out of bed for a dustpan and brush. But, as usual, he couldn't find it, so I had to get up. I was laughing so much, he started up. When we got back into bed, interesting things happened. We didn't care about the noise. I suppose, we have to thank Henry and Rose for something.

I have conquered, O Fuckoffey.

Wednesday 11th:

We got a plasterer in for the ceiling – not too expensive.

While Henry seems delighted, Rose complains about everything – the rain, the sun, the wind, even the expensive restaurant where they took us for dinner. This was an effort to repay us for the accommodation. I was thrilled not to have to cook, but Rose thought the food was "shit". We thought it delicious, and Henry ate it all but didn't say anything in rebuttal. I'm bearing up. But it seems like they've been here for weeks. Everything's a bit of blur. This morning, while the men were taking an after-breakfast turn

around the square, Rose came into the kitchen where I was washing up, a look of triumph on her face and a dead insect in her palm.
"A flea!" she shrieked.

I feigned ignorance. "It couldn't be. You don't get fleas in winter."

But, while I put it in the trash, she held up her other arm. "I got
bites, from that mattress yeh wanted us to sleep on."

"But you're not sleeping on it!"

"They got in our bed, too."

"You picked them up on the plane," I said flatly. "Now, the
water's hot, if you want a bath."

She looked puzzled. "It ain't always hot?"

I was patient. "This is Ireland, Rose. We don't have constant
hot water. We believe in saving the earth's resources for the next
generation."

I'm beginning to think the Greens have a point – Americans are
the main sinners in global warming. Finished washing up while Rose
had her bath. It was funny. She was in there for ages, but no taps
were turned on. Only heavy breathing. What was wrong? Finally I
knocked worriedly on the bathroom door. "You OK, Rose?"

A big moan.

"Rose!" I knocked harder. Had she slipped? Drowned?

She opened it, flushed. "I'm cleanin' the damn bath."

"It's clean, Rose."

"Filthy!"

"No, rusty. It's an old tub, Rose."

I'm going mad, mad, mad. When the men came back, Charlie
said Henry and Rose were going to the Aran Islands. GREAT, I
thought, when? But I said nothing. Apparently they're "disen-
chanted" with Dublin and want to see the West. Hope they won't
be too disappointed. Everyone dotes on the Aran Islands –
everyone in the world, but me. I went one summer years ago when

it rained non-stop. It'll be horrible in February – cold and wet. But I didn't want to put them off. No, it's just the place for them. "See Dun Aengus and die," Henry moaned.

"Where's that?" Rose whined.

Henry ecstatic. "It's a prehistoric fort in the Atlantic. I did it at the Academy."

"Shit, Henry! I don't wanna see some damn ruin. We came to see castles!"

"I gotta see ruins. And beehive huts, too!"

"I'm allergic to bees." She held out her arm again. "I already got a flea bite!"

Charlie laughed. "With all those cockroaches in New York, why worry about an Irish flea?"

"Yeh want me to get plague!" Rose shrieked again.

Can't stand any more. Now they're twisting our arm to visit the Aran Islands with them. Why can't Charlie make them go by themselves? He should be firm, but he allows himself to be walked over. We can't afford a holiday just now. On top of that, I'm worried the house will be robbed. The Peeping Tom will be around. But Henry and Rose keep reminding us they're family, and they spent "good money" coming to see us. How could we let them go alone? Easily. VERY.

Monday 16th:

In the end we all came west – leaving the fleas to fate.

I'm writing this in the middle of the night in a horrible B & B, the most awful I've ever been in, on Inishmore, the biggest of the Aran Islands. Still convinced my previous trip here was enough for one life. I'm not an island type, despite a fondness for Arthur Ransome. The place is bleak in February, and the rain has been ceaseless. But this morning the men rented a car in Rathmines, sharing the payment, as Henry suggested, and which used the last of our money, as I feared. Then we set out early for Galway.

Charlie drove, keeping up a running commentary. "Loose Chippings . . . now that's an unusual name for a town."

"Sure sounds English," Henry said.

Charlie's voice deepened. "You see those sheep in the field?"

Henry and Rose craned back at the woolly bundles.

"You've heard of the sitting duck," Charlie went on in full flight. "They're sitting sheep. The farmers cut their legs off to prevent them running away."

Henry and Rose wanted to report this to the ISPCA.

"It won't do much good." Charlie kept his voice steady. "It's agricultural policy here."

"Then Amnesty! The UN!" Rose screamed.

As we drove on, Henry suddenly chuckled chestily. "Why do I listen to yeh, Charlie!"

We stopped for a pub lunch halfway – a good lunch, but Rose complained, naturally. When we started again, Henry fell asleep, so she shook him, irked. "Wake up! Yeh can't come all this way and sleep!"

He jerked up. "I am awake!"

She nudged him sharply. "Yer missin' all the castles! Look!"

We were passing a castle, so I turned around. "Want to take a picture?"

She took some more photos. In the end, Charlie refused to stop any more. And by the time we hit the stone walls of the west, Rose was asleep, too. Me exhausted from the two of them bickering in the back. We parked on the Galway quays and woke her up. The plane fare to Inishmore turned out to be too expensive for Henry and Rose, so we caught the ferry. It was as bad as could be expected and took almost as long as the voyage to Wales. Several people were sick on the deck, including Rose, who moaned her usual refrain, "All men are bastards."

While ours drank in the bar, I tended her. Tried not to throw up.

Raining as we docked in Kilronan. On my last visit, the quayside was full of brown, wizened men with buggy whips. It looked like a masochists' retreat – but their horses and jaunting cars were lined up in the background. There were a few this time, too, and taxi-vans and bikes. But Henry and Rose refused to pay for transport, so we set out on shank's mare in search of accommodation. Despite some modernisation since my last visit, the island's right out of the past. There's horse shit on the narrow roads and a smell of turf – everything's primitive, even the greedy, grasping islanders.

Firstly, no room in the inn.

We went from house to house in the rain, Henry holding on to his tam in the wind and Rose wobbling in her heels. But nobody wanted one-nighters. They wanted people who'd stay for a week – *Deo gratias.* No profit in us. In the Aran Islands tourists are prey – at least, it seems so to me from our experiences today. But Charlie says I should look at it from their point of view.

I was homesick for city streets, so suggested we go home.

No luck.

Henry, too, disappointed. He did his "to be, or to be" thing. Rose told him to shut up.

He looked hurt. "Can we try one more house?"

We did. It was a whitewashed cottage with briars growing up the front, a slate roof and a pretty hill behind. But the *bean a' tí* was fierce. She had a moustache, a craggy island face and barked at us in Irish.

Charlie did his "*Masha deli*" thing.

She barked louder. "*An bhuil Gaeilge agat?*"

I reddened. "*Cupla focal. . .*"

Rose, shocked: "Peggy, you swore!"

"No, I was speaking Irish."

"You said *fuck!*"

"No, I said, '*I speak a few words.*'"

Luckily, I remembered some more Irish phrases. Haven't thought of it much since school. Charlie's right. My stupidity's a matter of shame. Like everyone, I've studied our language from age four to eighteen. That's fourteen damn years, so why can't I speak it? Fear, that's why. And a feeling of inferiority to all the *Gaeilgeoir* types, like our haggish landlady. Our room's awful, too. Dominated by a picture of a bleeding Sacred Heart. The duvet's torn and the sheets wrinkled and perfumey, as if unchanged since the last customer. But I didn't say anything – in case Rose went in search of pubic hairs. And it was so good to lie down. Afterwards we went to the American bar for an *aperitif* and then dinner. The men ordered Arthur Guinness, while Rose and I had our usual vodkas. In the background, Johnny Cash croaked that he'd walk the line.

I'm certainly walking it lately.

Finally we staggered back out into the turfy-shitty dark in search of a restaurant. It'd stopped raining and stars studded the clear night sky. The dark was mystical, overwhelming. Suddenly I was happy. I can't explain the feeling – joy, I suppose. It's enough to make you believe in islands. Or something.

Then Rose twisted her ankle. "Shit!"

Henry ran back. "Hon, yeh OK?"

She lay on the ground, moaning. "Shit!"

Henry knelt down beside her, tenderly massaging her ankle. "Is this a bad one, hon?"

Rose grimaced in pain.

"Is that better, sweetie? We need ice, or cold water."

Charlie ran back to the pub.

Me amazed. Whatever about his bimbo, Henry seems to care for

Rose. You never know about someone else's marriage. They were in love again. It wasn't just sex. Maybe they stimulate each other by shouting? That's why they have such a good sex life. Any time Charlie and I shout, it ends in tears.

Charlie returned with a wet tea cloth and a pair of the barman's trainers. Henry bound Rose's ankle, and she put on the trainers and hobbled on, supported by the two men. The restaurant was closed – a notice said service was limited in winter. Relieved that we didn't have to waste good money on a bad meal. Instead went back to the B & B, hoping to order a high tea – maybe a slice of ham and some brown bread.

But no landlady.

The whole house had gone, either to mass or a *céilí* – she'd said they were going somewhere but it didn't register with me. The fire was out, too, and the only welcome was the raised hand of the Child of Prague statue on the kitchen mantel. I was hungry but feared helping myself from the fridge.

Rose's ankle had swollen badly, so we all went to bed. There's nothing more miserable than going to bed early in a B & B. They're bleak places on the whole. Stay home unless you can afford a hotel is my motto. A hotel, at least, has a bar to drown holiday sorrows. Full of them tonight. Also worried about our house being robbed. I can picture Packy peeping, realising we're not there and robbing us. God.

Hugged Charlie's back. "I'm starving."

He was stoical. "Try and sleep."

Then thumping through the thin partition – Henry and Rose at it again. They seemed to be on the floor this time.

"D'yeh hafta do it *here*?" Rose wailed.

Henry breathed heavily. He's definitely oversexed for his age. How could he? And Rose in pain now from her sprained ankle.

"Stop it, Henry!" she hissed.

"I hafta do twenty more push-ups, Rose!"

"And I hafta live like a fuckin' nun!"

Then the truth dawned on us. I nudged Charlie's back, as he laughed gently. His stepfather wasn't a sexual athlete after all, only trying to get fit, probably for his precious golf. The men had filled up on Guinness, so were soon snoring. Vodka does nothing for me, so I can't sleep. On top of that my tummy's rumbling with hunger. I'll see in the dawn and tomorrow will be a write-off. But I'm trying to be still and not to wake Charlie.

Rose's breathing told me she wasn't asleep. Also her tossing and turning and groaning. After a while, she tapped the thin wall. "You awake, too, hon?"

"Yeah," I whispered. "How's your ankle?"

"OK. Took some Tylenol. Can't ya sleep, hon?"

"I'm too hungry."

"Want some cookies from the flight, hon?"

"No, you eat them."

But she hobbled to our door, giving me a cellophane-wrapped ginger cookie. In her nightie she looked old and vulnerable. She had curlers in her tatty hair and her face was a white creamy mask.

Me touched. "You sure?"

She put the cookie into my hand. "Eat, hon. I got more."

Rose collects all sorts of things – sugar and salt packets in restaurants, little sachets of ketchup and mustard which she scroogily presses on friends. Normally I hate it, but that crumbling cookie has eased my hunger. Or maybe it was bonding with Rose. Think we have at last. I'll try and sleep now.

Next Day:

Didn't sleep at all. Charlie did, but badly, with me tossing and

turning. Of the four of us, only Henry slept well. Went groggily
into breakfast. Everything in the B & B more cheerful than last
night. The room was bright and sunny now, and a group of young
people babbled happily in Irish at the big centre table. A smaller
table was set with four orange juices.

Henry was intrigued by the Irish speakers. "Yeh guys speakin'
Gaelic?"

They invited us to join them. Introductions were made and we
all sat down, chatting away, with a few of Charlie's "*Mash Deli*"
phrases thrown in. But then our hag came in, slammed down
plates of porridge and waved us grumpily away. "Not there!"

We were startled. Even Rose was cowed.

"Here!" She rattled a chair at the smaller side table with the juice
glasses. "This is for the old people."

Old people? We weren't that old. But, seeing the deflated look
of Henry and Rose, I said, "But there's space at the big table."

"It's for the *young* people!" she roared. "The Irish speakers!"

"I speak Irish," I lied.

She sneered marvellously.

As we sat at the other side of the room, Henry watched the big
table like a child left out of a party.

Our hag had one hand on her aproned hip. "Do youse want a
full Irish breakfast?"

"What's an Irish breakfast?" I asked to be difficult.

"Bacon, egg, sausage, tomato," she recited.

I ordered porridge and a soft boiled egg.

She glared at me.

The others had full Irish breakfast.

"And we'll like homemade brown bread and coffee. Is it brewed,
by the way?"

"It's coffee!" she leered.

It was real, but stewed. Drank it anyway. And after breakfast checked out with relief.

Hag grabbed her money, waving us off. "I'll see youse in the next world, please God."

"I hope not," I said – one world was enough.

Henry tried to give back the barman's shoes, but he kindly said to keep them, which made me feel better about the islanders. Maybe we just met a crone? It was just our luck. Our ferry wasn't due to leave for a while, so Henry hired a jaunting car to "do" the island. After all, he'd come to see Dun Aengus. He couldn't go home and tell his Brooklyn friends that he hadn't seen it. There was the usual fuss getting Rose aboard, as she seemed to frighten the horse. And once on, she shivered and moaned as of old. "Jesus, Henry, I'm cold! Where the fuck are we goin'?"

"You'll see, Rose. To be, or to –"

"Shit, Henry!"

"To God's own country. . ." He looked dreamily ahead.

As we bumped along the rough roads with our jarvey, the salt wind cut our faces, and the misty rain tangled my hair. I was frozen to the marrow. We all were. Finally we stopped and, clutching our coats around us, clambered over some rocks to the old fort with Rose bravely limping after us. Dun Aengus hung over the Atlantic like a cliff. It was spectacular. Amazing. A prehistoric fort, built by the Celts or someone else; I forget. The ocean roared cacophonously beneath. If only I were a musician, I'd copy the sounds. I'd compose beautiful music. Suddenly I saw our place in the scheme of things. Horrible landladies and perfumey sheets don't matter much. Nothing does. Not compared to this.

"See Dun Aengus and die," Henry prayed, clutching his tam.

"Aw, drop dead, Henry!" Rose elbowed him from beneath her shawl.

But she was mesmerised, too. They'd come to Ireland in search of ruins and found a beautiful one. Will they die happy now? No, they'll go on bickering into the grave. But I take back everything I said about islands. There's beauty on that forsaken rock, in that indifferent ocean. It's amazing. Before Christianity was heard of, people came here. Then monks prayed for their world, which would disappear. Everything ends. Cruel forces are at work everywhere. The whole island will one day be devoured by the sea. Disappear like us, like everything. But for the moment there's only imperfect love. Are Charlie and I going to be in love at Henry and Rose's age? Despite everything, they have each other.

Then Charlie took my hand. "Reminds me of 'Dover Beach'."

Me puzzled. "Where's that?"

"It's a poem by Matthew Arnold," he said pointedly, as if to an idiot. He always does this, talks down – irritating. "Oh, love, let us be true to one another..."

Luckily we read Matthew Arnold for the Leaving, so I finished: "And we are here as on a darkling plain..."

Charlie went on:

"Swept with confused alarms of struggle and flight

Where ignorant armies clash by night."

The poem's about loss of faith. I'm worried about Charlie losing his – not his religion, but faith in our life together. Why else was he quoting it? It ain't too cheery. Still, better than anything by T. S. Idiot – although I didn't say so. Anything for peace, which should arrive in about two days time when Henry and Rose catch their flight home – God willing.

"Henry, yeh fucker!" Rose's voice carried over the roaring ocean, as we clambered back over the rocks to our pony and trap and the ferry home.

"What is it, hon?"

"Goddammit! I've sprained my other ankle!"

She'd fallen into a rock crevice.

No joke getting her home, but that's another story. Hope we get a breather from visitors for a while now. Feel I've done my bit. House intact when we got back. Philomena hasn't been burnt out yet. Tree still there, street calm and peaceful. It's so good to be home. Charlie asleep beside me, so all's well with the world.

MARCH

Monday 16th:

March blissful so far – no visitors. Mainly spent working on house. The only problem now is Fuckoffey. Charlie's in good humour which makes me suspicious. He still goes out to the library most days, while I tip-tap away in the small bedroom. Is he meeting her for lunch, tea, drinks, *miscellaneous activities*? Otherwise things OK. Work going well. Except my energy's not what it was. Is this a sign of the upcoming Big M? Read in a magazine that HRT's the biggest medical bungle of the century. It's actively dangerous and offers no health benefits at all??

Only other problem is Sweetie. He/she won't stop using our stoop for a toilet. It drives Charlie crazy. He goes around the corner and barks at her – which makes things worse. I've read that dogs think humans are other dogs. A barking human only confirms this to Sweetie.

Two letters this morning – the usual epistle from Fuckoffey, which I wasn't permitted to see. But I'm telling myself to be sensible – if they were meeting daily, there'd be no necessity for letters, would there? Other letter from Henry. As usual, Charlie read this silently, then handed it to me.

> *Dear Charlie and Peggy,*
> *Thanks for your hospitality. I've seen the Aran Islands and*
> *feel renewed in every way. I can now die happy. It worries*

*me that you guys are so poor and I enclose fifty bucks to go
to a fridge. It isn't hygienic to be without one these days.
You guys need to watch the hygiene.*

*I always regret that I didn't see my way to helping you,
Charlie, old pal, in your efforts to go to college and feel that
your present poverty is a reflection on me. Thank you,
Peggy, for all your meals and the kind use of your bed. Rose
sends her best and will add a PS.*

Fondly,

Henry.

*P.S. The SOB wants to go back next year! I'm getting a
wet suit! Strained my wrist getting off the plane. Shit!*

See you guys!

Rose.

Another visit's something to look forward to. Like Lent.

Asked Charlie what Henry meant about college. Charlie has a
doctorate and started life as an academic.

He shrugged. "Wars of yesteryear."

He always says this. Charlie is really a very sweet and forgiving
person and never harbours grudges.

Tuesday, 17th:

Paddy's Day nothing over here, compared to New York. Oh, I
suppose the parade has improved since my youth, but it was
freezing, as always. Can't remember one fine Paddy's Day, ever,
when it wasn't cold here. Walked across Dublin to the Mater
Hospital by myself afterwards – Charlie went home to work. My
mother died there. For years couldn't even think of it. But coming home has made me able to face her sufferings again. Thought
of Uncle Tommie, her brother, who took me over to New York
after her death. He seemed old then, must be in his late eighties

now. Came home and wrote him a St Patrick's Day card. Better late than never.

Sweetie attacked Charlie in the lane today. He's bought some extra strong scotch tape and plans to muzzle the dog – at both ends, he says. Told him to be careful. Mona might call the ISPCA. Charlie said what about dog's cruelty to man? Hope he's not going crazy. He went for a long walk today, while I worked.

Fuckoffey called while he was out. Had to ask her in. We sat in the kitchen over coffee. Then she got alarmingly matey. As an "older woman", could I advise her about going on the pill? Nearly fell off the chair.

She blinked innocently. "Have you ever taken it, Peggy?"

I said yes, fuming inwardly. (What if she wants to take it for Charlie?)

"It didn't give you cancer?"

"Oh, yes!" I snapped. Couldn't help it.

Her eyes filled with concern. "Peggy. . ."

"I was joking."

She looked relieved. "They say there's a risk."

Told her everything's a risk. You can choke to death on an apple pip.

"A friend has cancer," she said worriedly.

I said I was sorry.

She looked at me in concern. "At your age, you must be on HRT, Peggy?"

"No, I'm not!"

It gets me – this "your age" crap. But she looked so hurt at my tone that I had to say I was thinking about HRT, and she shouldn't be afraid to take the pill. It's safer than getting pregnant. Terrified she wants it for sex with Charlie. But, if so, would she be discussing the topic with me? Probably not. Hate being an older woman.

She's the most ageist little cow I've ever met. There I am, calling another woman a cow. But can't help it. Why didn't I tell her to shut up? Charlie wasn't even here. Because I'm Irish, that's why, and have a low self-image from being slapped in childhood. Everyone Irish of a certain age has been abused – like everyone was exposed to TB. It wasn't just the orphans, the whole country was traumatised by the harsh spirit of the thirties, forties and fifties. There was no glimmer of light till the sixties.

Wednesday 18th:
Mrs Murphy rang the door yesterday to say she was worried about Charlie.

"He was running up the lane, barking," she said.

"Probably chasing Sweetie," I sighed. "The dog irritates him."

She said Mona'd go berserk if anything happened to her dog. Warned Charlie of this later. He growled at me. Is he cracking up under the strain of a girlfriend on the pill? Erin isn't good for him; she's a downright bad influence.

Thursday 19th:
Bad news – cork tiles rising. Floor's too damp. Charlie says we'll put down quarry tiles. Didn't say I told you so. We went down to a tile shop on the quays and bought enough for the whole ground floor in a sale. They sold us some glue which is used for swimming pools – should do the trick.

Charlie started today – I hate him hammering. He has to cut some of the tiles. It fills me with anxiety that he'll knock his thumb off or something.

"Shit!" he yelled at mid afternoon.

I ran downstairs, expecting disaster.

He was stuck in the tile glue. It was right out of Abbott and

Costello. As he swayed, I couldn't help laughing.

"Grrr!" He threw the paper towel roll, but missed me.

I escaped upstairs.

In the end he stepped out of his slipper-socks. They were ruined, of course, but somehow he got the kitchen done. Floor looks nice.

Later:

The community guard has settled the row between Philomena and the Peeping Tom's parents. It threatened to get nasty, but he managed to get people to shake hands all round. Wonderful; now we can sleep easily in our beds.

Tonight Charlie was reading a book about beating cancer.

Panicked and asked him if anything was wrong?

He looked at me nervously, like he had something to hide.

My heart stopped. He's had his check-up, but was there something he didn't tell me? Has he another lump? What kind of marriage have we, if he won't tell me things?

"Someone I met in the library – eh, she sits on the front desk, has a friend who has leukemia," he said calmly. His voice always gets deeper and calmer when he's lying.

I asked who, but he said no one I knew.

"Charlie, you should tell me if anything's wrong."

"Stop worrying, Peggy. I'm reading this for hints," he said. "So I can help, the, uh – librarian . . . to help her friend."

Her friend. Who is "her"? Is she Erin's friend, too? I was so mad about her reference to my age that I forgot to find out more. I asked Charlie if he'd heard about her friend having cancer. But he gave me a funny look, so I said nothing more – Charlie isn't meant to have any stress either. I was told that by the doctors at the time of his illness.

APRIL

Wednesday 1st:
Good news – a judge has thrown out the Paula Jones lawsuit against Clinton. I heard it on the news and, like Clinton, thought it was April Fool's Day. But it's true. Always thought her a gold digger. Monica Lewinsky's another matter, although Bill denies the relationship was "inappropriate". Fuckoffey's inappropriate, I'm sure. Beginning to think Rose has a point – men all the same.

Thursday 2nd:
House in chaos – lots of cursing and gnashing of teeth. Quarry tiles v. hard to lay. Charlie has progressed to the sitting room and is laying siege to himself in there. I don't know how he'll get over the loose tiles to exit the room.

Friday 3rd:
My cousin, Margot (silent *t*), rang from Oregon, saying her fifteen-year-old daughter, Shevawn, wants to visit for Easter. She's adopted – a Chinese-American child, who saw a film about Ireland and fell in love with it. I foolishly said yes. I've no sisters and, despite my fondness for cats, would love a daughter. Girl-talk's a thing I miss.

"She keeps a journal," my cousin added. "She's gonna be a writer. I gotta get you two together."

I said Charlie's the real writer, a poet and publisher to be exact.

I'd wanted to marry someone with a fondness for fiction, but had to make do with poetry. You don't get everything in life.

"That's great, great!" she yelled down the line, not getting my joke. "Shevawn likes poetry, too. And U2. Have you heard of 'em?"

Even old fogies have heard of the famous band, but didn't say this. Then reality hit. What to do with a teenager for three weeks? I have my work – money to make, bills to pay, bread to keep on the table. Charlie's too busy contemplating T. S. Idiot and probably Erin. So, while Margot babbled on that Shevawn was no trouble, a model child, I finally got a word in: "But Margot, she might get bored." I know it's a common teenage malady.

Margot stopped short. "Peggy, she *loves* Ireland!"

"But there's nothing much here – for a teenager."

"She's already packed," my cousin said flatly.

Me gobsmacked. How'll I entertain her?

"Don't they have museums in Dublin?" Margot shrieked. "Art galleries? Maybe she can find a horse somewhere?"

Do fifteen year olds like art galleries and museums? Although childless, I definitely doubt it. And where'll she find a horse? No riding schools near by. The only horses I ever see around here are the occasional travellers' ponies, trotting up and down the Rathmines Road. Now and again a traveller delivers coal and turf to our street. We call him the one-armed man, 'cos he's lost an arm somewhere. There are riding schools in the Phoenix Park, but they're expensive. But I'm getting off the point. I'd serious doubts about Shevawn's visit, so tried again to dissuade her mother.

But Shevawn had bought the last air ticket to Ireland – out of her own money. The very last? What could I say? But it's only April now. Have they run out already? Will Ireland be black with tourists this summer? Dublin's the latest fashion for drunken stag weekends. The city isn't ours any more. But our visitor's only a child. I keep telling myself, and my cousin's had a hard time. She recently divorced her husband, Ramon (pronounced *Ramón*), and went back to nursing to support herself and child. But Shevawn's going to take up time – mine.

Saturday 4th:

Charlie's furious because I walked on a tile before they're set. Also annoyed with me for hemming and hawing about Shevawn's visit. He says I'm hard, mean-spirited, ungenerous, don't like children. All untrue. That's marriage for you – I'll have the task of cooking, cleaning up after and entertaining her. Didn't remind him of Henry and Rose. No, you get more with honey than with gall. Calmly explained that my relationship with Margot's remote. We share common great-grandparents. We're cousins, named after the same ancestor, a Margaret, but with different abbreviations. Her grandparents emigrated – mine took the soup and stayed. As children we were pen pals. Then we met one summer, briefly, in our twenties. We now only write at Christmas. Or she rings out of the blue, in the middle of the night, for advice on her marital problems.

Charlie frowned. "Irish-Americans have a strong sense of family."

I was stung. "She must – sending a child across the world to someone she hardly knows."

"They grow up quickly these days."

"That's what I'm afraid of."

"Peggy, you're mean!"

He thinks we're running a holiday camp. "We'll be responsible for her."

"Look, she's adopted. Her father left. Can't we give a poor orphan a holiday?"

All this fuss about poor orphans typical of Charlie. What about me? I'm an orphan of fifty. Now I've to cope with a young visitor.

OK, so Charlie's nicer than me – I admit it. And more generous – we're to spend all our money publishing poetry. Charlie's given Fuckoffey back her typescript with some suggestions for a rewrite, so that's still on the cards. So is she. Charlie's quite infatuated, I'm sure. See what comes of wearing a black polo neck?

Later:

I've got it: Shevawn's visit will keep *me* busy. Too busy to worry about Fuckoffey. That's why Charlie wants her. But he's said nothing more about her visit, so neither have I. I suppose it won't kill me to help a kinswoman in difficulties. I admire Margot for adopting a child. Besides, I don't know any young people, so it'll be good to get acquainted with the new generation. And she'll be a change from Henry and Rose's gripes. But I've heard nothing from my cousin. Maybe Shevawn won't come after all?

Sunday 5th:

Floor finished. Looks wonderful – Charlie bought champagne to celebrate. Q: Can we afford this? A: Definitely not.

Someone's vandalising Charlie's tree. A branch was pulled off this morning. Charlie's mad. Very. We think it's the local boys. The main suspect is Packy, the peeper. Charlie's convinced he's the tree culprit. So last night he sat in a kitchen chair on the street, wrapped up in a sleeping bag, with an old sword he bought in an antique shop. He says he's going to catch whoever's attacking the tree. He's going crazy. Even the neighbours stare at him warily. And Mrs Murphy gives me nervous looks and says this is what comes of being an intellectual.

Monday 6th:

No attacks on tree last night. Vandal seems to have given up. Tree has survived – minus two branches.

Wonder when exactly our Chinese-American Hibernophile's coming? No letter from Margot. If she's to be here for Easter, she'll have to come soon. Rang Margot last night.

"Yeah, I wrote," she said tiredly. "Didn'tja get it? Her flight's next Wednesday – April 8th."

Two days away.

I got busy. Moved my computer into a corner of our bedroom and painted my small study white. We bought a futon mattress, and a new duvet in Dunnes, a pretty pink floral cover with matching curtains, suitable for a young girl. I found a small chest of drawers secondhand and painted it pink to match. My untidy study's gone. Everything looks fresh. A perfect teenager's bedroom.

"You think she'll like it?" I asked Charlie.

He gave me a funny look. "That's a change of heart."

I suppose it is, but children weren't on our list. When we met, Charlie already had a daughter, and there was my age. Looking back, thirty-five wasn't that old. It wouldn't be nowadays. But, no regrets. Still, maybe I've missed out. Virginia Woolf said never pretend that things you haven't got aren't worth having. Well, I don't – but neither am I foolish enough to think Shevawn's going to like me.

Tuesday 7th:
Margot's letter came – no flight number and some strange instructions.

> *Dear Peggy,*
> *I'm so glad you can take Shevawn. She's a sweet little thing and clings to me terribly. The truth is that I know nothing about her origins. She was abandoned at birth, so is very family oriented. Please make sure she meets the extended family and visits our great-grandmother's grave.*
> *Love and thanks,*
> *Margot.*

Stared at the letter. What extended family? I don't know where
our ancestor's grave is. Looked for it once in Glasnevin, but
couldn't find it. This grave thing's carrying family feeling a bit far.
Does Shevawn need roots that badly? And, if she's so family ori-
ented, why not send her to China?

Wednesday 8th:
Bussed to airport to meet Shevawn – traffic terrible. But we needn't
have worried – her plane was late. While Charlie smoked calmly in
the coffee shop, I paced nervously up and down in front of the
flight monitors. Airports make me emotional. They remind me of
other journeys – my flight from Ireland long ago. I'll never forget
a weeping young nun in Shannon airport. Seeing her heartbreak, I
cried myself. How's her life gone? I was so nervous on that flight
that I kept my seat belt on all the way and my head in the
emergency-landing position. I was afraid to leave my seat. I still
worry about flying. What if Shevawn's plane crashed now? What
would I say to Margot?

We waited at the barricade as the passengers came through. The
flight was Delta via Atlanta, so they were tanned and dressed for
summer. All nationalities – blond Swedes, swarthy Latins, untidy
Americans, pinkish Irish, but no Chinese-Irish-American fifteen
year olds.

At last a small Asian girl appeared. She wore a baseball cap, outsized white T-shirt and sloppy orange shorts. White slouch socks
showed up the brown of her thin legs, and she was dwarfed by a
backpack. She was in the care of a freckled male flight official, who
pulled her small wheeled suitcase. He had a nasty crew-cut and an
ID on his lapel.

I walked over. "Shevawn? I'm Peggy, your mother's cousin."
She squinted quizzically. Didn't look fifteen. Maybe twelve.

I bent to kiss her.

She pulled away awkwardly. Damn – rushed things, presumed an intimacy we didn't have. Have to admit it: children scare me.

Turned to official. "We're meeting Shevawn."

He looked me over suspiciously. "You have identification?"

I hadn't. You don't in Ireland.

"I need identification!" he barked.

Did he think we were white-slave traders? I showed him Margot's letter. "My name's on the envelope – Peggy O'Hara."

He checked with his envelope and shook his head emphatically. "It says here, Peggy McCarthy."

"But I'm Peggy *O'Hara* McCarthy."

Luckily Charlie had an American driver's licence.

"In future, carry identification!" The official handed me an envelope of travel documents.

Shevawn still didn't make eye contact. Her eyes were glazed with tiredness as we found our way to the taxi rank. Charlie put her bags in the boot of a free cab, then we got in back and he sat up front with the driver.

As we moved off, I babbled awkwardly. "How was the flight, Shevawn?"

She yawned, but didn't answer.

I tried again. "Any turbulence?"

She shook her head silently. Then closed her eyes and was soon nodding in sleep. Dammit, I'd tried too hard again. The child was too tired to be bothered with silly questions. Whispered this to Charlie, who craned back, smiling and saying she was flat out.

At home he carried her upstairs to bed. From the doorway I watched her lithe bronzed young limbs sprawled in that deep sleep of youth. She looked so beautiful with her thick blue-black hair falling over her face. "Poor little thing. It was a long flight."

Charlie squeezed my arm. "Tomorrow she'll be full of chat."

Then he went off to the National Library, while I worked at the computer. Around five that evening, I went swimming as usual in Rathmines pool. I didn't want my young visitor to awaken in a strange and empty house, or to be awake all night, so I roused her with some difficulty and took her with me. On the way, I made several more efforts to talk to her, but she still said nothing. Odd behaviour for someone who desperately wanted to meet me. She had no interest in swimming either. She just sat in the noisy changing room, beautifully turned out in new Nikes and Levis, her shiny blue-black hair out of the ponytail now and hiding her face. While unruly young Dubs shrieked and horse-played around her, she was lost in her novel.

Later:

Philomena called in to borrow some salt. She's out of work for three months now and living on social welfare. She seemed cheerier and said she'd taken my advice about hobbies and tried bridge but didn't like it. Instead she took up ballroom dancing. Asked me to go to a tea dance with her. Told her I didn't dance. But she said I wouldn't have to dance, just sit and have tea. But never could stand dancing, so said I was busy with Shevawn – thank God for the child. Introduced them, explaining we were extended family.

Made pizza for dinner, but Shevawn took one bite and went to bed. It ain't fair, everyone likes my pizza. It's famous – extra thin and crispy with anchovies, olives and double cheese.

Margot rang about eight. "Peggy, is Shevawn enjoying herself?"

I said she didn't talk much.

"Peggy, she never stops talking! Put her on."

I called upstairs to the girl.

"What's she been doing so far?" Margot quizzed me. "Has she met any relatives yet?"

What relatives? They're mostly dead. We have a distant cousin in Kerry, did Margot mean her? "There hasn't been time, Margot. I went swimming, but she didn't want to."

"Why not?"

"She's probably tired. She's slept most of the day. Uh – she didn't eat her dinner."

"Peggy, she eats like a horse!"

I was doing something wrong.

"She likes soup, Peggy. Give her tomato soup."

Then Shevawn came and chatted yawningly and *sotto voce* to her mother. From the kitchen I couldn't help but overhear: "No, it's a small house, Mom . . . Much smaller than ours . . . Kinda dingy. They got books everywhere. Naw, haven't met any relatives yet, only a man called Charlie. I think he lives here, too. And a funny woman called Philomena lives next door. Yes, she's a relative, I think – extended family." Then she yawned loudly again, hung up and went sleepily back to bed.

Later:

Shevawn very quiet, almost timid. Very cooperative about Charlie's ludicrous rule about wearing no shoes in the house. It's an Asian habit, too, apparently. In bed told Charlie what Margot said: Shevawn ate like a horse and never stopped talking. What am I doing wrong? He said I worried too much. She's a kid and shy. I'm to relax. Trying to.

Thursday 9th:

Shevawn didn't get up this morning. About eleven I opened her door, and she was still out cold. But she'd settled in nicely, putting up a poster of the latest teen idol, Leonardo di Caprio, on the wall, and on the chest of drawers beside her bed a smiling framed photo of her dad, Ramon. He met Margot in the US navy, where they were both nurses. They seemed happy enough until lately. Last Christmas, Margot called me in New York to say that he'd left her. "He wants to be happy!" she'd screamed down the line at four in the morning. "Who the hell's happy? Are you happy, Peggy?"

Said I was. Thought Charlie was, too. She was angry then, but has mellowed since. At least she hasn't mentioned the divorce recently. Odd Shevawn has no snaps of Margot. Maybe because she lives with her? Shevawn ate no lunch. She stretched sleepily and had a glass of water. Then sat at the kitchen table, her shiny raven hair over her face, writing in her journal. What was she writing? Obviously her opinions of Dublin. And us.

"You're not hungry?" I asked.

"Uh-uh." She flicked her wonderful hair. Everyone has a characteristic gesture, a gesture which gets them, and that haughty flick's hers.

She ate tomato soup for dinner – to my relief.

Afterwards she sat at the kitchen table, again studiously writing in the journal. I hovered around, cleaning up the kitchen and racking my brains for something to say. "Mom says you like U2?"

No answer. Her beautiful almond eyes glittered in irritation. God, was she mute?

"Whatja think of their latest record?"

Nothing.

I kept trying. "What other bands do you like?"

She bent her head again. "Dunno."

A word, at last. "That's no answer!"

She registered surprise, then looked back into space.

"Mom said you saw a film about Ireland?"

Her eyes glittered again.

"What was it?" I persisted.

She shrugged again, bent over the journal and wrote furiously.

Washed my teeth in the bathroom. When I came out, Shevawn had gone upstairs and the journal was left unguarded on the table. I glanced at it quickly.

The inside cover was full of rude *bon voyage* messages from her classmates. Things in big print: DEAR SHEVAWN, I HOPE YOU ENJOY YOURSELF IN IRELAND. I HOPE THEY HAVE BIG DICKS THERE AND YOU GET PLENTY OF FUCKING IN.

It sounded like plenty of sightseeing.

I stared in horror. She's only a child. But obviously I'm out of touch. This is modern youth.

I flicked to today's entry.

> *The flight was boring. Mom's cousins are Americans, not Irish. The man's young OK like Dad, but the woman's old like Mom. She has gray hair, frizzy and grown out like Mom's and talks LOTS. So far I've met no Irish people. The house is not a thatch cottage, but very small — the smallest I've ever seen. Everyone here's poor. It's not in the country or by the sea. There are no islands near.*

Then Shevawn's footstep on the stairs. Snapped diary shut – just in time. She ran in, glancing suspiciously at it, then me.

I looked quickly away – my face on fire.

She flicked her hair haughtily, grabbed the book and ran back up the stairs to her bedroom. Her door slammed shut.

She knows, I'm sure. How could I've done it? Plumbed the depths of depravity, by reading a poor orphan's diary. How'd I like someone to read this? Not at all.

Friday 10th:

Good Friday. Always hated it in childhood, but it's completely different nowadays. Not the same penitential atmosphere at all. Almost festive. Still, had to spend the day working. Behind with my work. I'm always behind with it, but I've a deadline to meet and had to waste the best part of one day at the airport. So asked Shevawn would she mind entertaining herself for the next couple of days, then I'd be free to do things with her. As a latchkey kid, she took this well, muttering the American "uh-uh" for no. Along with "hm-hm" for "yes", it's the gamut of her vocabulary. She throws in the odd "dunno", too. Mostly she sits on the front windowsill, reading and munching. She's discovered Mrs Murphy's shop and buys endless bags of crisps and Cokes from her. Except for Packy, our pale Peeping Tom, the kids on our street are polite and well-brought-up.

Later:

I hoped Shevawn would pal up with the family of girls opposite, but they're too young for her. Instead she's found Packy — or he's found her. Hell! He's taken to loitering eternally outside our door. As well as "peeping", Packy's been "inside" in some youth prison for breaking that elderly neighbour's little finger, so this alarms me. He's about fifteen, too, but old in the ways of the world. He's responsible for the rude graffiti in the street, I'm sure. I once caught him scribbling obscenities on a wall and stared in disapproval. But he'd yelled, "Whatcha lookin' at? Ye mad-haired granny!"

Mad-haired? (Not bad) But *moi?* A granny?

I didn't reply. As well as his other talents, Packy's famous for his goalie skills in street football — hence he's named for Packy Bonner. Now his favourite spot's right outside our house with his team in attendance, chatting up Shevawn as she sits dangling her skinny slouch-socked legs on the sill behind our tree. She snacks all the time. No wonder she hardly touches her meals.

Packy gives me the willies, considering the *Bon Voyage* messages in Shevawn's journal. Charlie, of course, says I'm exaggerating. Packy's a tree-violater, he says, but otherwise harmless. He's paid his debt to society and should be forgiven and accepted back. That's typical Charlie – seeing the best in people. But he hasn't read Shevawn's journal. And I can't admit to such a foul deed. (What kind of person am I?) When I describe Packy as pale, I mean it. His face's totally drained of colour, kind of luminous. Must be from being locked up in solitary. But his muscles are alarmingly developed, and lately he's dyed his blond hair a garish orange and wears a safety pin in one nostril.

Sunday 12th:
Philomena took an overdose. Spent today, Easter Sunday, in St Vincent's Hospital A & E waiting room. We were meant to take Shevawn out to Howth on the DART, but Philomena knocked on the door just as I was carving the lamb for Sunday lunch. Her voice was wobbly and she staggered. "Peggy, can you-ou-ou help mee?"

Thought she was drunk. But no. She took an over dose of Valium and half a bottle of whiskey. Called an ambulance immediately and went with her to the hospital, taking all the empty tablet bottles in her house.

At the hospital the nurse asked me when she took them. I didn't know exactly, and she was completely gaga by now, but she'd muttered something about two hours ago. So they said it was too late to pump her stomach. She lay there with tubes out of her and very red in the face. There didn't seem to be any other treatment. I sat in the waiting room with all the cut fingers and broken arms.

Hours passed. At one point I went to her bedside and a child-doctor said Philomena might go into a coma.

"You have to fight, Philomena!" I whispered frantically.

"Ye-e-s, Peggy!" she wheezed. "I wanta be like you, Peggy."

An hour later, no sign of a coma – Philomena just rather groggy. As soon as she started to come round, she begged me for a cigarette. The nurse said OK, so had to go across the road to the Merrion Centre for them. But left her feeling better and having tea and toast. Came home emotionally exhausted. Is this all Packy's fault for looking in her window? No, it's the result of loneliness. There are so many lonely hearts in the world. Why didn't I go tea-dancing with her? It wouldn't have killed me.

Other awful news – on the way home, from the top of the bus, saw Charlie walking along Merrion Road with Fuckoffey. Suspect the worst there. Confronted him in bed last night.

He was defensive, as usual. "If I explained you wouldn't believe me."

How's that for an answer?

Am I unreasonable? When have I ever not believed him?

Later he told me Erin has a boyfriend, so I have nothing to worry about. Could this be true? The truth is often stranger than fiction.

Monday 13th:

"Packy's in the IRA!" Shevawn babbled to Charlie at lunch today. She still never addresses me. Not directly. What's wrong with me?

Charlie bristled. "Nonsense! He's just a petty criminal. The IRA wouldn't have him!"

Her eyebrows shot up. "A criminal?"

"Yes! And a coward! He attacks trees."

"Trees?"

"He tore a branch off mine. Have nothing more to do with him!"

Shevawn smiled into her tomato soup. She has a habit of smiling conspiratorially when speaking to Charlie, who treats her like a doting father. He wagged a warning finger. "I'm serious now. Stay away from him!"

She flicked her blue-black hair and went on pretending to eat.

It's a public street, after all, and we can't ban Packy from loitering outside our house. Maybe we could, but we don't want to try it. We might get a few stones in the window. But I can forbid Shevawn to sit on the the sill. This afternoon, I'd had enough and went outside. The two young people hovered on the pavement, arms linked romantically.

"Shevawn, inside immediately!" I ordered. "And Packy, go away!"

I'm still amazed at my courage and amazed that he stared at me somewhat sheepishly – yes, that's the word. The look didn't go with his appearance. He wears the uniform of modern youth: drainpipe jeans, outsized check shirt and fat squeaky trainers.

I waved my arms. "Go away, now!"

He slunk off, his shirt flapping loosely on his taut frame. Shevawn flounced inside, ran upstairs and banged her bedroom door. She sulked there all day. Or I thought she did – I was deep in my work.

At dinner time, I called, "Shevawn! Dinner!"

We were having frozen pizza for the second night running – I discovered she likes it. Charlie came in from the sitting room, peering hungrily at the table. "Hmm, pizza again?"

Said I was busy. I pointed upwards, whispering, "She won't eat my pizzas."

"Oh . . .!" Charlie smiled cheerfully and called up the stairs again. "Shevawn!"

Again no answer.

Shevawn wasn't in her bedroom.

Charlie and I ran frantically out to the street and searched the neighbourhood. Finally we ended up in the local park, a Victorian square which once served the families in the big terraced red-bricked houses. But now it's a public park, laid out in flower beds and bushes. There are plenty of benches and swings, but for some reason the neighourhood children are not allowed to play there, which is a pity. But there's been a murder near by. Still, other, older youths mass there regularly, smoking and drinking cider. They were there today, at the edge of the tarmacadamed playground. Packy was among them – and Shevawn.

Charlie walked right up to her. "Home, Shevawn!"

They were eyeball to eyeball. The cluster of youths stared aggressively. All boys in jeans, sloppy T-shirts and the usual expensive trainers. Shevawn's shorts and baseball cap made her look like a smaller boy and much too young for them.

Her hands were defiantly on her hips. Her lower lip quivered. "What's up with you guys?"

The gang closed in. Packy moved to her side, his fists clenched menacingly. "Hey, old man, she can stay."

Charlie bristled. "No, she can't! Her dinner's ready."

This banality defused the tension.

The gang stepped back. Charles grabbed Shevawn's hand and started walking. I followed nervously. Would they follow us home?

But Packy only yelled, "See ya, Shevawn!"

We were half way across the park when Charlie turned. "And you vandals leave my tree alone!"

He's done it now. The tree's finished. So are we.

Tuesday 14th:

Have we been hasty about Packy? I don't think so – there's the matter of a broken little finger and Philomena's attempted suicide. But she's doing OK and should be home tomorrow. Shevawn's even quieter now and keeps to her room almost completely, only coming out for a nibble at mealtimes. She eats a little, but with no appetite. Afterwards she goes out to Mrs Murphy's shop for more packets of crisps or Cokes. I figure she's used to being on her own. But I want her to enjoy herself, so we brought her to the local cinema last night to see her hero Leonardo di Caprio in *Titanic*. She must've told Packy about this, perhaps when she went round to Mrs Murphy's shop, because as we started up the lane, Packy tailed us. Shevawn ran back to him, delighted. I turned to catch them holding hands romantically as they followed. What could I do? Forbid her to talk to Packy? I tried and so did Charlie. But she isn't our daughter.

At the cinema Charlie pointedly bought three tickets instead of four. But Shevawn strode up to the booth and boldly bought Packy's ticket. He, of course, took it, leering triumphantly at Charlie.

I was at the popcorn stand. "Popcorn, Shevawn?"

She nodded eagerly.

The attendant stared patiently at the young people. "Small, medium or large?"

Shevawn looked lovingly at Packy. "Large . . . and two Cokes."

"Small, medium or large?"

"Two large."

"Diet or regular?" the girl enquired.

"Diet."

Then Packy nudged her, whispering.

"Eh – sorry, one diet and one regular," she corrected.

The girl filled the paper cups. Then the giant tub of popcorn – almost bucket-size. Then the young people ordered Maltesers.

"Small, medium or large?" the girl enquired again.

Charlie boiling by now. Finally I got a small popcorn for us and paid for the lot, while the two young people hurried, laden down and laughing, into the dark cinema.

Titanic had just started – basically a melodrama with an awful lot of water. It went on and on. Charlie normally has a taste for popular culture, but we sat uncomfortably through it, aware only of Shevawn and Packy's popcorn-munching behind us. Then the crinkle-crackle of sweet bags being opened. Charlie fumed and I got a crick in my neck from craning back to make sure they didn't do any more than hand-holding. But luckily they were too busy eating and watching all those poor people drown.

Afterwards we walked home in silence while the young people trailed behind, laughing happily. At our house Shevawn lingered outside with Packy. He put his arm around her and was kissing her goodnight when Charlie shouted from the hall door, "No, Packy, not tonight! Off home with you now! Shevawn, inside!"

Packy in shock.

Charlie stood his ground. "Bedtime, Shevawn!"

I quaked inwardly. Now we're marked people. It's only a matter of time before Packy sets his gang on us. We'll be horribly robbed, mutilated. All our fingers broken, worse, chopped off.

Shevawn clung to him sadly. He kissed her tenderly.

"I'll see ya later, Shevawn," he said softly, squeaking off down the street to his house.

Amazing. Went to sleep glad of a dry bed.

Thursday 16th:

Philomena's home from hospital. Went in for a coffee with her. She promised never to do anything like that again. She had been taking medication for blood pressure, which brought a toxic shock reaction, which in turn brought on depression. I asked her to tell me if she gets depressed again. Also asked did she take my advice about taking up hobbies? She said she'd re-signed up for bridge classes. Told her to persevere.

Re: Shevawn – one week down, one to go. She hasn't seen Packy since. She talks a bit more to Charlie, but hasn't thawed to me. He took her into Trinity one day, another day to Swift's tomb in St Patrick's. In the evenings he always plays Scrabble with her, while I work. Coming into the kitchen last night, they were laughing over a Snoopy cartoon. My heart squeezed with loneliness. Why have I no rapport with the girl? Is it something subconscious? Some envy I'm not aware of? With no daughters, I've never experienced the dying queen syndrome, but now I do. Charlie's no Woody Allen. Whatever about Fuckoffey, he wouldn't run off with a child. No, it's the power young girls have over men. Youth is so beautiful, and Shevawn has such a coltish grace. Feel old, old, old. How many days till the big M?

Thursday 23rd:
Finished up my work. DON'T want Shevawn going home and saying she had a horrible time, so for the last week I've tried hard to entertain her. Margot said she liked horse riding, but I'm afraid to let her go alone to the Phoenix Park. Perhaps it's overprotective of me, but Dublin's become such a violent city. Yesterday was fine and sunny, so we took the bus to a riding school in Wicklow. It's called the Bel Air and is attached to a comfortable old-fashioned hotel, set in beautiful wooded countryside. All the way down the N11, Shevawn's nose jammed curiously to the bus window. She seemed mesmerised by everything.

"Enjoying the scenery?" I asked hopefully.

She dragged her gaze to me. "Hm-hm."

"Is that 'yes' or 'no'?"

She frowned. "I don't see any peasant cottages."

I was startled – she'd said something at last. But didn't she realise she was staying in a peasant cottage? Unthatched and two-storey, but a cottage all the same. "We'll see some soon – when we get off the motorway."

We got to Ashford, then made our way on foot through the village to the hotel. In the stable yard we were both lent hard hats by a horsey girl. My horse was huge and called Trampas. Shevawn's pony was called Lucy. As I watched in terror, she mounted lithely, grabbed the reins and trotted confidently off. With her hair spiking out from under the hard hat, she disappeared into a posse of other riders.

I was terrified of Trampas. Finally, with the help of a small wall and a few leg-ups from the instructor, I straddled him. A bad idea. I was miles from the ground. My head reeled in a sudden attack of vertigo.

"Please! Let me down!" I screamed.

But the instructor led my horse out of the yard. I yelled again. Still indifferent, she attached a long lead to Trampas's halter and led us after the others. Better, but still awful. Shevawn had galloped out of sight by now, so I had to go on. It's years since I've ridden, and I don't really know how – just thought I did. I bumped up and down in the hard saddle for an hour, following the others and too terrified to notice the scenery.

On the ride home, Trampas broke into an excited gallop. Clung to his neck in terror, wailing at the instructor, "Can't you stop him?"

She was unmoved. "He wants to get home."

So did I – alive.

Afterwards I ordered tea and scones in the seedy hotel lounge.

As I sat painfully on the edge of my chair, Shevawn, as usual, ate nothing. Instead she nibbled on something in her bumbag. Asked what it was.

She offered me some sort of dried meat.

I declined. Now I understand why she doesn't eat – she has her own supplies.

"Want a Coke, then?" I offered.

She nodded, so I hailed a passing waitress.

"Enjoy your ride?" I asked casually.

She shrugged boredly.

"You didn't like Lucy?"

Her shoulders still hung around her neck. "Hm-hm."

Yes or no?

My God, another week? I'm a total failure as a surrogate parent. As a bloody human being. Can't stand much more of this silence. If I hear "Hm-hm" or "Uh-uh" again, I'll strangle her.

Monday 27th:

Yesterday afternoon the three of us took the DART to Bray. It was a fine Sunday, so the esplanade was crowded with early summer trippers. While Charlie and Shevawn climbed the Head, I waited at the bottom, staring out at the blue hazy sea. The sun played with the water, and I was thinking about the genius of the Impressionists and imagining how I'd paint it. When they came down, Shevawn was tired and grumpy. I'm beginning to understand her moods. She gets cranky like a worn-out child – maybe low blood sugar. She's probably not used to so much walking. After all, her legs are smaller than ours, and at home her mother must drive her everywhere.

After candyfloss, she cheered up. Then a weird thing happened. I'd never have believed it, if I hadn't experienced it. We were sitting

on the esplanade wall, enjoying our last licks of floss, when two
louty boys came up and started urinating in the shelter beside us.
Foolishly I argued with them.

"Can't you use the public toilets?"

"They're locked!"

"Well, go somewhere else."

"Where?"

"A bush! The sea!"

"Are you suggesting we pollute the sea?"

Then they turned on us, shouting at Shevawn. "Go home,
chink!"

While Shevawn licked stoically, Charlie jumped up in shock,
shouting in her defence, "Clear off!"

"Fuck you, old man!"

I told Shevawn not to mind them. She flicked her hair back and
studied her candyfloss stick.

Then Charlie shouted at them again. They shouted back more
obscenities. Then two young girls ran up, shouting more racial
abuse. They were obviously sent by the louts. Finally we escaped
into the bumpers.

Shevawn and I shared a car. Before I could say anything more,
she grabbed the wheel and we took off after Charlie. He swerved
and bumped us. We caromed off the side and chased him, Shevawn shrieking and completely recovered from the previous
insults. God, what's Ireland coming to? What strange beast's stalk-
ing the land? They call it the Celtic Tiger, but it's some evil spirit
of racism.

Charlie bumped us again. "Gotcha!"

Shevawn banged him into the wall, almost jolting me out of my
seat.

She never offered me a turn, but I didn't mind. I was delighted to see her so spirited now, just as she'd been on the horse. When Charlie's around, she lights up. She's no longer the taciturn child. And he responds to her. The power of youth, which youth is so blissfully unaware of.

On the way home, told Shevawn they were bad boys. There're many Asians living in Dublin. Some run wonderful restaurants. Chinese food is Charlie's favourite.

She looked at me sideways. "I was scared I'd be the only one."

"Well, you're not."

I no longer saw a spoilt young girl, but a lonely teenager. A child adopted by foreigners and now dumped on more foreigners. Had she really wanted to come or was Margot just unloading her? As she was so discreet, I'd never know. One good thing – Shevawn's distracted Charlie from Fuckoffey. He hasn't mentioned publishing her poetry lately. Maybe the whole thing has fizzled out? Died the death?

Wednesday 29th:

Shevawn's last day, so took her into the city. The National Museum's running an exhibition on Viking Dublin. She wasn't too interested, but I insisted. She sat up front in the bus and I sat beside her. Who should we see as the bus swung round the top corner of Dawson Street? Charlie and that woman! They were talking earnestly. Then she kissed him goodbye!

Well!

Our bus roared to a stop at the end of Dawson Street. Shevawn hemmed and hawed about getting off. But I was firm. Her mother wanted her to see some museums. So I put Erin out of my mind and walked Shevawn firmly round the Victorian building. She looked boredly at the bits of our Viking heritage which had been recently excavated – canoes, weapons, rusty jewelry and other dingy artefacts. Another failure. Then a reconstructed house on stilts fascinated her. There were no tables and chairs, only a straw bed on the floor.

She studied it for a long time, saying at last, "It's like an Asian house."

I almost fell over. It was her second complete sentence – to me. "Oh, how's that?"

"Asians don't have tables."

I stared into the model house. "It makes more sense."

Her face animated. "You think so?"

I nodded. "Saves space."

She'd liked something at last.

In the Ladies, I remembered Margot's strange request. "Mom said something about you visiting a graveyard. You want to?"

She smiled secretly. "Uh-uh."

No – I decoded by her body language, the tone of her voice.

We went out through the museum shop, where she wanted to buy some presents. So I said I'd wait for her on the outside stone steps. My feet ached, which happens lately, despite my expensive Reeboks. Feet are the first body parts to give out. From too much use. Evolution hasn't caught up with the fact that we walk upright. We're all in the hands of nature. Even the menopause is part of the plan. Grandmothers are meant to help perpetuate the species by looking after the young. Packy's catcall was correct. I am a granny, but I've arrived at the state without going through the first step.

Half an hour passed. I watched the TDs walking in and out of the Dáil, trying not to think of Erin. She was kissing Charlie. But people kiss each other all the time. I kiss people all the time. It means nothing.

But where was Shevawn?

I went back to the museum shop, but no sign. Back outside

again – no. Where was she? Keeping calm, I searched back through the whole exhibition.

Nothing.

They were closing. But the officials hadn't seen a Chinese-American girl. Beginning to panic, I roamed up and down Kildare Street, then ran over to Dawson Street. No sign of her. All sorts of scenarios flooded my imagination. Abduction? Rape? Murder? What'd I tell Margot? Should I go to the guards now? Instead I rushed home. She'd surely be there. Yes, she'd gone ahead of me. That was the answer.

But the house was empty.

When Charlie came home, he didn't say it, but I felt he thought it was all my fault. I was too preoccupied to say anything about Erin. That seemed insignificant now.

We waited, but no sign of Shevawn.

Then Charlie broke his silence. "How could she disappear?"

I put my head in my hands. "She said she had shopping. I thought she meant the museum shop. I have most of her money."

He bit his lip.

"After all, she's fifteen." I pictured her brown young body covered with green slime being pulled out of the filthy Liffey. I saw Margot's accusing face. She'd never forgive me. Worse, I'd never forgive myself.

Then Charlie stood up abruptly. "Packy!"

We went to his house – a shabby single-storey cottage in the next street. His mother answered the door, friendly but curious. When I asked for Packy, she called into the house. "Packy! Packy!"

He shuffled to the door, barefoot – orange hair ruffled, safety-pin nosering dangling. He looked at us sulkily, then back at the floor.

"Have you seen, Shevawn, Packy?" Charlie quizzed him. "She disappeared in town."

He wrinkled his pale forehead, his blue eyes concerned. "Naw."

I told him what happened.

He shrugged. "She's probably just gettin' stuff. She'll be back."

We moved off.

"Wait!" Packy called after us. "The park. She liked it dere."

Amazingly, he came with us to search the park. Again my imagination ran amok. A park murder? After all, she'd gone there before, sneaked out when she was grounded. But no, she wasn't there. Packy chatted to the cluster of youths, but they hadn't seen her either. Had we misjudged him? He seemed genuinely concerned now and fond of Shevawn, whom he called "Sleepless" from the movie *Sleepless in Seattle*. I said she wasn't from Seattle, but Oregon, the next state. He informed me that she'd lived in Seattle, something I didn't know. Obviously he'd cracked her reserve in a way we couldn't. I should've invited him in, taken him to Wicklow, the bumpers in Bray, the museum, encouraged the relationship under supervision. He seemed a nice boy now. At least he entertained Shevawn. Who had she met up with now? The whole thing was miserable.

We went to Rathmines Garda Station. They took it very seriously and immediately alerted all patrols, which alarmed me even more. I went home to phone my cousin, inwardly rehearsing all the way: *I lost her, Margot. Took my eye off her for ten minutes. She disappeared in daylight Dublin.* God, would she ever be seen again?

But Shevawn was at the house when we came back. She was sitting patiently on our windowsill, dangling her brown legs. A big Blarney Woollen Mills shopping bag at her feet. Thank you, God.

I hugged her tearfully, while she stared in amazement. But this time she didn't pull away.

Charlie out of breath. "Now, young woman, explain yourself!"

Shevawn squinted at him, puzzled.

He looked at his watch. "You've been missing for three hours!"

It seemed like three years.

She flicked her hair haughtily, upset by his anger. "What's up with you guys? I went shopping. I told *her*!"

She pointed angrily at me.

"I gotta present for my dad." Her voice broke.

I was puzzled. "But I had your money."

She held up a credit card.

I must've mistaken her meaning – thought she meant shopping in the museum shop, when she meant an ordinary shop.

"It's a misunderstanding, Charlie – my fault." Crying with relief, I hugged her again – which completely baffled her. It was like no one had ever hugged her. Didn't Margot?

As Charlie phoned the guards, Shevawn shyly showed me the bulky white Aran she'd bought for her dad. She smiled secretly. "Like it?"

"It's lovely. Get anything for Mom?"

Her smile vanished. She shook her head no. I told her to pack for tomorrow. We had something to eat and went to bed exhausted. Never got the chance to ask Charlie about seeing him kissing Fuckoffey in Dawson Street. I'm afraid to. OK, so I'm an ostrich. Is there anything wrong with that? Anyway, it wouldn't be right to question him, after today's ordeal.

Thursday 30th:

Last night the oddest thing happened – someone left a new tree outside our hall door. It's an expensive evergreen in a big wooden tub. Has it been stolen from the Swan Centre? By Packy and Co? Probably. Trees have been stolen from the Swan Centre in the past. Charlie's checking with the security guard to see if they're missing anything. I knew it was a bad idea to accuse Packy, but never thought of this result. Now two trees block the pavement.

The three of us taxied to the airport this morning. As always, traffic horrendous, and we thought we might miss the plane. But we needn't have worried. Shevawn's flight was delayed indefinitely. So, as Charlie had a lunchtime appointment, I suggested that he go and I wait. No point in both of us wasting our day. He agreed much too quickly. Was he going to Erin?

He hugged Shevawn goodbye. "Don't turn into a crisp now."

She giggled, blushed and lowered her eyes. Then she watched him sadly, until his tweed jacket disappeared into the crush at the exit door.

I watched, too. Then distracted her. "Why don't we buy something for Mom?"

She shrugged boredly. Honestly, who'd be a mother? She's obviously Daddy's girl. The parent who stays doesn't score as highly as the one who leaves. But she had to get something for Margot. She couldn't go home empty-handed. "Come on," I said.

But Shevawn didn't move. She just stared at the empty exit door. Was she that fond of Charlie? Has he become a father figure?

I touched her shoulder gently. "We'll get Mom a scarf!"

She nodded and followed me to the silk shop. We picked a scarf with a Gaelic motif. While the assistant packed it, Shevawn mumbled nervously, "Think she'll like it?"

I nodded. "She will."

Her flight wasn't called till mid afternoon. I got her some magazines. We had tomato soup. Then crisps and Coke. Then more crisps and Coke. And more tomato soup. Finally we were told to board, and I was allowed into the duty-free and through the usually draconian US immigration to Gate 22, where we waited again with the other passengers in our usual contemplative silence.

Shevawn broke it. "Why'd he leave?"

"Charlie?"

She nodded, brushing teary eyes.

I was amazed. "He had work, Shevawn."

She bowed her head.

"Men have work," I went on gently. Then it hit me – if Charlie's Dad, maybe I'm Mom? I stroked her thick silky hair, thinking how much divorce hurts kids. Maybe silence is their way of expressing it? But the adopted have to take their chances like everyone else in life. How could I explain that to her? I haven't mastered the art of losing myself. I don't know what Charlie's doing all day, but suspect the worst.

"Into the West," she said suddenly after another bit.

I didn't know what she was talking about.

Her long lashes were still wet. "The movies I saw – one was called *Into the West.*"

"The film about the horse?" I laughed. "That made you want to visit us? Gabriel Byrne was in it. He's my favourite actor."

She nodded solemnly. "And *The Secret of Roan Inish.*"

"I didn't see that."

"It was about an island – I was hoping you guys'd live on an island."

"Ireland is an island. A big island."

"Oh . . ." She took out her journal and started writing earnestly. What was she saying about Ireland of the Welcomes? About Packy, who'd been kind to her? About the racial attack in Bray? About me? Charlie? Was she writing, "I'm staying with two people who love each other, but who are on the verge of divorce like my mom and dad." Did she realise already that love doesn't last?

I watched. "You keep that faithfully, don't you? Mom said you want to be a writer?"

She bit her lip. "Yeah – read it, if you like."

I felt a pang of guilt. "No – it's private. But thanks. Eh – I keep a journal, too."

This made her look up. "Anyone ever read it?"

"No. But you can some day."

She bent again over the journal, heaving a big sigh. "I'm sure gonna miss you guys."

I was stumped.

"You can come back," I heard myself say.

She looked right at me. "Next year?"

I cleared my throat. "Yes . . . but talk to Mom about it."

She stretched her thin arms happily. "Aw, she's too busy."

"She's busy all the time?" I asked.

She hesitated. "Yeah, she sleeps."

"Well – she's a nurse, she must be tired." I wondered what Shevawn meant – too busy to talk, or too busy, period? But didn't pursue it. "She'll be glad to see you again."

Her face broke into that secret smile I'd come to love. "You think so?"

"I know so."

The plane was boarding at last. As we stood up, I said awkwardly, "Can I've a kiss goodbye?"

Her downy cheek brushed mine. She hesitated, then whispered shyly, "You guys like the new tree?"

I understood. "Ah, so it was you?"

She glanced at me sideways again. Then, flicking back the marvellous hair, turned abruptly and disappeared down the boarding steps into the maw of the plane and the care of the Delta officials.

MAY

Friday 1st:
E-mail from Shevawn already.

> *Hi, you guys!*
> *I enjoyed Ireland so much. Thanks a lot. Mom says I can*
> *go back next year – if that's OK. She missed me lots. Dad*
> *did too. He got me a book of Irish Fairy Stories. I love*
> *them.*
>
> *Lots of love, Shevawn.*

Now, isn't she a well brought-up kid? Told Charlie she could, of course, come back next year. He smiled.

Saturday 2nd:
Haven't had too much time to miss Shevawn.

"CHARLIE! CHARLIE!" a man's shout awoke me this morning.

It came from the street. Charlie dead to the world. It was Saturday, so me in a blissful dream about the two of us dancing round a Maypole, but conscious, somewhere through a fog vaguely, that someone wanted Charlie.

He snored beside me.

"CH-A-R-L-I-E!"

Then, singing: "If I ever go across sea to Ireland . . ." wafted up to our bedroom window.

Damn – the clock said 6.30a.m. Put a pillow over my head. Maybe he'd go away. This was my morning for a sleep-in.

"Then maybe at the closing of each day. . ."

Our bell blasted.

This awoke Charlie. "Christ, who the hell's that?"

"Hey, Charlie? Y'all in?" The accent was American – very southern. I sat up.

The bell again – it'd wake the dead, the street at least. Charlie jumped out of bed. He always sleeps in his underwear, so pulled on his pants quickly and ran down the narrow stairs to the front door. I followed sleepily, tripping, as my toe caught in my dressing gown cord. Luckily didn't break my neck.

A man of middle years was on the doorstep.

"Hi y'all!" He was obviously a tourist and wore a ludicrous Kelly green jacket with matching cap. He swept it off, nearly smothering Charlie in a hug. "Charlie!"

Charlie rubbed his eyes. "Billy Boy?"

He's a greying, suntanned pin-up – handsome, if you like the brawny type, with piercing blue eyes. He could play a lead in *Cheers* or any of those American TV sitcoms. Despite the hour, he shadow-boxed Charlie. "Remember y'ole buddy? Flew into Dublin this mornin'."

"My God, come on in!" Charlie hauled his bag in from the street.

Our visitor followed. "Henry said I'd find y'all here!"

Charlie rubbed his eyes sleepily. "How's Henry?"

"Fine. He and Rose drove down to Atlanta last month."

Then Charlie introduced me. "Uh – this is Peggy, my wife."

He bowed slightly to me, with that quaint southern courtesy.

"Hi!" I held out my hand.

He cracked it. "Pleased ta meetcha, hon."

Thank God, I'm no pianist. But I have to type on the computer.

Why do some men break your bones? Is it a macho thing? A proof that sincerity goes with strength?

"You've heard me talk about Billy Boy," Charlie turned nervously to me. "We were in grade school together."

I nodded. Billy Boy's Charlie's cousin from Jacksonville, Florida. After grade school, they'd been Catholic Boy Scouts together. And, I must say it, he's the handsomest man I've ever met. He certainly has the most unusual eyes, sort of aquamarine. And a granite jaw, which softens completely when he smiles. That's another thing – his smile lights the world.

In the hall he thumped Charlie again. "Time ta visit with ma ole' buddy."

"You need a bed, Billy?" asked Charlie.

He waved dismissively. "Naw, can't putcha out."

Charlie appealed to me. "We have a bed, haven't we, Peggy?"

I nodded vigorously. "If you don't mind a futon. We bought it for our last visitor – a girl. So it may be too small."

"It'll be fine." Billy Boy looked from one to the other. "But y'all sure now?"

We said yes, and he said the Irish were so hospitable – to me. It's a bit soon after Shevawn, but a few days won't kill us. And it's Charlie's home, he can invite anyone he wants. I felt sorry for begrudging him Henry and Rose and was completely won over by Shevawn. She was such a silent, dignified child.

Billy Boy's the opposite – one of those exhausting, hyper people who always seem to be moving. He didn't rest after the flight – instead talked non-stop about old times. And over breakfast he showered us with presents – bourbon whiskey for Charlie and expensive Belgian chocolates for me. One bite meant about a hundred calories which is twenty lengths of Rathmines pool, but I nibbled guiltily as Billy Boy gave us family news.

Then I enquired, "You'll be sightseeing round Ireland, Billy Boy?"

Billy Boy smacked his lips. "Sure, gonna get maself hitched."

I thought he meant he'd come here to get married – to an already existing girfriend here, but no.

"Gonna find maself a pretty Irish colleen," he drawled. "A redhead."

He's come to Ireland for a wife – can't believe it, but it's true. I couldn't resist saying, "I know someone with red hair."

He lit up. "Ya do?"

I went on – spitefully, I'm afraid. "She's American though, a student. What about Erin, Charlie?"

Ignored his outraged look. Now I've absolutely no doubts there's something going on.

Billy Boy waved again. "Naw. American gals are all feminists."

The way he said it sounded like a dirty word. A pity. Erin would be an ideal candidate. But we haven't seen her lately as she's studying for exams. Charlie's publishing her book next month. Terrible of me, but hope no one buys it. Don't say this, of course. And I shouldn't hope, as it'll be a financial loss for Khyber Press – which is Charlie's name for his publishing company.

This afternoon:

Philomena's been quiet lately, but today she popped in to borrow some sugar. Gave her a cup and asked how things were going?

She took off her glasses. Her lower lip trembled.

I dread another suicide attempt. Asked what was wrong?

"I want a baby, Peggy."

"A baby? Well . . . you might have one. You're not forty yet?"

She shook her head dolefully. "No, but I never will."

I changed the subject. "Are you still going to the tea dances?"

"Yes, every Sunday. I live in hope of meeting someone like Charlie. But everyone's older."

Told her Billy Boy was looking for a wife, too, but he wanted a woman with red hair. Philomena's mousy, but said we'd invite her in for a drink sometime while he's here. She went away happy. You never know. Maybe she could dye her hair red? Menstruation, motherhood and menopause are the three life stages for a woman. Philomena's in the second phase, and I'm coming into the third.

Later:

Tried to invite Philomena for a drink this evening, but she was out. Spent the afternoon chatting to Billy Boy. Worn out.

Actually, I've heard *a lot* about him down through the years. He's a distant cousin on Charlie's father's side – the father who died young. But Charlie hasn't seen Billy Boy for years. It's the American mobile society – people up and go to the far side of the continent and never see their family again. Charlie moved to NY with his mother, while Billy Boy stayed in the south and married his high school sweetheart. But that marriage failed when he was drafted for Vietnam, where he flew a helicopter of all things. After the war, he went into the dry-cleaning business in Florida. Over the years he sent Charlie postcards, announcing his next two marriages. Number two wife divorced him on discovering feminism. Then he picked up number three in a nightclub. She wears a bra size 38DD, he'd scrawled over a little postcard sketch of exaggerated female breasts. I was shocked at this male chauvinism, but Charlie laughed it off, saying there was no harm in Billy Boy.

Then we didn't hear from him for a few years – at least ten. During that time, Charlie suspected his cousin might've gone bankrupt. This was correct. He'd tried to make a comeback by joining a syndicate of men growing marijuana for the market, but had been caught and did time in prison. Then we heard he was out, but divorced again, and doing better in another dry-cleaning business in Atlanta. Now he's here, in search of wife number four. Some people never give up. You have to admire his energy, his hope. Maybe Mrs Murphy is right – there's something in American water?

He wants to advertise in the papers. But I said to try the local discos and pubs first. He might be lucky there, and it's safer than advertising. But no, he's going down the country on Monday. I suggested Lisdoonvarna, although it isn't quite the courting season there yet. Not till September. But he said he'd give it a try. He plans to rent a car in Galway. He's terribly romantic and talked non-stop of his future life with a "traditional" Irish girl. It's a fantasy out of *The Quiet Man*. He imagines he's John Wayne and he'll meet Maureen O'Hara, milking a cow outside a thatched cottage, preferably barefoot. Can't believe he's real. Is he? Honestly, if you sat in Jury's Hotel, you'd see busloads of Billy Boys in green jackets. How come you never notice them in America? Why do they stand out so much in Ireland? It's one of life's mysteries.

Charlie tried to dissuade him – during tonight's after-dinner cigar. "Why not give it a rest, pal?"

Billy Boy waved at the smoke. "Naw, don't need no rest."

Charlie ignored the anti-smoking gesture. "I mean the *wife* business. Give that a rest. Take a breather."

He shook his head no – vehemently.

Charlie frowned. "But you've had *three*."

Billy Boy's eyes darkened, then lit up. "It'll be fourth time lucky!"

"Why not live in sin?" Charlie said.

"Naw, gotta git maself an Irish redhead. It's the prettiest darn colour in the world."

I couldn't help laughing. "Any other requirements?"

Billy Boy mused dreamily. "Well . . .?"

"What about smoking?" I asked.

Billy Boy glanced awkwardly at Charlie, who still puffed obliviously.

"Gives ya cancer, hon. But it ain't as important as good boobs. And she hasta be under thirty."

"Inches?" I enquired.

"Years!" he shot back.

For boobs, thirty's the slim side of good. Maybe I'm humourless, but the way he said "good boobs" got to me. Also, the reference to age. Men are awful.

But he smiled dippily. "Ah want little ones, Peggy."

He said it so tenderly, it made my heart miss. Does he realise how much care little children need? But this makes him a human being, not a chauvinistic stereotype, this very ordinary desire which his three ghastly wives have denied him.

Charlie looked worried. "But why an *Irish* wife, Billy? You'll find plenty of redheads in Atlanta."

Billy Boy sighed happily. "Saw me this ad, Charlie – for Irish Sweetheart Tours, an agency for American men in love with the natural charm of Irish women. Said Ireland was the place for the traditional woman, they're growin' on trees here. If ya sent a couple o' thousand bucks, they'd bring ya down the country in a bus an' find ya one. So thought to maself, hell, gotta cousin in the old sod, don't need no bus. Why not look up ol' Charlie – while ah'm gettin' maself hitched?"

Why not, indeed? But now it sounded like he was picking a brood mare.

"Kill two birds," he went on.

Honestly. Where's he been all his life? Is there any such thing as a *traditional* Irish wife nowadays? Someone who'll walk two steps behind him? A virgin, non-smoker, willing to bear children? Irish women have never been treated well. It's always been a misogynist culture. Women are brutally murdered all the time. There are daily reports of sexual abuse in *The Irish Times*. Are we now to be exported on the hoof?

"And no lip, hon!" he quipped.

I bristled. Did he mean me? "I'm not your *hon*."

But he smiled disarmingly. "Ah don't want no feminists, hon."

I hid my irritation. "She can't have a mind of her own?"

"Sure she can . . . just no feminism."

I cleared my throat. "That might be difficult nowadays."

But he looked genuinely sad. "Feminists an' me, we don't get on too good. No, sirree. Ma last three wives were all housekeepers – in a literal sense, hon. After the divorces, they kept the damn house. All three of 'em. Ah hadda pay alimony too. Ate dogfood for years."

Soon he'll be paying a fourth wife – and eating catfood. "Charlie's right – you should live in sin."

"Ah was brought up ta believe there'd be one lady in ma life, hon. But experience taught me different." He shook his head reflectively. "It sure as hell did."

I arched an eyebrow at Charlie.

He looked away. Does that mean what I think it does? Guilt about Erin? I don't know why he won't communicate with me. Tell me he's in love with her.

Sunday 3rd:
Glad Billy Boy's here. Despite his "hon-ing" me. It's good for Charlie to see someone from his youth. Having come to Ireland, we're more or less stuck, for financial reasons. Dublin's home now – it's not just the money, Charlie hates to travel. But he misses America – the food particularly: Bisquick biscuits, American bacon and

sausage, Campbell's chicken noodle and bean soup – which aren't available here yet, although they have other varieties. It gives me hope that we'll go back someday. He'll long for Campbell's tinned chicken noodle soup so much that we'll pack up and go home. Maybe it's a good thing it isn't here yet. When I went to America first, I missed Irish salad cream of all things, and Jacob's Cream crackers. It was the pain of exile, the perversity of human nature, always wanting what you can't have – wouldn't buy them now.

Charlie and Billy Boy talk endlessly about their childhood. In Catholic grade school, they went through a religious phase.

This morning Charlie laughed. "Yeah, Sister Immaculata told us that dirty books were an occasion of sin and we mustn't read any. So we decided to have a public bonfire. The only thing we could find, even remotely suggestive, was *The Call of the Wild*!"

I laughed. "You burnt Jack London?"

"We sure did!"

My husband a book burner? I couldn't believe it.

Billy Boy cackled chestily. "Charlie was pious then! None o' this 'livin' in sin' shit."

Monday 4th:
Billy Boy was wife-hunting – house blissfully quiet.

He put on his awful green jacket yesterday afternoon and caught the Galway train. He wanted to see the sun go down on the bay like the song says. He was sure he'd find his perfect woman there, staring out into the Atlantic. But he didn't have to wait that long. They were pulling out of the station when he spotted her sitting opposite in the train – right hair, age, "boobs", everything. And yes, the inevitable happened. He fell for her – instantly and for ever.

Well, not quite for ever.

He came back this evening – in a squad car.

An earnest, red-faced young garda accompanied him into our sitting room. He told us Billy Boy was picked up for harassing the young woman. He followed her home and stood outside her house all night. It's against the law to stand outside someone's house. I didn't know that, but it is.

Charlie explained that Billy Boy was harmless. A romantic American in search of love. Not a stalker.

The garda shoved up his cap. He was genial enough, but issued a warning. "It's a serious offence, sir. He'll be in trouble if it happens again."

Billy Boy put a hand across his heart. "Meant no harm, officer, honest."

So he was reprieved.

Afterwards we all sat silently at the kitchen table. Billy Boy's blue eyes seemed to have faded – they looked less intense, sort of bewildered. He's like some big hurt dog who doesn't understand that he's been too friendly.

"Ah just wanted to buy her dinner," he mumbled, running his hands through his thick hair. "Saw her on the train, so sat me down opposite. Sweet-talked her, but she wouldn't answer. Figured she was playin' hard to get, so grabbed a cab at Galway and followed her cab out to Salthill – always wanted to say, 'Follow that cab!'"

I swallowed nervously, afraid of what was coming.

"But she called the cops," he went on. "Oh, boy!"

He didn't do anything, but must've scared her badly. It's weird for a man in his forties to be picking up girls. She probably thought he was a sex maniac. A serial killer, responsible for the recent missing Irish women.

Saturday 9th:

I'm finding life difficult – crowded.

Billy Boy has no interest in the tourist trail, and he's so depressed by his Galway trip that he's completely given up his wife-hunt. I'm relieved about that. But he hardly goes out now and hangs around the house, dressed in a singlet vest and tracksuit bottoms. He sits in front of the TV all day, channel-surfing. He's happy if he finds some American sport and watches it, imbibing endless diet Cokes. Otherwise he plays endless darts in the kitchen with Charlie. Charlie's good with him, but Billy Boy takes up space in such a small house. His laundry's always airing on the heaters and his Cokes and half-eaten kebabs fill the fridge – kebabs are almost all he'll eat. Or boxes of takeaway fried chicken. Tonight I tried breaded pork chops and creamed cabbage, à la Julia Child, but he only picked at them. In future I'll make no effort. It'll be fried egg sandwiches for lunch and hot dogs for dinner. Charlie's the same if I try anything fancy.

Later:

Must keep my patience. If I feel confined, Billy Boy does, too. He started getting gloomy tonight and we had a row about Clinton – whom he HATES.

"Hope they get slick Willy!" he grumped. "Hope they roast his ass for droppin' his pants."

I said nothing was proved against Clinton. Paula Jones was a consenting adult and obviously a gold-digger from the start. The judge had thrown out her case. Monica Lewinsky was an infatuated child. I knew her type. A groupie who collected scalps. Didn't say we have one in our marriage.

Billy Boy cackled. "Ya mark ma words – he'll hafta pay up good."

I said it was a Republican plot.

He was irked. "That's sure funny, comin' from a feminist! Ah suppose y'admire Hillary?"

I nodded. "She'll be president some day."

"Pity she can't take care of her man!"

Can't stand much more of Billy Boy. And now Charlie's irritated with me for upsetting our guest. He's nicer than me, kinder to helpless things – dogs, cats and Billy Boys. But I can't help myself. Mankind has moved on from the cave days. The macho type will soon be obsolete. They're the dregs of evolution. Like that New Zealand bird which is dying out because it's forgotten how to adapt. I hate rednecks everywhere. A redneck bombed the government buildings in Oklahoma City and killed hundreds of innocent men, women and children. A macho culture produces the Timothy McVeighs of this world. And the Billy Boys.

Monday 11th:

Billy Boy still watches TV all the time. He still doesn't go out and, although I encourage him to see some of Dublin, doesn't seem to have any sightseeing plans or, thankfully, any more plans to meet his future wife. Charlie suggested again introducing him to Philomena. She's attractive in a dull way, but doesn't have the required red hair. Still, she's the right age for Billy Boy. So knocked again last night and luckily she was in. Asked her in for a drink last night, without hinting anything to Billy Boy.

Result: disastrous.

Philomena chatted chirpily. But Billy Boy seemed to guess what was on our mind and, although polite, was definitely *not* interested. He retired early and we were left talking to Philomena. Hard to think of things to say. She told me she was enjoying the tea dances and has met a boyfriend – aged eighty. They're doing a strong line. I was startled, but later on in bed, Charlie said don't discourage it. "He'll drop dead on their wedding night and leave her all his money!"

I said not to be heartless.

"Philomena'll never cope with life. And for him, it'll be a good way to go." This is Charlie's idea of joke.

Friday 15th:

This visit's getting me down. Sex is out for one thing – it's impossible with someone in the house all the time, waxing lyrical about Irish hospitality. Don't feel in the slightest hospitable. Feel I'm losing Charlie. When we were weekend shopping, I casually asked him how long Billy Boy was staying.

He was outraged. "That's awful of you, Peggy."

"Why, awful?"

"Turning my cousin out."

"I'm not – I need my room back – uh, sometime."

Charlie looked grave. "He needs support, Peggy."

Now I feel guilty. Am I getting to be a right old grump? Suggested we all go out somewhere. After all, Billy Boy's seen hardly anything of Dublin. He can't go home and say he's seen nothing. But he had no interest in the usual cultural grand tour – St Patrick's Cathedral, Christ Church, Trinity College. Nor do the galleries hold any interest for him. The theatre's out. Nor will he go to the movies. And he doesn't drink, so the pub's out of the picture, too.

"Like to come to a concert?" I suggested brightly last night. "Charlie and I have tickets for the National Concert Hall tonight. I can get you one. They're singing arias from famous operas."

He considered this. "Naw, ain't got much time left. Ah gotta find ma woman."

Alarms rang in my head. God, hadn't he abandoned that idea?

Does this mean another arrest? The guard warned him about harassment. What if someone else reports him? Billy Boy isn't a bad person, but lacks common sense.

I pressed him to come with us, while Charlie told him to do what he wanted. "It's OK, if you want to stay home, pal. You mightn't like it."

I elbowed Charlie sharply.

Billy Boy relented. "OK, Ah'll go with y'all."

The National Concert Hall is always relaxing. It has a wonderfully tranquil atmosphere. The music was lovely last night and the singing, too, but our guest was bored, because from the start he fidgeted nonstop. Still, he was polite about it – he's polite about everything, except the Clintons and feminism. So, at the interval, I suggested he give it a miss. We'd stay on, of course.

He frowned, relieved. "Y'all sure?"

We were – he's a grown man.

So he went in search of Dublin's nightlife.

Saturday 16th:
Billy Boy came in late last night. This morning he didn't appear for breakfast, so about eleven, I brought coffee and Danish to his room, as I wanted to start work. Then I could be uninterrupted till lunch – a good stretch of time. I have a deadline to meet.

I laid his tray on the bedside table. "How'd you get on last night?"

Billy Boy slapped his pillow and propped it behind his head. He sat up, looking happier than ever. "Met maself a sweet little gal called Sally. Now, ain't that a cute name?"

I agreed. As he sipped coffee, he told me it was the real thing.

Tried to ignore the nerves in my tummy. Is Sally a young girl in need of my protection? Does she know the conditions? How had things happened so fast? But it wasn't like the Galway fiasco. He hadn't been arrested. Or not yet. But I still worried. Then I heard myself say, "Want to bring her home to dinner?"

He put down his cup. "That'd be swell, Peggy. Ah want her to meet the family."

I was alarmed. "Oh . . . things have gone that far?"

"Peggy, ya're lookin' at a man in love."

We shouldn't have let him out of our sight. He's a buffalo in a china shop. "Where'd you meet her?

"By the canal."

"The Canal House?"

"Yeh. That's it. Ah stopped by for a drink. Peggy, y'know that song – 'Down by the Sally Gardens'?"

"Yes, it's by Yeats."

"He country and western?"

"No, he's an Irish poet."

"But it's a song. Ah got it on tape.

"It's *from* a poem." While he listened entranced, I recited a verse about the lover meeting his love, ending with –

"She bid me take love easy, as the leaves grow on the tree

But I being young and foolish with her would not agree."

Billy Boy was puzzled. "But where are these Sally gardens?"

"Nowhere, it's just a song."

"But who's Sally? She die or sometin'?"

"No one died. A sally's a kind of reed, I think."

"A *reed?*"

"Yes, it grows by the riverbank."

He sipped more coffee and nibbled on his Danish. "Ah thought it was a girl."

As I went out, he sang softly, "Down by the sally gardens, ma love and ah did meet . . ."

He sang it in the bath, and while shaving. He sang it all morning, then while dialling Sally's number to make the next evening's dinner date.

What kind of girl is she? A non-smoking, virginal, doormat? How can a man of Billy Boy's experience fall in love at first sight? Love's only instant in youth. It took Charlie and me years to love each other. I mean *really* love – the nitty-gritty and all that. Life is still a struggle for us.

Sunday 17th:

Billy Boy brought Sally to dinner this evening. They arrived at the doorstep arm in arm, both smiling happily. He'd certainly wasted no time in clinching the deal. "Peggy, ah'd like ya to meet Sally, ma fiancée."

The girl batted half-inch lashes at me, her eyes blue stars. "Billy's told me all about yez."

I shook hands and showed them into the sitting room.

I'm hopeless at guessing age, but I'd say Sally's about eighteen or nineteen – a Dub, like one of those kids in *The Commitments*. Big – the type Renoir would've been delighted to paint. A low-cut blouse revealed her voluptuous cleavage, and her long legs were shown off by high-high heels and a black micro-mini skirt. The impression was sexy rather than traditional, from leggings to soot-lined eyes. But she had the required red hair. Lots of it cascaded on to her shoulders, setting off clownish white-face make-up and red cupid lips.

"I wanta marry Billy and have his babies," she said first thing.

I blinked. Was she real?

She batted her long lashes again – they definitely weren't real.

"We want six kids," she repeated.

Billy Boy kissed her deeply. "Thanks, hon."

Afterwards she turned to me for confirmation. "Isn't he a beautiful man?"

I agreed.

They kissed again.

"Hey, break it up, you guys." Charlie came in with champagne. He popped it open and poured it into four glasses. It was too expensive, but Charlie's generous to a fault. Billy didn't drink his, just toasted the future with a sip, then handed me his glass. I have to admire him for this. It must be hard for an ex-alcoholic to watch others drinking. But he says no, he's made up his mind.

He's made up his mind about Sally, too. She's going back to Atlanta with him in ten days' time. He even rang the US embassy, who advised him that Sally didn't need a visa to visit. All she needs is her passport. If they're both free, they can marry later in the States. Then Sally can come back home and get her Green Card here. It seemed so easy. And so different from my emigration so many years ago. But then I wasn't getting married.

Sally isn't a doormat. She smokes, but Billy Boy doesn't seem to mind – a change from his attitude to Charlie's habit.

"In Dublin, we hafta have our fags and pints," she said, holding Billy Boy's hand as we sat around the dinner table.

Billy Boy laughed. He looked at her with such enviable love as she babbled eagerly about the clothes she'd need. She asked if she'd need shorts for Atlanta. I told her yes – and bring a couple of summer dresses. It'd be hot in the summer. And she'd need layers for winter.

She tossed back her red hair. "I won't bring me coat."

"You'll need it in winter," I said.

She was puzzled. "Winter?"

She didn't seem to know that there were seasons in America – even in the south. To her it's all a year-round Florida beach. All she'd need is sun cream and a bikini.

The dinner went well. Billy Boy, who'd previously spurned my cooking, ate it. Love suits him. We had fried chicken, à la Julia Child, a salad, potato salad, and cookies with McCombridge's Brown Bread ice cream and my special chocolate sauce for dessert. Sally loved the sauce, so I wrote out the recipe, then and there: condensed milk, brown sugar, maple syrup and cooking chocolate. It's on the cooking chocolate wrapper, but I didn't pretend.

Asked if she liked cooking.

She looked lovingly at Billy Boy. "So long's I've someone to cook for."

He kissed her hand. "Thanks, hon. But Ah'm gonna make no slave o' ya."

"But I wouldna cook for meself." She pronounced *cook* the Dublin way – *cuke*. Also *book* became *buke*.

Somehow the after-dinner chat got on to writing. I was explaining how I made my living – as a hack writer.

"I wrote a buke, too," Sally confided. "I showed it to a real writer. She said it was a mixture of Roddy Doyle and Maeve Blinchy."

"Binchy," I said.

"Yeah, Maeve Blinchy," she insisted.

I let it go.

Tuesday 19th:

Things seem to be off with Sally, because Billy Boy's hanging around the house again. If you ask how things are going he grunts. It's pretty depressing that he never goes out. He always wears the same tracksuit bottoms and a T-shirt vest. He hasn't seen Sally for a few days. What's happened? He looks and acts miserable. Today he's taken to his bed completely. It's only a cold, but he insists it's full-blown 'flu. He sneezes and coughs so loudly that he keeps us, and the whole street, awake. Last night I heard the old lady next door groaning in despair. Don't blame her. Her son looked at me curiously today. I'm not surprised – it's been going on for three nights. Mrs Murphy suggested Lemsips. Billy Boy took some and he's a bit better. At first he drank nothing but diet Coke, but today I brought him up chicken soup and crackers.

I knocked on the bedroom door. "These are a good imitation of American saltines, Billy Boy. The soup is homemade."

He groaned from under the blankets. "Thanks, hon, eh – sorry, Peggy!"

"It's OK. Call me hon if you want."

"Ya're good, hon. Ah ain't had homemade soup since Ah was nine years old."

"It'll do you good."

He heaved himself on to the pillows. "Ah'll never feel better."

I put down the tray. "Should I take your temperature?"

He shook his head, coughing long and loudly. His eyes were bleary and even his tan had faded in the few days. I wanted to call the doctor, but Charlie said no, so didn't. Charlie's right – Billy Boy's not that sick, just a bad patient, like most men.

Saturday 23rd:

It's all on again with Sally. I don't know the details – only that Billy Boy phoned her yesterday and disappeared for the rest of the day. He came back saying that she's going home with him in five days' time. He took us all out to dinner at the Shelbourne last night to celebrate. I've never been in the restaurant before. It must've cost a fortune, but he wouldn't take a penny's contribution from us.

"Ya guys've put me up, this is payback time," he kept saying, drinking in Sally with his eyes.

A wonderful meal. I had salmon. Charlie had duck *à l'orange*, Billy Boy and Sally a huge steak each.

Sally looked happy and beautiful in slinky black. Billy Boy looked the stereotypical Yank in his ghastly green jacket. While he listened, she told us all about her life. She's originally from a big family in west Dublin and hopes to be a model. Afterwards we all walked home by the canal. The full moon was reflected in its inky water and branches trailed the surface. All the ducks seemed to be asleep. Only drinkers laughed happily in the background. It was so peaceful, you'd never know you were in the middle of a noisy capitol. We were almost home when I remembered Sally lived somewhere else. In a flat? In west Dublin with her family? She'd have to get a taxi, but first I invited her in for a nightcap to finish off the evening.

The lovers sat on the couch. Her head was on his shoulder; he tenderly held her hand. His horrible jacket looked so wrong against her bohemian black. I couldn't help thinking of John Betjeman's poem, "In a Bath Teashop"; Betjeman's more human than T. S. In the poem a couple are having tea in a teashop. She's an ordinary woman and he's a thumping crook, but both are a little lower than the angels.

We had tea, too. Sally smoked, and we chatted on till late into the night. Billy Boy made no effort to take her home. He was in the flow state and lost to everything – except her. I had to work the next day, so finally yawned pointedly. "I'll have to go to bed."

"Can Sally stay the night?" Billy Boy's blue eyes pleaded.

I looked doubtfully at Charlie. The house was too small. I could cope with one, but not two visitors. There was no extra bed, or clean sheets.

Charlie went to the phone. "We'll call her a cab, pal."

Billy Boy looked so disappointed.

"Her parents might worry," I said.

This idea amazed Sally. She laughed, her blue, black-rimmed eyes puzzled. "Oh, no, Peggy."

Doesn't anyone worry about her? She's still young and out very late. But she told me she had her own place now, in central Dublin. A cab finally came and they both left. Perhaps I should've let her stay? Was it mean of me? Too middle-class?

Monday 25th:
Well, Billy Boy's found his red-headed woman. His *coup de foudre* seems to have stuck. For the last few days he's spent all his time with Sally. Sometimes he stays out all night. I'm so envious. I can imagine what they're doing – whispering sweet nothings to each other among the reeds of the canal. Or lingering in Stephen's Green. Staying in bed somewhere? The world belongs to lovers. Can't help remembering the time when I first met Charlie. Why can't it be like that now? It might be, but for Erin. Haven't seen her lately. Should I be worrying?

But too busy thinking about Billy Boy. It's none of my business, but Sally's barely twenty and he's in his mid-forties. What do her parents think? Will Sally enjoy Atlanta? They plan to go back down to Jacksonville for Christmas to meet the extended family. How'll she adapt to America generally? The climate, the lack of public transport, everything? It'll be very different from Dublin. What'll she work at? I wasn't told what she did here and didn't ask. Is she unemployed? There are plenty of jobs now, so why isn't she working?

We haven't seen Billy Boy for two days – relieved the house quiet again.

Tuesday 26th:
We've started getting nuisance phone calls. It's always the same – the phone rings and I dash downstairs to get it. Then a deep man's voice asks for Billy Moore. When I say he isn't in, he hangs up. It happens about ten times a day. It's quite disturbing.

Last night the doorbell rang.

A small, dark, muscular man was outside. He was dressed spivily in leather trousers and a leather jacket. "Is Billy Moore in?"

"No," I said. "Will I say who called?"

The man didn't move. "Expectin' him soon?"

I nodded cautiously.

I was about to add that he'd surely be back to collect his things before returning to America, but stopped myself. There was something sinister about the caller. The voice was the same as the phone. I hate to say it, but he might be a drug dealer, a money collecter or some sort of criminal. I certainly didn't like the look of him.

Charlie said I was imagining things. But today a car was parked outside our house.

I peeped through the curtain. "Look, it's him! The man who called yesterday."

Charlie again pooh-hooed my fears. "Billy probably met him in the pub."

"He doesn't drink!"

"He met Sally in a pub."

That was true. In The Canal House, he'd told me. But I'm not so sure the sinister man's harmless. Where has Billy Boy gone now? I'm worried after what happened before. But he's a grown man and should be able to take care of himself. Perhaps, while waiting for Sally's passport to come through, they've taken a trip west before departing for the States? That would make sense. Billy Boy's seen hardly any of the beauty spots like Killarney or Connemara. He's spent most of his holiday sneezing in our drab little bedroom or looking out on our drab little street. But why hasn't he let us know where he is? Most peculiar.

Thursday 28th:

Billy Boy's return flight's in two days, but we still haven't heard a word from him. Where is he? I steady my nerves by going into Mrs Murphy's for a gossip. Hate any other kind of shopping. She was in a doomy mood today – house prices rising, etc. Disaster on all our heads when monetary union finally happens. Our house has gone up, too, which will be good if we ever want to sell it. Otherwise it's just hard on first-time buyers. And what'll happen to the world if interest rates go up?

Later:

We got a call from Pearse Street Garda Station. They're holding Billy Boy – sounds serious this time. Oh, dear God, why did we let him out? Why didn't we heed the young guard's warning? What's Billy Boy done now? Despite everything, I'm fond of him. He's so damn vulnerable, he's his own worst enemy.

Charlie hurried into town.

He found Billy Boy locked in a cell. He had two black eyes and bruises all over his body. He'd been arrested for common assault, he was told. Allegedly, he'd assaulted Sally's "friends", who had beaten him up before reporting him. He got all the blame for the fight, but as he was soon departing, the guards agreed not to press charges for disturbing the peace. He was steeped in luck there. But Charlie had to promise to look after him and see him on to the plane tomorrow morning.

Again we all sat at the kitchen table.

I had a *déjà vu* feeling.

Billy Boy's stared into space. "Ya guys have been so hospitable."

I couldn't look at him. Those two black eyes haunted me.

"Ah shoulda taken ya advice, Charlie, ole buddy," he sighed.

Charlie was sympathetic. "Oh, I don't know about that."

"Taken a rest from women. Y'all were right."

No one spoke. What was there to say? Billy Boy attacked a man. Not Sally's outraged brother or father. No, her pimp. Sally's a "working" woman all right, one of the young prostitutes you see pacing up and down the canal or in Fitzwilliam Square – come to think of it, Billy Boy said he met her at "the canal". It didn't register with me. I thought he meant a pub. Anyway, nowadays prostitutes are driven indoors by new leglislation. They don't frequent the canal so much.

I'm cut to the heart. She's only a child and probably from a difficult background. Couldn't Billy Boy still love her? I asked him outright.

His eyes filled with tears. "Sure, I could."

"Then why not take her to a new life in the States?" I asked.

He shook his head. "She won't come. Her pimp got holda her, threatened her family."

It's a melodrama, something out of a nineteen twenties silent movie. But this is modern, near-millennium Dublin – I can't believe it.

I persisted. "But she wanted to go to America."

"She got scared, Peggy," he said.

So much for Irish Sweetheart Tours. For Irish hospitality. I suppose Billy Boy can't save Sally, if she doesn't want to be saved. But they seemed so good together. And now he won't have his little ones. Maybe love's too scary. At least Billy Boy's kind of love. I wonder did he know about her profession from the start, but didn't like to ask. He's a man of the world; surely he knew? I'd say so.

He hung around the house for his last day. I heard him singing in the bath, "If ya ever go across the sea to Ireland . . ."

Then, "The Sally Gardens".

Saturday 30th:

It's been the longest month of my life. A note from Billy Boy on the kitchen table when we got up this morning. It was written in the careful hand he'd learnt all those years ago in grade school with Charlie.

> *Hi Y'all,*
>
> *Couldn't sleep, so got a cab out to the airport. Don't worry, you guys, I'll be on that plane. Thanks for everything, y'all couldn't have been better to me. You're one lucky guy, Charlie, old buddy. Peggy's a great gal. You guys got it all.*
>
> *See you, old pal.*
>
> *Love,*
>
> *Billy Boy,*

We didn't hear a thing this morning. He must've crept out of the house like a mouse. He left me a beauty salon gift voucher for a facial and another bottle of bourbon for Charlie.

His note got to me. After all my griping, Billy Boy thinks I'm great. When I was so impatient with him – about his quest, his politics, even calling me "hon". Finally his very existence drove me crazy. He's a lonely man, that's all, thinking we have it all. We do have something. It may not be all, but it's something. Fed up with myself all day, so went to Rathmines library and checked the meaning of the "sally gardens" in the Yeats' poem.

"A sally: any of several eucalypts or acacias, resembling the willow." There are trees like that down by our canal. I'll think of Sally every time I see young lovers lying there. Or if I hear Roddy Doyle's name mentioned, or see the film, *The Commitments* – Sally with her smokes could've been one of its marvellous characters. But she's caught in an underworld of prostitution. How did she get sucked in? Was it because of drugs? You see evidence of this world in the banners hanging in certain parts of the city: ADDICTS WE CARE, PUSHERS BEWARE. But Sally didn't seem to be a user. Why then is she a prostitute?

Also checked on that soon-to-be-extinct New Zealand bird – it's a keria.

Later:

Today's post brought a letter from Uncle Tommie, my mother's older brother.

> *Dear Peggy,*
>
> *I was very glad indeed to hear from you. I'm getting old now and would like to see Ireland one more time before I die. I had hoped to see the four green fields united before my death, but that's unlikely to happen now. I'll try and come in the fall when the fares are down. Give Charlie my best.*
>
> *Your loving uncle,*
> *Thomas O'Hara*

We'll never hear from Billy Boy – he ain't the writin' type.

JUNE

Monday 15th:

No entries in the visitors' book this month. All quiet on the Khyber front, too. June wet so far. Rain day after day. Neighbours still say, "Lovely day," when you meet them.

I always agree.

Mrs Murphy says if the neighbourhood children don't get some sun soon, they'll develop rickets. She told me about her own childhood today, how on fine days her mother would walk them all down to Sandymount Strand for a day at the seaside. They'd bring ham sandwiches and milk in a bottle. They never had buckets and spades. Could listen to her all day. Life has been a struggle, yet she's always so cheerful. Ireland's so different from when she was young. People had a hard time then. A week in Kilkee was luxury for my parents in their youth. After I was born, my mother never went on holiday. Now everyone goes to Florida and Lanzarote.

Friday 19th:

Fuckoffey finished her exams. Asked Charlie was there any hope that she'd fail, but he was definitely not amused. Yesterday he launched her book in The Brazen Head pub. It's called *Msturbation* – no comment. We drove down there with about a hundred of the books to sell to any poor sap with money to waste. We got an old banger, an ancient mini – 1985, but in good condition for running round Dublin. (Mostly this means sitting still in traffic.) But today it wasn't bad and we got there on time. The pub had supplied sandwiches and Charlie paid for wine. About a hundred people came – mainly Trinity students and staff.

I watched from the edge of the crowd as my boyish husband introduced a young poet-lecturer from Trinity who did the honours. The lecturer praised Erin's freshness and vigour and wit and vivacity and sprightliness and passion and God-knows-what else.

Then she read the title poem – vigourously indeed, stamping her foot and ending each verse with with the line – "I fuck myself."

That's all I can remember.

What's she mean?

Have I been on the wrong track all this time? Up the wrong tree? Imagining trysts in seedy bedsits? No – across the room, Charlie was gazing too adoringly at her. But Erin's going back to America for the summer. So nothing can happen then, as he won't travel. But the thought sent me into a hot flush. God, it happens all the time now. Wine always makes me red in the face, but can't bear the thought of giving it up. Maybe I should give it up in social situations. Become a secret drinker when the colour of my face wouldn't matter.

After the reading, I chatted to a skinny young woman about the Northern Peace Process. It's in the news – Drumcree and all that marching and non-marching.

She looked outraged – what'd I said wrong?

"What'd you think of the reading?" she asked coldly.

"Well, it was good. Yes, vigorous."

"It was brill!"

My face on fire. "Yes, and she read it very well, too," I muttered apologetically.

The girl found someone else to talk to. I hid behind Erin's book. After a while she pounced over, bosoms bouncing, and beaming, as usual. "Peggy, dear! How sweet of you to come."

She smothered me in a kiss.

"Of course, I'd come!" I said.

"You look different!"

"I do?"

"Yes, you've got new glasses."

I felt they looked nice. "They were dear. The lenses are two strengths – one for reading and one for distance."

She grinned. "Presbyopia!"

"What's that?"

"Presbyopia. It's what you have – the first sign of middle age! What age are you?"

"Forty-five," I lied.

"Oh!" she grinned maddeningly. "Charlie said you were forty-nine."

The cad. But can't believe Erin. Watching her bound across the room, I couldn't help remembering the Jane Austen quote: "Imbecility in females is a great enhancement of their personal charms."

Why can't I tell Erin to shut up about age? I believe my theory of low self-esteem is right. It comes of having been slapped in school. This is all over the radio, newspapers nowadays. Everyone has been abused by someone, it's almost a necessity. Hate Erin. Hate her poetry. Hate her ageist comments. Hate the way she presses her bust into me when she talks. Is she trying to smother me? Most of all, hate the way she sucks up to my husband. She thinks stealing him's going to be a walkover. That I'm going to disappear, abandon the field to her. No, Peggy O'Hara's made of sterner stuff. I'm going for HRT tomorrow. Although I read in a magazine article there are awful side effects – breast tenderness or enlargement, depression, weight gain, lack of libido and increased blood pressure. Are women of our generation guinea pigs? Also, HRT's marketed as natural but comes from either pigs ovaries or the urine of pregnant mares. The poor things are put into foal to produce urine that can be sold for a huge profit. They're kept thirsty so the oestrogen levels in their urine are concentrated, and once the mare is too old to foal, she's sold to the knacker's yard. Don't know if I can go along with that. The article recommended diet and herbs.

Saturday 20th:
This afternoon Philomena dragged me into her house to see her wedding dress. It was Laura Ashley, a creamy satin, laid out on her couch with creamy satin-covered shoes. She's on a high, so the flag's flying for love. Mad about her eighty-year-old fiancé, Oliver – Ollie for short. The wedding's to be in a month. They're going to Portugal for the honeymoon. Afterwards he's going to buy her a coffee shop to run. Or else a delicatessen. Must say I like the sound of that. He sounds so practical.

We're invited to the wedding. Very touched.

She hugged me tearfully. "Thank you, Peggy."

I was puzzled. "I didn't do anything."

"You told me to live life. I'd never have met Ollie if you hadn't taken me in hand. You're a real friend, Peggy."

Felt better about everything. Philomena's got new glasses, too. Gold and nicer than mine. They make a big difference.

I'm slightly worried by her elation. Don't know why I said it, but did. "Love isn't the feeling when you eat chocolate, Philomena."

Her eyes bulged behind her glasses. "What is it?"

"It's more like porridge. A daily, solid thing."

"Like you and Charlie?"

I said nothing. My heart missed a beat. It does this all the time now. I wonder if anything's wrong? Maybe it's my age. Or worry about Charlie and Erin. I didn't say Charlie hates porridge. Won't eat it at all. But love isn't an infatuated "high". Just hope things work out for her. Said we'd go for a drink with her and Ollie tomorrow night. Charlie agreed. Still says he's going to buy Philomena some sexy underwear, then the wedding night will carry Ollie off and she'll be a rich widow.

Sunday 21st:
Met Ollie and Philomena for a drink. Charlie quite taken with him. He's a tall, thin, distinguished, white-haired man, quite presentable. They sat holding hands, sweetly, as we came in. He told us about his life in business. Apparently he's an entrepreneur and he's got businesses all over the place. Then the talk got on to poets. He thinks they all drink themselves to death. Charlie lectured him on this. Ollie puzzled that Charlie's semi-retired and makes no money from writing. Only from editing, which is starting to come in now. Much to my relief.

"My dry-cleaning business needs a manager," Ollie said.

Charlie thanked him profusely, but declined.

What a nice man. Philomena's problems may be over now. Marriage is the great stabiliser. Charlie now says he won't buy the sexy underwear. He likes Ollie too much. Invited them both to dinner instead.

Friday 26th:
Philomena and Ollie were expected for dinner today. Charlie bought champagne, and I cooked quail, grape and spinach tarts – got the recipe from the back of the quail wrapper.

You cook the spinach and drain well, then mix in the butter and add seasoning. Poach the grapes in a little water until warm; divide the spinach between the pastry cases and place a quail on top. Add the brandy to the roasting tin and boil rapidly for one min., then spoon over the quail. Garnish with grapes before serving.

They were ready by 8p.m. and smelt delicious.

At around 8.30p.m., Philomena came to the door, huffing and puffing and red in the face. "Oh, Peggy, I'm sorry, but Ollie won't come."

We were awfully flat. Apparently the man's getting cold feet. Feels too old to be a bridegroom and doesn't want to be a boyfriend. Very disappointing. Naturally, I assured Philomena it didn't matter. She could have dinner with us. But she wouldn't stay, so Charlie and I had quail tarts and champagne. It was a bit of an anti-climax.

Asked Charlie what he thought of the quail.

He mumbled something in reply – then ran for the bathroom with his hand in front of his mouth. Threw up. After all my efforts. The tarts were delicious, but that's what I get for trying to be creative.

Tuesday 30th:
This morning got the brilliant idea of hanging round the National Library at lunchtime to see if Charlie was having lunch with Erin. Well, I put on my headscarf and sunglasses, even though it was a grey day, and walked up and down Kildare Street for a while, around lunchtime. Charlie didn't come out. So finally I pretended to ask a guard outside the Dáil how I would visit the government buildings. At that point, just when I was caught in conversation and couldn't slink off without seeming suspicious, Charlie came out of the library gate. He was looking so handsome in his tweed jacket. My heart missed, as it always does when I see him unexpectedly.

He saw me immediately. "Peggy!"

"Charlie!"

"What're you doing here?"

"Eh – nothing. A coincidence. I came out for a walk."

He looked at my scarf and sunglasses, puzzled. "You're dressed for the weather?"

"I thought it might be hot."

He pushed up his hornrims and looked looked upward. "Hmm. Well, this is a nice surprise. Come and have lunch!"

We had a lovely lunch in Kilkenny Design. Am I going cracked or what?

Later:

June gone. Except for the rain it's been unremarkable. This morning brought another letter from Uncle Tommie.

> *Dear Peggy,*
> *I'm making arrangements to come to Ireland in the fall. I am keen to find our family's plot in Kerry, as I want to be buried there. I suppose you will know where it is, as you will have buried your mother there. If not, will you make enquiries?*
> *Your loving Uncle Tommie.*

What's it with Americans and graves? Mother's buried with my father in their own grave in Glasnevin cemetery. I've only visited it once, although I think about them every day of my life. Especially my mother. A relationship doesn't end because a person dies. It's like they've gone into another room. A cliché, but true. Charlie still has that anti-cancer diet book by his bed. What does this mean? He still won't eat salads, but he's making more of an effort with fresh vegetables and fruit. He has a grapefruit every morning. At least that's something, but I'm still worried. I don't believe all that bilge about a friend of a friend in the library.

JULY

Wednesday 1st:

Nothing much happening. Erin's gone home to New Jersey for the summer, but Charlie still gets twice-weekly epistles from her. It's getting me down. He seems to think this is quite natural and I'm mad to object. He says I'm turning into a jealous, suspicious person and I was never like that. Am I? No, I'm an anesthetised patient on an operating table who feels the pain of the knife but is unable to shout, STOP!

Also, getting more hot flushes.

Went to the doctor who said I was perimenopausal – sounds like some sort of seaweed. Prescribed HRT patches. But is this modern medicine making a disease out of middle age? And I'm not that happy about the ill-treatment of mares. Prefer natural remedies. So went to the health shop in Swan Centre for herbs. A girl there helpfully listed the physical and psychological symptoms of menopause in store for me – excessive sweating, palpitations, joint pains, cramp, headaches, fatigue and reduced libido. Then she recommended alfalfa, kelp and St John's wort for anxiety. Agnus castus for hormonal misfunction. Sage for hot flushes. Motherwort for help with palpitations. Eleutherococcus or Siberian ginseng for energy levels.

Ended up getting HRT patch.

No ill effects – so far. Except last night in bed couldn't find it. Then discovered it stuck on Charlie.

"What's this?" He pulled it off his leg.

I grabbed it back. "My oestrogen patch."

"Jesus!"

"It's OK – prescribed by the doctor."

"For you!" He jumped out of bed, wailing, "Now I'll grow breasts!"

Told him not to be an idiot. After he'd calmed down, he said he hoped they knew what they were doing. I said there's no history of breast cancer in my family. Asked again why he was still reading the cancer health books – how to lick it, when he had. Was everything OK with him? Had he any new symptoms? He kissed me good-night and said not to worry, that he was still advising that friend-of-a-friend who has leukemia. Sounds fishy. Never known him to take the slightest interest in health matters. Even his illness didn't make him give up smoking. Should I be worried?

Saturday 18th:

No breasts for Charlie, but more visitors for us – this time just for dinner. Phone went at 7a.m. this morning. I staggered down the stairs to get it.

It was my friend, Bobbye Ann Gross.

She and her husband, Tom, are old New York neighbours. We once lived in the same upper West Side apartment building. They've stopped off from a tour of the British Isles and are in Dublin for a few days. On Tuesday they're meeting a coach in London to do the Lake District and Scotland – lucky dogs. Never been to the Lake District or Scotland, but there's not much chance this year. Not with our mortgage repayments.

They're not staying with us – absolutely their own choice. So, invited them to dinner tonight.

Firstly I was late home – a bad start.

I had to deliver some work to Drumcondra. Then it took me about two hours to drive back to Rathmines. I'd have been as well off on a bus. Or better still, on foot. Still, I had everything planned and under control: if you're entertaining, keep it simple, according to dear Julia — then relax and enjoy your friends. So I'd popped a free-range chicken in the oven, instructing Charlie to turn it down as soon as it started sizzling. Of course, he forgot, so smoke billowed from the kitchen as I got back.

Almost smothered at the front door.

Held my breath and ran into the kitchen to turn the oven off. Our guests were being entertained by Charlie with aperitifs and pre-dinner snacks in the sitting room, so obviously hadn't noticed.

I opened the kitchen window and smoke cascaded out. As I took out the charred chicken and put it on top of the stove, my eyes smarted and my breath caught.

Charlie came in then, oblivious. "What happened? I was worried."

I swiped at the air with a tea towel. "Traffic! Pity you didn't worry about this!" I pointed to the burnt bird. "You didn't lower the oven!"

He blinked vaguely. "Was I supposed to? Is it OK?"

"It'll have to be!"

Charlie slunk away, muttering apologies. Couldn't start a row. Hate people who quarrel in front of guests. But, honestly, if I don't write everything down (things like "turn off the oven, if the house appears to be on fire"), I can forget it. Charlie won't cook either — he'll only complain about my cooking. He'd probably starve to death if I wasn't here. The chicken was dried-out but looked edible inside — the smoke was mainly from burning fat. It was too late for something else, so I carved it up and put it on a serving plate — "what the eye can't see" and all that.

Then I noticed the gin bottle half empty.

Charlie'd bought an old expensive London Dry bottle from our local pub and filled it with some cheap Irish gin to fool Tom – who claims to be a gin gourmet, but never notices the difference in martinis. I never knew it, but gin varies enormously. As does beer. And Scotch whisky. We were visiting the Grosses in their New York apartment once, and Tom showed Charlie his large collection of single malt whisky – there were about fifty different bottles in a press. I never even knew there was such a thing as single malts either. It tasted of something funny – musty water, or smoky turf, or maybe unwashed socks.

Charlie was back. "Need help?"

He was on gin martinis. I pointed to the bottle. "This was full."

He frowned. "S-so it was."

"Well, don't get drunk!"

Charlie put on his look of injured innocence. He always does when he's guilty. Oh, he doesn't have a drink problem – yet. I just worry that he'll get one. It was my fault for being so late. But why martinis? They always make him drunk – he's a whiskey man.

I greeted our guests in the living room, apologising.

It's a May-December relationship, a second marriage. Tom's older, an English professor from Columbia, who's written a series of best-sellers on prose style. And Bobbye Ann's in her thirties, the author of a charming children's book – she's from somewhere in South Carolina or Virginia. Maybe that's why she insists on spelling her name in this odd way. (I suppose one book makes you a writer – she has an agent and all.) Tom's huge – about six feet four with thick, yellowing white hair and a goatee beard and horn rims. He'd be handsome except for his dewlap. Mostly he reminds me of a gigantic Burl Ives and bulges out of his outsized clothes. He always wears the rumpled garb of an American academic – button-down Oxford shirt, navy blazer, grey slacks.

He bear-hugged me. "Hi, Peggy."

There was drink on his breath, and his kind spaniel eyes were bloodshot. Tom had obviously hit the martinis, too.

Bobbye Ann was on G & T.

"Peggy!" She kissed me, smelling of expensive soap. Her apple-pink cheeks were soft. "You're so good to invite us."

Bobbye Ann's a small, perky woman who, even in high heels, barely comes to Tom's elbow. She's a twin-set and pearls type and wears expensive label clothes. She doesn't bother to dye her already grey spiky hair. It's cut in a short pudding-bowl style and she wears thick, round, milk-bottle-type glasses for terrible sight, and has *terribly* strong views on everything.

But I love her eccentricity. In New York we met weekly for cappuccino and chat. She can discuss all the latest women's fiction. In that area, she's about the best-read person I've met. And she'd brought me a beautiful silk paisley scarf. That's another thing about the Grosses – their generosity.

I took it out of the box. "It's beautiful, Bobbye Ann."

Charlie got a bottle of single malt Scotch – something he could never afford himself. We chatted briefly about old times. Then I went to see to dinner. Bobbye Ann offered to help, but the kitchen's too small. If there's anything I can't stand, it's being crowded in my lovely little kitchen. So declined.

As I left, Charlie offered more drink.

Tom was already drunk, so I looked warningly at Charlie. "Dinner's nearly ready."

He ignored me, collecting glasses. "Then we'll have a half one."

Bobbye Ann put a hand over hers. "Not for me, thank you."

Charlie went to Tom. "Let me replenish yours."

"Well," said Tom owlishly. "It's not noffen we're oudt."

I went oudt – to the kitchen.

Charlie followed with the empty glasses.

I was about to warn him about drink again, but Bobbye Ann tip-tapped officiously after us. "I'm checking the menu, Peggy," she said.

"It's roast chicken." I was nervous she'd see it was burnt.

Bobbye Ann's allergic to everything – milk products, onions, you name it, the list's endless. But the chicken was free-range, and I'd strictly excluded onions from the stuffing, milk products from the mashed potatoes and gravy, so hoped everything was OK.

As I coped with the sizzling gravy, Bobbye Ann peered disapprovingly at the charred carcass. I thought she'd say something about its semi-edible state, but no – she asked what it had been fed on?

I hadn't a clue.

She peered through her thick glasses. "Not wheat?"

"Wheat? I doubt it. It's free-range, Bobbye Ann. Maybe grass?"

She sniffed. "Never heard o' chickens eatin' grass. Back home they're corn-fed."

I remembered those jaundiced American chickens, because Charlie refused to eat them, insisting they'd been doctored. It's another one of his cracked notions. Impossible to persuade him that they'd been fed on yellow corn and hence their colour. But what do they feed Irish chickens? Didn't know. But didn't want Bobbye Ann having one of those bad reactions you read about, so offered to get something else – a little fresh fish perhaps? The shops were still open.

But she stuck with chicken.

I made the salad dressing. I'd bought more of Rose's expensive Balsamic vinegar. At over three pounds a bottle, it's gourmet, but I wanted the best for our guests. As I got ready to douse the salad, Bobbye Ann freaked. "You're not putting *that* on my salad!"

I was taken aback. "What's wrong with it?"

She peered belligerently at the brown mixture. "The vinegar."

"It's the best!"

"Fermented!"

I read the label, puzzled. "It's gourmet, Bobbye Ann. Look, red wine vinegar."

"It could kill me!"

I stared at her. "K-kill you?"

"I'm allergic to fermented vinegars, must have distilled."

"Distilled?"

All this vinegar stuff is news to me. How can you live for fifty years and not know that there's a basic difference in vinegars of all things? It varies, the same as gin and whiskey, as Bobbye Ann now informed me. Luckily Mrs Murphy was still open, so I dashed to the shop. She badly wanted to chat. The news about another paedophile priest had just broken, and she was having difficulties believing it. She's terribly disillusioned with the Catholic Church, which is understandable, considering a new horror story breaks daily.

True, but said I couldn't stop now. I'd talk to her in the morning. And when I asked for the distilled vinegar, she looked at me crossly. She was about to say that she hadn't any of those fancy American things and I ought to know that by now, when I pointed to the shelf behind her. "There it is!"

"Where?" She turned to the row of white Cross and Blackwell – *distilled* malt vinegar bottles.

I laughed, saying she thought she was a neighbourhood grocery, but was a gourmet shop all the time.

But she muttered crossly, "Americans will be the death of me."

"Me, too!" I grabbed the bottle and ran.

This vinegar would take the paint off doors, but Bobbye Ann

wanted it. Her dressing turned out to be breath-catchingly acidic. Tasted some on a teaspoon, coughing, as I passed it to Bobbye Ann. "Should I add sugar?"

Bobbye Ann sipped the teaspoon officiously. "Certainly not!"

"You're diabetic?"

"No, but sugar's toxic."

A scientist once told me it was the purest food, by which he meant no additives. As Bobbye Ann washed her hands, I began to worry about the chicken. Poked around in the bin and retrieved its plastic wrapping – damn, it'd been fed on wheat! God. What now? Would Bobbye Ann choke? Asphyxiate, like I'd once seen in a movie? But nothing I could do now, or the men would be completely plastered. So when everything was on the table – the salad bowl, the two dressings, the carved up chicken, the stuffing in a dish, the vegetables in another dish, the Ballymaloe Cranberry sauce spooned out – I called the men in.

"Yes, dear," Charlie called back sweetly. Then joked *sotto voce.* "Hurry now, Peggy'll be angry if the meal gets cold."

He always says this – it's completely untrue. But they came quickly, looking at me guardedly.

Charlie held a chair for Bobbye Ann.

He was holding his drink, but Tom swayed alarmingly as he sat down, clumsily clattering the chair on the hard kitchen tiles. He's older and had to be tired from the long flight the previous night. Then the flight over here from London. But he garrulously ate a big dinner, admiring my cooking all the way. Inwardly I thanked Julia Child – she's helped me more than anyone in the world, and I never had the chance to thank her. She's dead now. But it shows the power of a book. Your influence can live on.

Dinner turned into a disaster – hope it won't be their last with us.

It went on for hours. The chat was loud and raucous – just like Tom – and focused firstly on Clinton's problems. Whether or not Monica would testify to having an affair with him. We talked about sneaky Linda Tripp's tape.

"It'd never be admitted in a court of law," Tom said. "It's illegal to tape people without their consent."

Strangely, Bobbye Ann thought Linda Tripp a patriot. She's terribly politically correct and used to write to the *New York Times* about the use of the word "black", rather than "African-American".

"Clinton needs to be stopped," she announced, looking to me for support. "We women have had enough."

Torn between my liberal values and my personal predicament, I said, "I'm sorry for Hillary."

"Ah, now wait a minute," Charlie held up his hand. "Bill's being persecuted, not prosecuted."

I stared him down. Of course, he'd have sympathy with Clinton, being in the same position himself. Erin/Monica, they're two of a kind. Sex-groupies. Marriage wreckers. Ageist tramps.

"Honey," Tom drawled in my direction, "Clinton's doing what all men do, given the opportunity."

"All men?"

"Sure, honey."

I glared at Charlie.

He looked away.

"It ain't the first time there's been ass in the Oval Office, honey. Most presidents have had a bit there."

I was getting hot. "Most?"

"Except Nixon."

Me hotter. "How do you know?"

Tom shook his dewlap. "Didn't have the balls, honey."

So that was it – a matter of balls. I was about to say something else, but Charlie changed the subject to Tom's latest opus; *A Guide to Better Style* has just come out. Tom sent Charlie an advance copy. The first of the guides, *A Guide to Good Style*, was a Book of the Month Club choice and sold over two million copies. The irony is that Charlie doesn't think it's good at all. Naturally, he doesn't quite say this to his old pal and drinking neighbour, Tom, although he teases him about his writing standards. But this doesn't make one whit of difference to their friendship. Tom's a sweetheart who just laughs at Charlie's impossibly (he says) high standards. He calls Charlie an egghead, and too intellectual for his own good. But if we ever go back to America, Tom's recommendation could get Charlie a JOB. He's that BIG in publishing circles. Not that this would ever occur to my darling Charlie. So we had to show them a good time. Apart from that – they're old friends and we wanted to.

Anyway, Tom believes good writing's colloquial – whatever you say is good – a let-it-all-hang-out American dream of instant success. But Charlie says good style's something you work for. And if you want to read up on how to attain it, you don't go to Gross's Guides, but study Fowler, Partridge or Wilson Follett.

Charlie was in full flight on this theme last night. "American vernacular depends on the empty repetition of vague thought, the breakdown of syntax. . ."

Tom chuckled. "You're an egghead, Charlie, but I love ya."

Charlie went on. ". . . the flat and colloquial diction that depends heavily on cliché."

I'd heard it all before, so studied Bobbye Ann for symptoms of allergic reaction. She looked OK, maybe, like me, a little irritated at the men for hitting the martinis so hard. But there was no sign of a swelling neck or the bulging eyes of asphyxia or of any other bad reaction to the chicken.

We had strawberries for desert – Irish. Nothing like them for flavour, but as I carried them proudly to the table, Bobbye Ann quipped, "You're trying to kill me!"

Me in shock.

She gripped her throat. "Strawberries!"

They looked a little on the unripe side, but OK otherwise.

"You have to be careful of Peggy," Charlie elbowed Bobbye Ann, whispering, "Don't get on her bad side."

As the visitors exchanged nervous glances, I wanted to hit Charlie. It seems strawberries can send Bobbye Ann into toxic shock, bring about instant anaphylactic death. She can't eat cheese either. It clashes with her depression medication. She risked decaff. The men did, too, generously pouring brandy into theirs. I eyed Charlie again to stop drinking, but he ignored me.

After dinner we retired to the sitting room.

The men had more brandy and talked more about old times. Finally Charlie got up, stammering, "I'll walk ya home, Bobby-T-Tom and Ann."

Bobbye Ann bristled – like a cat with fur rising. "It's Bobbye Ann!"

Charlie hiccuped. "Yes, I mean Bobbye-T-T-Ann and Tom!"

I swore to kill him.

Then, as we all stood up, Tom was footless. He reeled drunkenly against his minuscule wife. As he fell on the couch, she jumped back, screaming. Her glasses were knocked off, and she waved the air, squinting blindly. Luckily Tom wasn't hurt, but lay on his back, flapping his arms like a huge upside-down turtle. Charlie, suddenly sober and no longer fooling around, got him up. "Come on, old son. Hippy-hop! Upsy-boopsy!"

I found Bobbye Ann's glasses.

She grabbed them, barking. "Thank you!"

God, was she mad with me? It was all Charlie's fault for fixing such strong drinks – he always does it with Tom. Charlie now had his shoulder under the older man's arm. Tom towered over him and reeled drunkenly, nearly falling over again, but steadying himself at the last minute. "I wanna thank ya, hon."

He kissed me wetly.

How would Charlie get him home? I felt OK but was over the limit for driving. And Charlie wasn't going near the car. I suggested a taxi, as the older man's eyes bulged alarmingly. "D-don't n-need no taxi, hon."

"Trust me, old son," Charlie coaxed, as they swayed to the front door.

On the street they bumped into Poopdeck Pappy. He was loitering outside our house, weaving drunkenly, too, and singing that there were empty saddles in the old corral. Tom hugged him and, digging for his wallet, gave him twenty pounds. Why didn't Charlie stop him? Poopdeck would only get drunker now. But the three of them zig-zagged off up the terrace to Mount Pleasant Avenue and the square, with Bobbye Ann tip-tapping crossly in the rear. Although thirty years younger, she definitely wore the pants in the relationship. Charlie's Freudian slip was accurate.

I did the dishes, swearing to murder Charlie when he got back. But my anger evaporated as the hours passed and he didn't return. Where was he? Had he run into Erin? No, she was meant to be in New Jersey. But what if she wasn't? And was it true that all men are at it, except poor, ball-less Nixon?

Time passed. Where was Charlie? He'd only gone round the corner to Belgrave Square. If the Grosses were staying with us, I wouldn't have had the worry. I did ask them, but they wrote, asking me to check out a small hotel there, so I did. I must admit to relief about this. After Henry and Rose, I'm nervous of couples

– particularly American couples. They're all too gourmet and used to too much, and Khyber Place, much as I love it, is a bit of a culture shock.

An ill-favoured thing but mine own.

Oh, we have ice now, plenty. A coffee machine and a cappuccino maker, but that's about all. We still don't have a microwave, dishwasher, washing machine, dryer, shower, food processor or kitchen weighing scales.

I blamed myself for the evening's disaster. I invited the Grosses for dinner and was late. I'd promised we'd do things together – after all, they've come all the way from England to see us, and Tom's very fond of Charlie and vice versa. It's probably a bit of a father-son thing. Charlie helped him get his first book published – he actually introduced Tom to his ex-employers, who published Gross's Guides, as they're called all over the States. It's hard to describe the stature Tom has. He's a sort of writing guru. He gets asked on to chat shows, etc., and people in America revere him in the same way as they revere the late Joseph Campbell or that man in England who writes about empty raincoats – I forget his name. But then Tom doesn't get drunk on TV.

Finally went to bed, but couldn't sleep, imagining the worst. Charlie'd been arrested for drunkenness. He was hurt. They'd both fallen and Tom had crushed him to a pulp. Why hadn't I gone with them? Called a taxi? I was about to ring the guards when Charlie fumbled with the key in the lock. As I came down the stairs, he stumbled in. Thank God, he was OK.

He smiled drowsily. "You still up, sweetheart?"

I was so relieved. "Where *were* you?"

"Got Tom as far as the square, but he fell again there. Couldn't get him up. Bobbye Ann was no help – all she did was gripe."

"I don't blame her. Was Tom hurt?"

Charlie grimaced. "No, God looks after drunks. But I strained my back."

"Seriously?"

He shook his head and, sighing, sat down on the bottom stair. "Luckily an off-duty guard saw us and helped get him to the B & B and into bed. Well, we got chatting and had a pint . . ."

"He didn't arrest you for drunkenness?"

"Don't be mad."

"You could've phoned."

"Sorry. On my way home, I stumbled over Poopdeck. Had to get him to his house. It's a t-terrible mess. We should go down and clean it up."

I married a drunk, but a kind one. "You're two of kind."

"C'mon, gimme a kiss."

I did and went back to bed.

Charlie sat on the stairs, murmuring sleepily, "I'm tired, Egypt, tired."

Fell asleep and dreamt of Nixon. Maybe we misjudged him?

Sunday 19th:
Things worse.

Overreacted last night – see that now. Charlie hardly ever drinks too much. Yesterday he was badly hung over and sorry, I knew, although he didn't say so. His back still hurt, so I said nothing more. The strain of visitors made him overdo the martinis.

Well, I'll begin at the beginning – the Grosses appeared on our doorstep about noon. Tom looked fine, and Bobbye Ann was chirpy again. After lunch *à la moi*, they said they'd take us out to dinner that evening, so we suggested Bray. Being on the DART, along with Howth, it's become a port of call. I love the Victorian seediness of the seafront, and the children playing on the strand with buckets and spades bring back my childhood. Tom's another Joycean and wanted to see the James Joyce home at the end of Martello Terrace, so they agreed to go there. The house appears in *A Portrait of the Artist as a Young Man*. The famous Christmas dinner row was set in the dining room. I'm not a Joycean, but it was something to do before dinner.

Because of Tom's size, we didn't all fit in the mini – so Charlie drove Tom, who hates walking. His knees were almost coming through the roof of the tiny car, and his weight tilted it alarmingly to one side as they took off toward Mount Pleasant Avenue, Ranelagh and the N11. Bobbye Ann and I bussed down to the DART. She wanted to see the famous sea views from the train. For the first time, we seemed to recapture our friendship and started discussing recent novels we'd read. I'm particularly fond of Alice Munro's short stories, but Bobbye Ann didn't share my enthusiasm about her latest collection – said it conned the reader. Shocked – couldn't say anything, except the woman's a genius. New York seemed a world away. We had to wait for a train, and this irked Bobbye Ann. All the way out she grumped about the wet Irish climate, insisting that her hotel was damp.

I was surprised. "Ask them to turn on the heat."

"I don't need a steam bath."

Why was she complaining like this? Could it be that bad? I checked the hotel myself. It was fine – comfortable without being luxurious, clean and new with en suite bathrooms. I actually tried the beds – firm – and there was a TV lounge in posh pink Regency style. It's not my taste and won't be the Grosses, but they're only sleeping there. I listened patiently until we came out of the tunnel at Dalkey and saw the spectacular view of the bay. This distracted Bobbye Ann for the moment.

The men were already at the Joyce house. As Tom raved about

it, Charlie claimed that the famous Christmas Day quarrel had
happened somewhere else – in a house called Leoville on Carysfort
Avenue. Charlie isn't quite as fanatic as Tom, although he knows a
lot about literary Dublin.

"But they walked around the Head before dinner," Tom argued.

"Yes, but the Joyces lived elsewhere. The story's dated from the
death of Parnell when they'd moved from here."

Tom knocked on the hall door and, when a young man
answered, drawled, "I believe James Joyce lived here once?"

"And we do now!" the young man quipped. But he invited us
into the front room, where the famous quarrel had taken place.
There were photographs of Joyce and a big mahogany dining table.
I walked around it, thinking of the famous novel with its sumptu-
ous description of roast turkey. We all signed the visitors' book.

When we came out, the weather had changed and a chilly wind
whipped up the waves. The men were keen to play golf on the
Head, so we walked up the Esplanade. A small group of
Romanian-looking men were playing some lively gypsy music –
certainly bringing colour to the place. Bobbye Ann grumbled
about it being off-key or something – if she wanted music she'd
play it at home. Then our men left us at the foot of the Head,
while we women went on to the Cliff Walk.

I remarked the everything was so beautiful, and Bobbye Ann
agreed. She pointed to the cross on the Head. "What's that?"

"A cross –"

"I can see that! Who put it there?"

"It was erected in Holy Year, I think."

She wrinkled her nose. "Hmm, a pity Ireland's so Catholic."

"Only the south," I reasoned.

"It's such an intolerant religion."

"But getting more liberal."

Amazed at myself sticking up for the Catholic Church – spent my life running away from it. And actually I'd often thought if only the IRA could blow up the cross on Bray Head, it mightn't be a bad thing. It dominates everything – like the Papal Cross in the Park. It couldn't be good for ecumenism. But walked on in silence. Bobbye Ann puffing and huffing and obviously unhappy about something else.

"You OK?" I asked nervously.

"It's too hilly for me!" she panted.

We were on the flat, and she wasn't out of her thirties. I asked did she have asthma, but no. "Let's rest on the grass then."

"That's too damp!"

I suggested a bench, but that was too cold. "I'm sorry Charlie poured such strong drinks last night," I said.

"Yes, I'm pretty mad with him. Tom, too!"

So that was it. I shrugged. "My fault. I was late with dinner."

"They're grown men, Peggy."

At least we'd cleared the air. Bobbye Ann was alarmed by the vandalised sign – BROKEN FRIDGES, FALLING SOCKS – but assured her there was no danger. Cliff Walk beautiful – the sea's bluer and wild flowers more plentiful than anywhere else. And all so accessible to Dublin. But lost on Bobbye Ann, who seems bent on hating everything. When we all lived in New York, she'd talked of nothing else but visiting Ireland one day. Now she's here and hates it. Why did she come?

She stopped, shivering, at the wall. "The sea looks icy. How can you stand this climate?"

"I'm used to it." You don't come to Ireland for weather. Why hadn't she gone to Madeira or the Greek islands? The Canaries? I suddenly had a vision of Bobbye Ann falling over the cliff. She lay on the rocks below, her expensive Burberry raincoat spread out like a batwoman's cape. The sea roared over her prone and tangled body. Was this wishful thinking? Did murders happen like this? Was I a killer? Or a crime writer *manqué*?

We finally returned to the golf course and waited for the men. Bobbye Ann shivered, although it wasn't cold, and spoke to me in monosyllables. I gave up making conversation and waved with relief when I saw Charlie and Tom at the last hole. As they gave back their rented clubs, I knew by Charlie's glum face that all was not well.

"My score was 96 – ten strokes worse than last time," he moaned. "Tom had a hole in one."

Tom put an arm around him. "You got fresh air, pal. And exercise."

"I've never done anything for the exercise!"

We squeezed into the car and drove to the Chinese restaurant in Bray's Main Street. I'd picked it because it was good, without being too expensive. The Grosses are rich, but we didn't want to stick them for an expensive meal. We were all comfortably seated in a booth and contemplating one of those all-in dinners for four, when Bobbye Ann snapped her menu shut. "I can't eat any of that!"

We both looked at her, as Tom kept studying his menu.

"I'm allergic to monosodium glutamate," she announced.

It gives her a rash or something. So she had plain grilled sole. I had my usual, sizzling prawns with cashew nuts, Charlie had his Peking Duck and Tom ordered a combination dish, plus a side order of duck with pancakes. We all had soup to start. All sorts of noodley stuff floated in it, and Tom thought it very good. He told the waiter it beat anything in the States.

I was relieved. Our old friends were enjoying themselves at last, the idiocy of last night forgotten. The meal was going well and the wine had a warming effect on us all. Despite her early grumbling and griping, Bobbye Ann appeared mellower and seemed to eat her fish without any trauma. The conversation lulled a bit, so during the main course, I brought up the topic of political correctness in publishing.

Bobbye Ann blinked behind her thick glasses. "It's about time they cleaned up their act."

She argued strongly for political correctness.

But Charlie disagreed with her.

Basically I think people should be called whatever they want to be called, but Charlie has strong views about freedom of speech. He believes that PC is a right-wing conspiracy. A sort of inverted insult to whoever you're trying not to insult. It's just his opinion, but Bobbye Ann was shocked.

"I don't believe this," she kept muttering. "You don't approve of PC?"

As Charlie shook his head, she was about to explode.

I nudged Charlie, trying to change the subject, but it was no use – he was in full flight. "They shouldn't bowdlerise masterpieces like *Huckleberry Finn*."

Bobbye Ann put down her fork. "You mean African-American children should hear a member of their race being referred to as *Nigger* Jim?"

"You'd prefer Black Jim? African-American Jim?" Charlie was polite, but his eyes glittered. I know that look. He'd give no quarter now. Being anti-PC had got him into trouble in his old company. It was one of the reasons we left – besides his health and the old man's murder.

Tom looked worriedly at his wife. He offered the Chinese pancakes around, but no takers.

I had to get Charlie and Bobbye Ann away from the cliff-edge of a quarrel, so chirped in with. "What about Conrad's *The Nigger of the Narcissus?*"

Bobbye Ann pursed her lips. "That's highly offensive?"

"What's offensive?" Charlie snapped.

Bobbye Ann shuddered. "That *word*."

Charlie laughed shortly. "Nigger had different connotations in those days. The book's a masterpiece."

All this time, Tom was eating silently. Now he turned to Bobbye Ann. "I taught it in class once, and a black girl walked out."

Bobbye Ann outraged. "You never told me that."

He tackled his duck pancakes good-humouredly, rolling one skillfully around the duck, sauce and spring onions. "Honey, I can't remember to tell you everything."

She bristled like some mad cat.

Oh, God, I prayed, don't let them quarrel. I hate quarrelling, so tried desperately to save the day. "Before going to the States, I thought it was just another slang word – you know, short for being of African-American heritage."

Bobbye Ann frowned. "I'm deeply shocked, Peggy."

"But . . ." I'd made matters worse. "But what about *Paddy*?"

"That's not offensive!"

I tried to joke. "Maybe the Irish have more humour, despite having so many Catholics."

This didn't go down well at all. Bobbye Ann picked up her fork, then put it down again and pushed her plate away. "This discussion has taken away my appetite."

Charlie and I looked despairingly at each other. We'd done it now. Yesterday was bad enough, but this meal wouldn't mend matters. I thought of the Joyce house we'd visited – the scene of that other famous political quarrel a hundred years ago. Now we were in another quarrel.

Tom turned kindly to his wife. "I think you're overreacting, my dear."

"But I'm offended!" She pushed her plate away and refused to eat another thing.

We finished up in silence.

Dead silence.

What is it with visitors? I was doing my best, but losing again. Some people aren't any good when out of their own environment. Bobbye Ann is like one of those turtles washed up by the Gulf Stream. She feels threatened and out of control when in foreign waters. This would never happen if we were all safely back in New York.

Finished our meal. Then Charlie drove them back. The car was even more lopsided now with Tom and Bobbye Ann's weight and, afraid the four of us wouldn't make it, I took the DART. I wanted to be by myself for a time. I felt so badly about everything. Sorry that Bobbye Ann hadn't enjoyed her walk. Guilty about upsetting her in the restaurant. We should've kept off certain topics.

When I got home, Charlie was in bed, reading Tom's latest guide book.

"Did they calm down in the car?" I asked.

"No."

"It was my fault for bringing up the subject."

"Rubbish."

"Bobbye Ann doesn't seem happy. Yet she has all the power in the relationship."

Charlie humphed and went on with his book. "This stuff's like giving someone a paddle boat to cross the Atlantic!"

I undressed tiredly and got into bed. "It's too colloquial?"

"It sure is! Listen to this: 'I say it's not getting much better in Russia because in lots of ways, the situation is worse since the fall of communism. For instance, this very problem of inflation and other problems. I think there is a tough job ahead, the toughest of

them all, I think, as far as Russia is concerned, is the problem . . .' "
He broke off. "Peggy, you're not listening to me."

I was, but only with one ear. I was falling asleep, thinking of my
hallucination of Bobbye Ann falling over the cliff. Maybe I should
write a murder mystery.

He went on reading. "Listen to this – 'Yes, the toughest job we
have to do is cope with rising inflation.' My God!" He threw down
the book.

Almost asleep, I drowsily confessed my murderous fantasy.
What did it mean?

Charlie was matter of fact. "You wanted to kill her."

I sat up, horrified. "What?"

"And I'll watch my back from now on!"

"But, Charlie –"

He laughed loudly. "Pity you didn't shove her over!"

I started to say something else, but he wouldn't listen. "Go to
sleep!"

I couldn't. Lay awake for most of the night. If the Grosses had
stayed in New York, Bobbye Ann would still be my best friend. I'd
have the most happy nostalgic memories about all our conversa-
tions over cappuccino on modern fiction. Now everything's
changed. And worse – I'm a potential killer.

In the middle of the night, I got up and read some psychology
in one of Charlie's encyclopaedias. Jung was consoling. We all have
murderous moments, but recognising them is a way of controlling
them. Only suppressed urges are dangerous. I imagined all mine
spilling out like the insides of a couch. Still, Bobbye Ann was probably safe enough.

Monday 20th:
Afraid we've lost a friendship – after all our efforts at being nice.

Tom'll get over the quarrel about political correctness – he'll laugh it off with Charlie – but there's a bitterness in Bobbye Ann. My mother always said, if you're nice to people when they come and nice to them when they leave, they'll forget what happened in between. This is my hope for the Grosses. In an effort to mend matters, Charlie and Tom spent the day at the races. Tom won a hundred and fifty pounds, while Charlie lost fifty. GRR!! He didn't take Tom's advice on a tip. Honestly, Tom doesn't know anything about Irish racing, yet he backed all the winners. Bobbye Ann entertained herself sightseeing in Dublin and came back full of praise for the National Art Gallery and the Book of Kells. She liked something at last. Amazing. And she acted as if she wanted to be friends again, inviting us both out to dinner. It went OK, kept off any dangerous topics. Fences mended, I think.

Tuesday 21st:
Charlie drove Bobbye Ann and Tom out to the airport this morning. They're catching an early plane and meeting their tour in London. I stayed home, writing this. I'm beginning to think visiting doesn't work. Why? Is it the cultural shock? Or did Bobbye Ann have PMT or something? Was it all my fault?

Same old story – terrible traffic. I dreaded Charlie being in a bad mood, but when he got back, he was in great form and hugged me, laughing with relief. We have our lives back. We could go back to our non-gourmet diet of boring gruel. He could watch his cowboy films in peace. But he looked solemn. "Guess what Bobbye Ann asked me in the middle of O'Connell Street?"

I couldn't.

"How could I stand living with so many Catholics?"

I was puzzled. "What'd you say?"

He squeezed me tight. "Told her it was hard. They don't wash and they breed like rabbits, but they have a natural sense of rhythm!"

I laughed, too. "Not this one."

He rock-and-rolled me round the kitchen.

How's that for PC?

Charlie very loving. Maybe he's seen that a younger wife doesn't always bring happiness. There's something about an old wife. Sometimes another marriage helps you to see your own more clearly. At least I can thank the Grosses for that. We have a good one really and hardly ever quarrel – except for Erin. Am I wrong about her? Wonder how her ghastly book's doing? Didn't ask and wasn't told. Only one review so far – a consolingly ghastly one in *Books Ireland*. Yippee! Still, wonder what tomorrow's post will bring. More epistles?

Wednesday 29th:
Monica Lewinsky's back in the news. She and her mother granted immunity from prosecution. It looks bad for Clinton if she tells all. Honestly, I hate the way Clinton's being hounded. Yet feel very sorry for myself at being in the same position as Hillary – married to a groper. Am I? Now that Erin's away, nothing's happening, but she'll be coming back in the fall.

Thursday 30th:
July very wet on the whole. No other news. The other day Mrs Murphy knocked on the door. She looked very worried. Told me Charlie's barking up the lane again. Was he OK?

I said to ignore him.

Can't help wondering sometimes if he's quite sane.

Friday 31st:
A letter from Charlie's grandson this morning.

He read it silently and passed it to me – the handwriting was childish, but neat.

> *grandpa,*
> *i won't call you "dear," cos it's a dumb convention, and you may not be such a dear. also i don't know you. if you care to redress this bad scene, i can visit this month. please reply soon, cos mom says i need to make reservations. she's well and says hello.*
> *yours etc.,*
> *jake foley*

We'd always known him as Jacob. I remember him as a fat, square baby, who screamed for his mom every time I went near him. It was very disconcerting. But he's fourteen now and apparently a bit of an intellectual like Charlie. Feel a bit weary, but it'll be interesting to see how he's turned out.

Charlie looked at the letter again. "He doesn't seem to approve of capital letters . . ." He read from it slowly: " 'you may not be such a dear.' Hmm . . . what's he mean by that?"

He was hurt – I knew.

I read over his shoulder. "I suppose 'dear's' a silly convention. It is really – everyone you write to isn't a dear, or dear to you."

"But I'm his grandfather!"

Even though it was so long ago, Charlie still feels guilty about the failure of his first marriage. Children are hostages to fortune: whoever said that never said a truer thing. He always supported his daughter Molly through college and often helped in adult life. But he still thinks the break-up had a bad effect on her. Although he remained friends with her mother, Lisa, it still took Molly years to settle. She'd had bad luck with men and was married twice – both times disastrously. The first husband tied her up and beat her. The second was a drug addict who stole to maintain his habit. The current boyfriend does something in television, so he's a better prospect. She's still poor, but things are looking up – the American family's alive and well.

A first family's a delicate subject of conversation. As a second wife, I'm always cautious about saying anything which might be taken as interference or criticism. I feel I'm treading on eggshells, so tiptoe round the topic. But after breakfast, I reminded Charlie gently that he hadn't seen that much of Molly or Jake since they went to Texas, so he couldn't be too surprised by the letter.

He looked sad. "But I can't stand the place. It's all big hats and cowboy boots."

If it's anything like the soap opera, *Dallas,* I understand.

"It has more people on death row than any other state," Charlie went on. "General Sherman said that if he owned Hell and Texas, he'd rent out Texas and live in Hell."

Charlie takes great dislikes to places. New Jersey is another no-no. And a visit to California would make him come out in a rash. Molly went west after college when Jacob was five or six. She got a job offer, which later fell through, but they stayed in Dallas. They came back to New York one Christmas years ago when Jacob was eight. It went well. He was a lively, curly-headed little boy then. Not whiney, but very chatty indeed. I gave him a Roald Dahl novel which he loved. After that Charlie visited a couple of times over the years, stopping off on business trips when he was wearing his editorial hat. But he hasn't seen Jacob for a few years now and not at all since we came to Ireland.

I'm nervous of boys.

Honestly, after the experience of losing Shevawn, I'm nervous of all youth. But Charlie was touched by the letter and immediately sent the fare. I suppose this makes me a stepgrandma – only six months to M day now. Resignation is the only thing. Nothing to be done about either state – being menopausal or a stepgrandma. Fate didn't make me a mother, but I can be part of nature's plan to ensure the survival of the race. *The Irish Times* had an article recently by some woman historian who agrees with me that the US family's alive and well. Despite the rising divorce rate, Americans keep getting married. Most do it twice. Some even oftener. They have multiple wives and children at all ages. They're often parents when they should be grandparents and grandparents when they should be parents. But if you father a child when you're seventeen and this child gives birth at fifteen, you can be a grandparent at the ripe old age of thirty-two.

Charlie was.

So can't complain about my new state.

AUGUST

Monday 17th:
Jake's here.

Charlie met him at the airport on Saturday – the day of the Omagh bombing, which has devastated everyone. It'll be like Kennedy's death – people will remember what they were doing the moment they heard the news. I was cleaning the kitchen when it came on the radio. Terrible. We've had the murder of the Quinn boys, now this.

But now we must think of Jake's holiday.

At first I was amazed at his size – v. small for fourteen. He looks more like twelve, which is odd, because his voice is breaking and wobbles up and down eerily. He could pass for Italian, a Renaissance page-boy – except that he's a modern American, with a huge helping of Charlie's brains.

He's a pint-sized Johnny Depp actually, with his hair sometimes loose and sometimes in a thick black ponytail, and a gold sleeper in one ear. And his voluminous red-and-white-striped Bermudas and outsize black T-shirt emphasise his slightness. He's odd in lots of ways. He refused to shake hands for one thing.

"It's Jake, not Jacob," he barked, first off.

He corrects me all the time.

And dazzles me with his knowledge of everything from Romantic poetry to Greek myth. He's well read for his age, for any age –

twenty, fifty, seventy or ninety. He'll hold forth knowledgeably at the slightest instigation. He's already informed me of the origins of the month of August – called after Caesar Augustus. Also, I've been instructed on the basic difference between Keats and Shelley. This lecturing seems to irritate Charlie, but I'm grateful Jake's so talkative. I can communicate with him much more easily than I did with Shevawn. So my confidence is up – maybe I'm not such a freak of nature and can relate to children.

He brought hardly any clothes and, to match the Bermudas, wears old battered Docksiders with no socks – he says socks are dumb and Einstein wore none either. They get holes in 'em and darning's a waste of time. I suppose that makes sense for Texas, but Ireland can be cold, even in August. But he's pretty definite in his opinions and hard to dissuade.

This ruffles Charlie.

Before bed last night they had a spat about what Jake should read. Charlie tried to give him Arthur Ransome's *Swallows and Amazons* – a favourite of his and mine. But the child scanned a page, then handed the book back. "Kid's crap, Grandad."

Charlie was taken aback. "It's a classic, Jake."

"Yeah, classic crap!"

While Charlie fumbled for something to say, Jake stretched up and took Bertrand Russell's *History of Western Philosophy* from the shelves, almost collapsing under its weight. He opened the tome. "I heard o' this guy."

Charlie smiled at me. "You'll find him a bit heavy going."

But Jake took the book to bed. I put out his light at midnight and found him asleep with it open on his chest.

At breakfast today they clashed about the IRA of all things – they're in the news now, calling themselves something else. Jake knows all about Sinn Féin and the Peace Process and wanted to go up to Rathmines to buy *An Phoblacht*. I told him it wasn't sold there, he'd have to go into town for it. We could go later on, perhaps this evening after dinner. But Charlie adamantly opposed this. "That rag's not coming into this house!"

Jake went pink, so, to distract him, I asked how he'd heard of it.

"A friend in Texas, ma'am."

I felt like a schoolteacher. "It's Peggy, Jake."

"Peggy, ma'am."

"You can forget the 'ma'am'".

"Sorry, uh – Peggy. I gotta pick it up for my friend."

Probably for Molly's new boyfriend who does something in TV. Anyway it seemed a harmless request, but Charlie still wouldn't budge. Any mention of the IRA sends him into a tizzy – because of Omagh. He held up a warning index finger. "No!"

"A newspaper can't do any harm," I pleaded, noticing the child's disappointment.

But Charlie wouldn't budge. He's ridiculous. The whole country's still traumatised, but I tried to argue that it was nothing to do with Jake. No use. So I winked at Jake, implying we'd get it later.

Charlie caught me. "No, Peggy. He could be arrested going back through US customs."

Arrested? Our waifish grandson? The US customs are awkward, but would they really think this child in short pants was in the IRA? Was remotely connected to Omagh? Ludicrous. But, as usual, Charlie got his way. Instead of *An Phoblacht* Jake bought a selection of sweets in Mrs Murphy's shop – Witches Brew, Fruity Frogs, Jolly Joggers and Blood Balls. He's particularly partial to Blood Balls, which are a type of chewing gum. He chews them non-stop. Hope he doesn't ruin his teeth.

Tuesday 18th:
Jake still wets the bed.

He fussed in great embarrassment and confusion when I went into his room this morning. Even wanted to make his own bed, but I insisted on helping him and fortunately discovered the stain. He blushed and looked so timidly apologetic that I wanted to hug him. But a child who doesn't shake hands wouldn't want to be hugged. So I didn't.

He put a hand over his face. "I'm sorry, Peggy."

I whisked off the sheet. "It doesn't matter at all, Jake."

But he was about to cry.

I smiled cheerfully. "Don't worry. I'll put the sheets in the wash and the futon in front of the heater. It'll be dry by tonight, then we'll turn it over."

He still hung his head.

"Now, listen Jake, the futon is inexpensive. I was thinking of throwing it out when your letter came."

"You were?"

"Yes, it's had it."

It wasn't true, I'd bought it for Shevawn, but didn't want him upset.

"Don't tell Grandad," he mumbled.

Promised not to, but told him Grandad wasn't an ogre. He'd been a boy, too. Accidents happened to everyone. I was incontinent till the age of nine, so knew how he felt. But there was no need to be embarrassed. He was with his own family – 10, Khyber Place was his home.

This afternoon bought a rubber undersheet in Clerys. Bed-wetting's a classic sign of disturbance. Is Jake insecure with us? Or is something wrong at home? Is Molly's new relationship working out? He's said nothing about her and won't be drawn.

Wednesday, 19th:

Took Jake on one of those open-top bus tours of Dublin. We sat upstairs, inhaling the benzine cocktail of car fumes as the chatty guide pointed out the sights. Jake intrigued by Swift's tomb. The president's candle in the window for returned emigrants. Also the guide's description of the various Dublin statues of Molly Malone, Oscar Wilde, and Anna Livia – the Tart with the Cart, the Quare in the Square, and the Floozie in the Jacuzzi. Came home feeling sick. Hope I haven't given myself lung cancer. Where, just where, do all the tourists come from? Why are they all coming to Dublin?

Charlie and Jake had a run-in about washing hands before dinner. Jake doesn't like to wash too much – not at all. Then Jake tried to lecture Charlie about Swift's tomb. So, over the washing up, without mentioning the bed-wetting, told Charlie that Jake was vulnerable.

He poo-pooed this. "He's a pain in the ass. A show-off."

The kid needs love. Why can't Charlie see that? If Jake's showing off, it's for attention. But Charlie humphed and said I was imagining things. He loves Jake, I'm sure, but they're two of a kind. Both stubborn intellectuals. You can be an intellectual at fourteen. I know that now, having met the dazzling Jake. He's kept Bertrand Russell in his room and endlessly explores Charlie's library, when he's not talking his head off. It's hard to keep up with him.

After dinner Jake was deep in a book and going on about Shelley's poetry again, quoting "Ode to the West Wind" – a poem I like and, as we did it for the Leaving, was actually able to quote, too. Think this surprised Jake, as he looked at me with a new respect. As a kid I loved the bit about falling upon the thorns of life and bleeding.

A heavy weight of hours has chained and bowed
One too like thee, tameless and swift and proud.

It captures adolescence perfectly, which one so completely forgets and which is exactly Jake's state now, and which we mustn't forget. I think Charlie does.

Jake then asked me rather pompously what I thought of Shelley's essay on *The Necessity of Atheism*. Naturally, I hadn't read that, so the dear child informed that he *had*, also that he was an atheist, too, and didn't want to go to church while in Ireland. I said we didn't go either and certainly wouldn't make him.

"Shelley's cool. He tried to convert the Irish," Jake went on portentously. "To birth control."

Charlie was irritated. "Yes, Jake."

"That's why I came."

"To tell us about birth control?"

"No, I came, 'cos Shelley did."

Charlie was put out – that *he* came *second* to Shelley, I think. Well, you can't win 'em all, can you? He was being silly. Jake was only showing off. It made me love him even more.

Then they had another spat.

Jake sat on the couch, his spindly brown legs just reaching the floor, lecturing us on Shelley's *novels*.

"Shelley didn't write novels!" Charlie used his Ph.D. voice. He hates to be called "Doctor", but he's a bit pompous sometimes, although I don't dare point this out. Well, hardly ever.

Jake paled. "Yes, he *did!*"

"No, he didn't."

"He did."

"Didn't."

Charlie reached up to our bookshelves for the *Oxford History of English Literature,* edited by Ian Jack. I didn't know we had it – we've so many tomes. He put on his reading glasses and perused the bibliography. "Ah, yes . . . here he is. Shelley, Percy Bysshe.

'Ode to the West Wind' . . . then it lists his other poems. And *Cenci* his verse play. Sorry, Jake, no novels."

Jake read over his shoulder, trembling and pushing back his heavy locks. "But he did, Grandad."

"Sorry, son."

Then, with a triumphant shriek, the boy pointed. "Look, there they are! He did!"

Charlie looked down the page, puzzled. "Where?"

With black hair falling on his flushed face, Jake read out. " 'Shelley published the following prose works: *Zastrozzi, A Romance*, by P. B. S. 1810; and *St Irvyne, or The Rosicrucian, A Romance*, by a Gentleman of the University of Oxford, 1811.' See! I'm right! I'm right!"

Charlie blinked at the book. "Hmm . . . so you are. Now, where'd you learn so much about Shelley?"

Jake shrugged casually. "In the library."

"Hmm . . . That's good, *very* good, Jake."

The boy went pink with delight.

Round two to him.

Later:

Before bed tonight Charlie and I discussed Jake's education. I wondered, should we consider sending him to some special school for gifted children? But Charlie said the public school he's at now isn't doing a bad job. Had to agree with this, but Charlie's going to write and ask Molly if he can do anything to help. Charlie's terribly proud to be in some way responsible for his existence.

Thursday 20th

Jake's had no more nocturnal accidents.

Last night he told me all the veins and arteries of the human body add up to twice the width of the equator – something like that. He seems happy enough and spends a good deal of time reading Bertrand Russell's tome in his room, while chewing Blood Balls.

This morning I found him smoking pot there.

I recognised the smell immediately. I'd tried it once or twice, but was a lot older than Jake at the time. And like Clinton, I didn't inhale.

"Jake, where'd you get pot?"

He went pink. "In school, Peggy."

"In school?"

"Yeah, they sell it there."

I asked no more about that, but kept looking stern. "You carried it through Irish customs?"

He nodded sheepishly.

"You know that's illegal. You could end up in jail."

"Yeah, Peggy."

"Give it to me, Jake."

"All of it?"

He dug into his backpack and pulled out a packet of grass wrapped in white tissue paper. Then handed it over reluctantly. "Ya gonna tell Grandad?"

"If you promise not to smoke again while you're here, I won't."

"Can't – you got it." But he looked relieved. "Uh, thanks, Peggy."

I hid the package in my handbag. Didn't tell Charlie. There's no point in making trouble for the boy. He acts tough, but he's sensitive – I can tell by the way he blushes. And I don't know how Charlie might react. He's a veteran of the sixties himself and has tried it, I know, like everyone else from that era, but he was so reactionary about the Sinn Féin magazine, he might blow his top about this. I fear he's turned into an old fogie. Except for his interest in Fuck-offey, but she's out of the picture at the moment. Although Charlie still gets those idiotic letters. He still insists it's just an intellectual crush. That no one else will talk to her about poetry. Maybe, but I'm too busy with parenting Jake to think about her. I wonder what kind of a mother I'd have made. I think we'd have done a good job, Charlie and I. I'd be the good cop and he'd be the stricter one.

Later:

Ever since I found the pot, Jake keeps offering to help me in touching ways. Like yesterday, he carried all the shopping home, then chopped stuff for a pizza. I've discovered he likes Sinéad O'Connor – amazing, and a bit of a relief that he has some normal teenage interests. He asked me if she lived in Ireland, but said I thought not – as far as I know she lives in London, but I'm not really sure. I could show him where U2 lived in Killiney, but he has no interest in the famous band.

I offered to buy him Sinéad's latest tape, but he declined, saying he didn't like to accept presents from anyone but his mother. I said he could accept from a stepgrandmother, but he gave me a funny look. Then I asked tactfully about his mom.

He shrugged. "She's OK, I guess."

It's a bit puzzling that he never mentions her. Is Molly pregnant again? Could that be the reason for all the identification with Shelley's birth control preaching? It's such an odd topic for a boy to be obsessed with. I asked where she was working now; but he hemmed and hawed and didn't really answer. He clams right up about her. I think from his old clothes and worn out shoes, they must be really poor. I'm getting him a decent pair of shoes, if it's the last thing I do on this earth.

As usual, Charlie's busy with his damn T. S. Idiot book – very convenient. But I have to be supportive, or the book will never get finished. So we take it in turns to entertain Jake.

This afternoon I took him to the National Gallery. It was hot and full of summer visitors. I'm proud of the way it's been done up, and His Highness seemed impressed, too, because he walked through the high, light-filled rooms, exclaiming loudly about the qualities of the different paintings. Jake has a real eye and is quite knowledgeable for a boy – for anybody. His favourite painter's Salvador Dali, and he never stops talking about surrealism. Particularly Hieronymous Bosch.

We wandered from room to room, stopping whenever Jake wanted to. When we came to the Italian room, I couldn't help thinking Jake looked as if he'd walked out of one of these paintings. He frowned in disapproval at a Madonna. "She doesn't have a baby."

"Jesus was probably grown up and left home," I said.

He swayed backwards, his thin arms folded. "I hate babies!"

I thought Molly must be pregnant.

"Know what I love, Peggy?" he croaked.

"What?"

"In Punch and Judy where they bash the baby." He giggled nerve-wrackingly. "It's so *funny!*"

He cracked up, laughing. His eccentricity reminds me of a character in a novel by John Irving who said everything in capital letters – *A Prayer for Owen Meany*. It was enjoyable, even if I've forgotten most of it – except, of course, the eponymous character who talked so loudly.

My feet ached and I had galleryitis. I can only last about half an hour in an art gallery without feeling tired. I sat on a bench, telling Jake my feet were worn out.

He looked knowledgeably down. "The average person walks about sixty thousand miles in a lifetime."

I asked him where he'd read that.

"Encyclopaedia. That's twenty times across the Atlantic. You've probably walked forty thousand miles in your life so far – which means that you've walked the equivalent of the Atlantic . . . about fourteen times."

It was definitely time for a curative cup of tea. I headed downstairs in the direction of refreshments, but Jake called after me, "Hey, Peggy!"

At least he'd dropped the ma'am.

He was still at the painting of Our Lady. "Say, what's the Assumption?"

I came back and stood behind him. In the painting the Madonna was being assumed into Heaven. It was like a holy picture from my youth. Our Lady wore a wispy blue cloak and white veil. Her eyes rolled piously upward, her bare feet floated nebulously over a rock. An innocuous serpent stared up at her. I remembered my catechism. "Mary was born without original sin, so she was assumed into Heaven."

He looked sceptical. "Ya mean sorta beamed up?"

I had to laugh. "That's a good way of putting it, Jake."

"Hmm . . ." He squinted at the painting, supporting an elbow with one palm and cupping his chin with the other. He tapped out a tune on his upper lip. It's a characteristic gesture.

Then I remembered more dogma from my indoctrinated youth. "Our Lady didn't suffer death. She was the best person who ever lived."

He stared silently at the painting.

"She was born without sin," I added.

He humphed. "But she fucked God, didn't she?"

It was a bomb going off. The group of French tourists stopped talking and stared. The uniformed attendant was stony-faced.

"Jake . . ." I whispered crossly in the shocked silence. "Keep your voice down!"

Ireland isn't Iran, we don't stone people for saying outrageous things. But despite TV programs like *Father Ted*, it's still Holy Ireland. He looked hurt. "I'm sorry, Peggy!"

I was sorry, too. He was a harmless child from a different culture – there was no need to overreact.

He offered me a Blood Ball, but I refused.

We both stared at the painting, ignoring the attendant. After a bit I said, "It wasn't quite like that, Jake. You've seen paintings of Mary with an angel?"

He nodded, cupping his chin thoughtfully.

"Well, the Angel Gabriel came and gave Mary a message that she'd get pregnant by the Holy Ghost."

He tapped on his upper lip again. "The Holy Ghost?"

"Yes, it was a miracle." I hurried to the next painting, my feet aching badly. "What about our cup of tea, Jake?"

"You want one *now*?"

I nodded wearily.

"OK. But I gotta see that Caravaggio."

Afraid to leave him on his own, I trailed after him. He strode past another bored attendant to the famous *Taking of Christ* by Caravaggio. What would he say next? I was expecting the worst. Would he accuse Christ of being a homosexual? The first gay libber in love with the apostle, John?

We studied the depiction of Christ's betrayal in the garden: His beautiful face, the despair of John, the brutal strength of the soldiers. I told Jake the story of its recent discovery in a local religious house. I tell all our visitors the story of how it was first thought to be an imitation, but then discovered to be genuine. "I think it's fifteenth century –."

"Late sixteenth, early seventeenth," Jake boomed.

"Oh . . ."

He pointed to the painting's title and date.

I peered at it. "Yes, well, of course. He was an early naturalist, I know that much. Famous for his use of light and dark."

"Chiaroscuro."

"What?"

"The word's chiaroscuro, Peggy." He rolled his r's like a native Italian.

"Hmm . . . of course." I tried again. "Well, Caravaggio was killed in a duel."

"He was exiled for murder and died of malaria." Jake swayed backwards on his battered Docksiders.

I was dazzled again. How can a fourteen year old know so much? It isn't natural. "You know a lot about Caravaggio. Have you seen other works by him?"

He shrugged. "Sure – in art books. We got 'em in the library."

In the gallery restaurant we sat beside the atrium. Jake had a Coke and two slices of carrot cake, eating while talking non-stop. His appetite, at least, is OK – he'll eat so long as it's American food. We've had fried chicken several times and made a few trips to the Swan Centre McDonald's, despite Charlie's protests about junk food.

While he demolished the cake, I told him George Bernard Shaw had funded the gallery with royalties from *My Fair Lady*.

This intrigued him. "But he's British."

"Irish."

"His plays are in English."

I nodded. "But he's Irish."

Jake wouldn't concede defeat. "He's in a dictionary of British writers. I read it."

"That may be so, but Shaw was born in Dublin. We'll pass his birthplace on the way home."

That shut him up.

As we walked home via Synge Street, I pointed out the house and told him all I knew about Shaw, impressing on him that his Grandad knew more about the writer than I did. Jake listened for once.

Friday 21st:

Told Jake to take a bath tonight.

He grumpily agreed, going into the bathroom without a towel.

When I knocked to give him one, there were frantic scramblings and hysterical shouts of, "Don't come in, Peggy!"

"I won't! Just want to give you a towel."

Big sigh of relief from inside.

Then the door inched open and a furtive brown hand reached out and grabbed the towel. Door slammed shut.

"Wash your neck, Jake!" Charlie shouted.

"OK, Grandad," he answered meekly.

Charlie made a face at his title.

"It can't be helped," I joked.

"What?"

"Being a Grandad."

He smiled wanly. Charlie isn't a Werther's Original grandfather and never will be. But he's very fond of Jake. We both are.

Saturday 22nd:

It's a bit of a strain, thinking of ways to entertain Jake. I'm not on vacation, so can't do things with him all the time. He says he's quite happy reading, but he should be doing things in the fresh air like a normal boy. Today I brought him into Mrs Murphy, who gave him some toffee apples. He's quite hooked on her sweets now, which must be terrible for his teeth. But Mrs Murphy's quite taken with Jake and suggested that he get to know some of the local boys. Wasn't too enthusiastic, thinking she meant Packy. I know Packy turned out OK in the end re Shevawn, but Jake's so small and so eccentric, he might get bullied by rougher boys. Anyway, Packy's too old for him. And no one around here's going to be able to argue about Shelley's novels.

But today a nice boy knocked on the door and offered to take Jake cycling to Sandymount Strand. I've seen him around in a St Mary's, Rathmines, blue school blazer. I was a bit hesitant, but Charlie said yes immediately. Jake wasn't a china doll, he boomed. We couldn't wrap him in cotton wool.

I suppose that's true.

Today Jake wobbled off on Charlie's old black bike.

I'd lost my ewe lamb. And what'll we tell his mother if anything happens?

But needn't have worried.

Jake back in half an hour.

His face was pale and he was breathing heavily. I helped him wheel the bike into the hall. He didn't tell me what happened and I didn't ask. Probably, the nice boy knew nothing about chiaroscuro or Shelley's novels. Or maybe they had a fight. Who knows? Anyway, I can't imagine Jake relating to any normal boy his age. I wonder if his mother knows how gifted he is? Does the school know? Talked to Charlie again about trying to find a special school for gifted children. Charlie said it was up to his mother.

Later:

Something awful happened.

I went into town later today to meet Mary Daly, an old school friend, in Hodges Figgis bookshop – at the coffee shop which is a nice quiet spot. Well, I was late, and there were guards at the top of Dawson Street and the street was blocked off – unusual for Dublin.

Told I couldn't walk down the street – because the Mansion House was cordoned off as a security measure for some celebrity. Explained I was late for my appointment and needed to take a short cut. A nice young guard said yes, but he'd have to check my handbag. I opened it, immediately remembering Jake's pot. Of course, it was still there. "Hell," said the Duchess!

As I trembled, the guard peered into my mess of Tesco receipts and old bus tickets. Then he found Jake's pot still wrapped in the see-through tissue paper.

God.

Controlled my shaking, but felt ready to faint. What would Charlie say? I could just hear him – "I married a drug addict." I could see the next day's headlines: WOMAN CAUGHT WITH DRUGS. I who had hardly ever even smoked a cigarette in my life.

The guard peered suspiciously at the white packet, feeling it without taking it all the way out. It looked like dried herbs. "Now what's that?"

I tried to joke. "Whatja think it is?"

Felt like someone about to be hung. All was lost.

But he shrugged and zipped the bag shut. "A typical woman's handbag."

I walked shakily on.

I'm still shaking.

Afterwards hid the loot behind the Irish fiction section in Hodges Figgis. My friend didn't turn up. No doubt I'll hear why. Must be a mix-up.

sunday 23rd:

Ursula and Gudrun Thomas invited us to lunch in Greystones today. I was delighted as I couldn't face another cultural Sunday, walking round Dublin. You can get enough of art galleries and museums. They're two retired Anglo-Irish schoolteachers and old friends of ours from way back. They knew Charlie first, then they became friendly with both of us when we came back here on holidays over the years. We often go down for Sunday lunch. Their late father was an academic, one of the first D. H. Lawrence scholars and published by Charlie's ex-employers. Charlie was his editor, so the relationship goes way back.

The car's clutch has been acting up, so took the 84 bus down, catching it at Donnybrook church. We jogged along, getting a great view from the top of the bus, Jake in the front seat, us across the aisle. Halfway, I noticed he was pale and unnaturally silent, so asked if he was OK.

He nodded miserably.

I opened the window. Poor mite. He looked awful. He's only a kid, despite his big ideas. We should've taken the DART to Bray — then taxied from there.

At Bray Town Hall, I looked over again. He was now green. "We're nearly there. Can you last another fifteen minutes?"

"Y-yes, Peggy."

Even Charlie was concerned and went over to his side, hovering like a nervous mother hen. "OK, old pal?"

"Y-yes, Grandad."

The bus climbed Bray Head, then roared down the hill to the

suburban seaside town. It's a lovely view down to the sea, and we got there without Jake vomiting.

Ursula and Gudrun live in an old house in the heart of the Burnaby. It has croquet lawns and trees and a frog pond. They're both incredibly kind, sort of theatrically Anglo-Irish and flamboyant. Ursula has short white hair and pink cheeks, while Gudrun has long white hair in a bun and a paler complexion. As usual, both were dressed sensibly in slacks and twinsets, etc. They were instantly taken with Jake and kissed him exuberantly – he has that effect on you. Brings out the mother.

But he pulled back abruptly. "I HATE KISSING!"

Charlie cleared his throat awkwardly. "Jake!"

But the two women laughed happily, completely unfazed. I laughed, too. Poor Jake was pink with embarrassment again. But he recovered quickly enough and wanted sherry when it was served before lunch in the fadedly elegant drawing room. Had no interest in Club Orange. The two women were delighted to oblige, but Charlie frowned in disapproval. I said it was OK. After all, French children drink from an early age. Then we all sat down at a huge mahogany table in a big formal dining room. They'd laid on an absolutely marvellous lunch of tender roast beef and Yorkshire puddings, roast potatoes, peas – all typical Irish Sunday-lunch fare, which both Charlie and I love. But Jake picked at his food, pushing it around the plate.

Ursula noticed he wasn't doing well and teased him in her theatrical accent. "You'll have to do better than than, Jake, if you want to grow big and strong."

He looked small and weak behind the big table. "I'm not hungry, thank you, ma'am."

Gudrun joined in. "Don't you want to grow as tall as your grandfather?"

Charlie looked over. "Yes, Jake, eat up."

Jake ready to cry.

I came to his defence. "He's a bit upset from the bus."

He looked gratefully at me. He wasn't a good traveller. Also the food was too un-American for him, and in the end he left most of it, except the trifle. He managed two helpings of that. During lunch the conversation somehow got on to Jake's favourite authors. Ursula and Gudrun are bookish and thought Jake would like C. S. Lewis, or someone like that. But he said no. Grandad had given him an Arthur Ransome and it was crap.

"Well, Jake, who do you like?" They both eagerly awaited his reply.

"Sacher-Masoch." He looked matter-of-factly from one to the other.

Charlie nearly choked.

But the name seemed to make no impression on our friends. At first I thought this was out of politeness, but Gudrun beamed innocently. "He's an American children's author, Jake, dear?"

Jake pink now, eyebrows up. "Naw, he's for adults, ma'am."

Ursula joined in cosily. "And what books did he write, dear?"

Jake thrilled at the impression he was making. He looked earnestly from one to the other. "Say, haven't you guys heard of masochism?"

Ursula looked vague. "Masochism? I don't think so, dear."

"Is it something to do with masonry, dear?" Gudrun enquired politely.

"No, it's sexual pleasure in –"

"Jake!" Charlie roared.

"Pain!"

"Jake!"

"But, Grandad . . ." Jake was about to cry.

"Well, well, we'll have to look out for his books." Ursula went out to the kitchen for the coffee, calling blithely over her shoulder, "Gudrun, write down the name. We'll ask at the library."

Afterwards we all played croquet in the garden. Jake looked so funny as he swung the too-big mallet, like some weird Beckett character. Charlie's old anorak made him look even smaller. And every time he hit the ball, it went past the hoop. He'd hit it back and miss again. Poor kid was mortified. I played worse – which seemed to console him a bit. Men are so competitive, even boys like Jake can take consolation from being better than someone. Charlie played like an experienced person and won, beating even the ladies.

We got home late – tired but fairly happy. In bed, Charlie gave out yards about Jake's reading matter. "Why doesn't Molly supervise him?"

"She's a working mother."

"I'm calling her!"

"Oh, he was only showing off."

Charlie turned his back to me. "If we'd had children, it would've been a disaster!"

This got me. "Why?"

"You'd spoil them rotten!"

I was upset by this – unreasonably. But Charlie kissed me goodnight. "You'd make a wonderful mother."

Saturday 29th:

It's Jake's last few days, so we decided to take him to Acton's in Kinsale for a CIE weekend break. It's a great deal – they bussed us down and put us up in the lovely old-world hotel. The journey was a chance for Jake to see some of the Irish countryside, too. This time he survived the bus OK. We stopped for the loo halfway at Cahir, and Jake was very excited by the huge Butler castle.

"It's cool," he kept saying, waving excitedly at the tourists peering over the ramparts.

He wanted to go in but there was no time. It was lovely to see him interested in boy's things at last – castles rather than Shelley and Sacher-Masoch.

And he loves the old town of Kinsale.

The three of us are sharing a room – as our "child", Jake got in free. The breakfast this morning was super, but I'd great trouble getting Jake out of bed for it. I called him and called him, but he wouldn't budge. I'd never seen anyone in such a deep sleep, so decided he must need it. At last he staggered down and looked sleepily at the long menu, as the waiter patiently asked him what he was having.

Jake rubbed his eyes, peering over the top of the menu. "Whatja sellin'?"

The waiter coughed politely. "Full Irish breakfast or a continental, sir."

Jake put his hand across the top of the menu. "I'll have from there down."

The waiter raised his eyebrows in surprise, and I thought there was going to be conflict, but Charlie actually laughed. And Jake ended up with a full Irish breakfast – plus. Naturally he didn't eat it all, but he made a good dint in it, despite the bacon being uncrispy.

This afternoon we walked around the old military forts. Jake in heaven and a real boy, exploring and climbing the castle ramparts. Charlie had told him all about the Battle of Kinsale and the days when the fort was the home of the English redcoats. He lapped it up, asking endless questions about Irish history, the different battles, and who won what.

Charlie's worried about Jake's shoes leaking and we were

discussing getting him a new pair, when suddenly we didn't see him anywhere near us. Where had he got to?

Charlie searched around. "I don't see him."

He'd vanished.

"Jake!" he called worriedly. "Jake!"

Then we saw him – on top of a high tower.

"Hiiii!" Jake waved. He seemed to sway as his funny Bermudas ballooned in the wind. "Grandad! Peggy!"

Charlie ashen-faced. "Jesus, he'll fall!"

I froze, too, as Jake crawled carefully along a balustrade. If he slipped, it was instant death. My imagination ran riot: phone calls, an autopsy, long distant flights, tears, a funeral. It brought me back to when Shevawn was lost, except this was worse. He really was in danger. This time we wouldn't be lucky.

"Be careful, Jake," I coaxed, noticing how he'd got there. A ladder had been left by some repair workers. The fort's stonework was being repointed. He must've climbed up.

"Come on down now," I called again, keeping the panic from my voice.

He waved back excitedly. "Hey, you guys, come on up! The view's cool."

Charlie looked terrible. "GET DOWN!"

"Aw, Grandad!"

"Jake! You heard me! GET DOWN! NOW!"

Charlie and I held the ladder while Jake made his way slowly back down. At each hesitant step, he looked down, almost missing once. My heart pounded deafeningly. I could almost hear Charlie's. But in the end Jake reached terra firma.

He hung his head, chagrined, expecting Charlie to explode.

But Charlie immediately hugged him. "You scared me, Jake. Jesus, you scared the hell out o' me!"

Jake blinked childishly. "Sorry, Grandad."

Charlie ruffled his hair, laughing aloud with relief. Tears weren't far away. "Don't *ever* do that again!"

I was shaking.

Charlie still held him. "You hear me, son?"

"Yes, Grandad."

For once Jake's big voice was muffled by Charlie's bear hug.

Sunday 30th:

For our last night's dinner we splashed out on one of Kinsale's gourmet restaurants. As always I stuck to seafood. Jake expertly scanned the long menu, his black hair flopping over his eyes. In the end he ordered the same as Charlie: a starter of frogs' legs of all things, then duck for an entrée.

I doubted either of them would be able to finish both, but said nothing. Man and boy seemed to have a rapport at last as they exchanged views about the deliciousness of frogs' legs. Maybe the ladder incident helped. Released inhibitions. Anyway, they're the best of friends now.

Charlie even allowed Jake a glass of wine with dinner.

During the entree, he asked about Molly, what she was doing for the summer and that. I know he hadn't liked to bring up the subject before, because of Jake's reticence. We thought she'd probably changed partners or was pregnant again. Something was going on, but we didn't like to pry.

But in the intimacy of the restaurant, Jake confided in us. "She's in jail, Grandad."

"Wha-a-t?" Charlie nearly choked on his duck.

Me on fish. Why hadn't he told us? Was it true?

But Charlie kept his voice light. "Why's she in jail, Jake? And how long?"

I was imagining the worst.

Jake shrugged. "Aw, it's only some dumb driving thing, Grandad. She forgot to renew her license. In Texas they putja in jail."

Charlie was relieved by this. "Why didn't you tell us?"

Jake shrugged. "'Cos . . . well."

I smiled to myself. He came to us because there was no one to look after him at home. Oh, he could've gone to his grandmother's family, but no, he came to us. At least it was nothing to do with Shelley's Irish visit. And I know Charlie's pleased that he came. That we could help in some small way. Sometimes good comes out of bad.

Monday 31st:

We're back home. Charlie immediately rang Molly, who assured him that she had indeed forgotten to renew her driving license and was caught on the highway. The jail sentence was only for a week because she was late for a court hearing and got sentenced for contempt by a cranky, right-wing judge, who didn't like the look of her. She was well and looking forward to seeing Jake again. Charlie vastly relieved and went out and bought her a watch. He told me to get Jake a pair of shoes before he goes back. I tried, but the stubborn boy didn't like anything in any of the Rathmines shops today.

I pointed to his old Docksiders. "You can't wear those, Jake."

"Why not?"

"They're worn out."

He shrugged. "But my mom buys me stuff."

"A grandfather can buy you a pair of shoes, Jake."

But no use.

So I got him *An Phoblacht*, warning him not to mention it to

Charlie. He hid it in his rucksack, then shyly said, "Thanks, Peggy."

Wanted to hug him, but afraid. Asked if he'd come back again next year, but he said quite solemnly that he didn't know his plans for next year yet.

Later:

Jake's gone – he's going back to school immediately after Labour Day. Both very sad. I tried again, but he still wouldn't accept a pair of new shoes. So I got him Sinéad O'Connor's latest tape and hid a pair of Air Nikes in his rucksack – I got a size bigger than he's wearing. If they don't fit, he'll grow into them. Charlie sent Molly a cheque.

All quiet on the Khyber front. Realised today I hadn't seen Packy for a while. Mrs Murphy told me he's robbing somewhere else now, so we can have a rest. The good news is that Philomena's wedding is next week. Grey in fashion this year, but it doesn't suit me. Never know what to buy. If I get a suit, I'll only be able to wear it once. In the end, got myself a new black dress in Marks and Sparks sale. Charlie says I look like a nun, but I can always wear black again. And it won't be funereal, 'cos I'm wearing it with a white jacket. Charlie's wearing his good tweed jacket and a new white shirt. I got him a new red woollen tie.

SEPTEMBER

Tuesday 1st:

Philomena's wedding off.

Last night she came to the hall door, all red-eyed and alone, and told me the whole story over a cup of tea. She's been jilted. I can't believe it – his children objected to the marriage. His children? How could they? Can they? Do they have the right?

"It isn't fair," she kept sobbing.

Thought it odd when her fiancé didn't come to dinner with us that evening. Obviously he was getting cold feet then. Invited her in, asking how could he still have children? I mean, do you in your eighties? When are your off-spring considered grown-up, flown the nest? You can't send them back, but can't you ever unload them? Be on equal terms, so to speak?

"They're threatening to cut him off from the family if he marries me." She started crying again.

I was still mystified. "But what age are they?"

"Fifty-five and fifty-six."

I made her coffee and we sat miserably at the kitchen table. "Maybe he'd be as well off without them."

She sighed. "No, he'd miss his grandchildren too much."

Did my best to console her. She said Ollie's children are all settled in life – he gave them all houses and loads of money years ago. But he's still wealthy and they're jealous because some of his wealth

185

might go to Philomena on his death. It's crazy. What were they upset about? He had discussed everything beforehand with them and her. His practicality was what I liked most about him. There was to be a prenuptial agreement about the deli shop. She was to get her start in business, and they were to get everything else – everything. Yet they still threatened to cut him off from his grand-children, who are in their teens. So he called the wedding off. Philomena wept all the time she was telling me this. Didn't know what to do.

"What'll I do with my Laura Ashley dress?" she wailed.

That got me. I was crying, too. It's a lovely cream cotton dress with lace – sort of broderie anglaise on the bust. "You can still wear it to parties."

"I never go to parties."

I just looked at her.

"I wanted to be like you, Peggy."

"Me?"

"You're so lucky with Charlie."

I said we have problems, too – things are difficult for everyone. Hope she won't end up back in hospital. Don't want to spend Christmas in Vincent's A & E – Easter was bad enough.

Thursday 3rd:
Didn't have to wait till Christmas.

The phone rang yesterday. Philomena said to come quickly, that she'd taken another overdose. I ran next door to find her lying on the couch, gaga.

"How many'd you take?" I held the empty bottle in front of her bleary eyes.

"The lot!" she moaned groggily.

"When?"

"H-h-half . . . h-half . . . h-hour ago."

I called an ambulance.

Great consternation in the street as it screeched up and she was carried out on a stretcher. Several neighbours, including Mrs Murphy and Mona, stood about anxiously.

"A pain," I said tactfully. "We're just taking precautions."

They nodded knowingly.

I went with her in the ambulance, the siren sounding all the way to St Vincent's. The same baby-faced child-doctor was on duty. This time they pumped her stomach, as it was under the two hour limit and not too late. It was a ghastly experience. I felt so sorry for Philomena that my anger dissipated completely. She was hooked up to some machine which was bleeping steadily. No sign of a coma this time. When she came round, I went with her as they X-rayed her chest. Afterwards they gave her oxygen, then tea and toast, which this time she didn't feel like eating.

"I'm sorry, Peggy," she sighed in the safety of the psychiatric ward.

"Now, now," I patted her hand.

"I didn't want to live."

"I know."

She sat up in bed. "Would you get me cigarettes, Peggy?"

I was getting to know the routine. No cigarettes in the hospital. So ran out and got her some from the Merrion Centre. Also bought her some Lucozade and a tub of Häagen-Dazs and a couple of doughnuts. She's being discharged today. How on earth will she manage without Oliver? Life is hard for some people. Hard and lonely. She has a married brother in the country, but they don't get on too well.

On the bus home saw Charlie walking up the Merrion Road again. Why is he always in the hospital vicinity?

When I asked him, he said he was out for a walk and decided to walk in the hospital direction to see the friend who has leukemia. He looked for me in A & E, but I wasn't there. Told him I had probably gone to the psychiatric ward by then. But this is very odd. Why is he so secretive about this person who has leukemia? And why didn't he ask in A & E? But that's a madhouse where no one knows anything.

Friday 4th:

People talking of nothing else but the Starr Report. It's in all the Irish papers. Clinton lied on oath. Now it's lies, not sex, which will sink him. Republicans talking about impeaching Clinton. As a Democrat, find myself outraged at this overreaction. It's totally Clinton's business whom he gropes. Both he and Monica are consenting adults. The only person who should be upset is Hillary. Feel enormous sympathy for her.

Then Charlie and Fuckoffey are consenting adults, too. It's a bit inconsistent of me to think they don't have any rights, but I can't help it. Erin's still away, so my problem's shelved for the moment. I fear the worst, as Charlie still refuses to discuss things with me. Still claims it's an intellectual friendship, implying I'm not an intellectual. If Charlie was a character in a book, I'd make him more talkative. He's always been taciturn. Are all husbands like this? The trouble is, you never know about anyone else's marriage. In fairy stories, the prince always kisses the Sleeping Beauty, but there's never any mention of after-dinner chat. Or pillow-talk. To be happily married, you need to be a mind reader. Or an expert in body language. I'm both. And I know he's being unfaithful in his mind – even if he hasn't done anything yet.

Thursday 10th:
Charlie's to be in a movie.

Can't believe it.

His ex-wife Lisa's making it next year. She's staying here at the moment, so we have another house guest – our sixth this year, according to my calculations. What does that say about us? That we're kind? Or stupid? Or maybe we subconsciously seek visitors because we're afraid to talk to each other? Think that's probably the truth.

Lisa phoned last week full of plans to visit, and Charlie hadn't the heart to refuse her. She arrived yesterday evening, via London and British Air, laden down with bags, expensive cameras and equipment. She's making a preliminary documentary – sort of a trailer to raise funds for the real thing next year, as far as I can gather. Lisa's a wizard at raising funds.

She's very ebullient and talks all the time about money and the movies. Her film's to be George Moore's "Homesickness" – a short story about a returned Irish emigrant at the turn of the century. In the story a character called James Bryden comes back to Ireland from the Bronx to recover from an illness, falls in love with a neighbour called Margaret Dirkin, but leaves without marrying her and spends his whole life regretting it. The story sums up the human condition – regret no matter what. If James Bryden had married Margaret, he'd be regretting someone else. She only became the love of his life because he lost her.

Maybe if Charlie lost me, he'd love me?

No time to think of that now. Too busy with Lisa, who talks about funds all the time. She's a tiny, hyper Irish-American in her mid-forties, like Charlie. She has wild, permed, white Afro curls, a pale complexion and a long thin face. She dresses with great taste – leggings and floaty silk shirts mainly. She sort of steals my

thunder a bit – oh, not for being so dynamic and Charlie's childhood sweetheart. No, it's not that. It's just that she's Jake's *real*
grandma. I'm an impostor. That's what really gets me. I can say it
here in the privacy of a diary. No one would understand.

Asked how was Jake first thing.

But Lisa waved me into silence. "That kid never stops blabbin'!"

"Yes, he's a bit of a genius," I said.

Her eyes opened widely and her forehead wrinkled – this expression is typical. "At what?"

"W-w-ell . . ."

"Blabbin'?"

"Yes, talking about great art and literature. He knows so much.
I couldn't believe it. There can't be too many boys like him."

But Lisa wasn't to be drawn. "Sure can't!"

"He might be a great writer some day."

"Hmm . . ." She was deep in some letter about fund-raising.

I didn't say, Jake must take after you, Lisa – talking all the time.
How could she not want to talk about him? Has she got eyes in her
head? How can she not be dazzled? But she isn't. It's The Film and
fund-raising for same, non-stop, from morning to night – which
gets on Charlie's nerves a bit, naturally.

He says he remembers now why Lisa and he parted: her endless
chatter. But actually she left him – which is why I'm here, so for
that I should be grateful to her. Her second husband's a dream – a
house husband actually, does all the cooking now and looks after
the two teenaged children, while Lisa brings in the bread. They
could take more interest in Jake, except they live in California and
it's a good bit away.

For the day job she has a small film company – mostly bread and
butter stuff: documentaries, ads, commercial videos for rock
groups – the sort of thing I know nothing about. But it's all very

highpowered – she goes to places like China, Japan and the White House, and has even filmed Hillary and Bill, which she takes with amazing casualness. She knows the Clintons by their first names, she says, and it's a strong marriage, despite the rumours. And all the latest non-rumours.

Tried to draw her out on this topic, but she was too obsessed with the movie.

But I don't mind her chatter.

Not at all.

Although she follows me everywhere, even into the bathroom, babbling endlessly about her numerous projects – she knows everyone in the movie business and goes to Cannes and places like that. She's even on first name terms with some famous actors. Last night she was talking about someone called Bruce. I thought it couldn't be Bruce Willis, it must be some other Bruce. But couldn't show up my ignorance. Asked Charlie later and he said it was Bruce Willis. Imagine. Lisa's almost famous.

We got a break to sleep last night – although Lisa didn't rest at all. For the first few hours after we turned out the lights, she was on the phone. (I quake at the thought of our phone bill. The first thing she asked, coming in the door, was the code to the States.) Then, as dawn broke, she was still at it. Talking to herself? Or into a tape-recorder? She must've been – there was no one else there and it was coming from the sitting room and not the hall where the phone is.

At breakfast she started up again.

"Now, guys, we could try for Nicholas Cage and Patricia Arquette for the leads. Or we could go for Tom Cruise and Nicole Kidman. But I prefer the fightin' Penns for the main parts."

Again, me ignorant. Asked who were the Penns?

Lisa wide-eyed in amazement, brow wrinkled. "But you've heard of the Penns, Peggy?

Had I? "Uh – no."

"Tut, tut, Peggy."

I looked at Charlie.

"Sean Penn," he said. "You've seen him."

I do vaguely remember the actor's name. It was just the way Lisa said, "the Penns", like they lived next door or something.

Lisa was still in her robe, waiting for the bathwater to heat, and had a fat Filofax diary on the table in front of her. "Sean Penn and Robin Wright! Where've you been, Peggy? You've seen 'em in plenty of movies."

Had I? Maybe, but at that early hour I couldn't put names on faces. I could only put Shredded Wheat on the table.

But Lisa pushed her bowl away. "I never eat breakfast."

No wonder she's so thin. She looked even more petite in the white flowing robe.

"Orange juice?" I enquired. "Tea, coffee?"

"Naw, coffee dehydrates the body. Any green tea?"

I said no.

"Pity, it detoxes the system. I'll take some OJ, then." She got out her vitamins and swallowed a handful. Then offered them around.

We refused.

"I take one gram of vitamin C a day, a multi-vitamin and mineral capsule along with a B complex," she said. "Plus a calcium supplement and 50mgs of Evening Primrose Oil."

Charlie raised an eyebrow. "Peggy's the same. What's wrong with food?"

"Food's depleted!"

Was this a hint about the Shredded Wheat? Charlie doesn't like cereal too much either – except for cornflakes – but it's what most people in the world eat for breakfast. And actually, I'm not the same – I take a multi-vitamin pill now and then, and a vitamin C when I feel a cold coming on. I try to persuade Charlie to do the same – sometimes he does and sometimes doesn't. But I can't really grind them up and put them in his food, can I? A, C and E are the essential detox vitamins, I've read. But I'm not like Lisa. Lisa's a fanatic. Bobbye Ann was a bit the same about her allergies, but Lisa's cheerier. This obsessiveness is very American, but you don't notice it so much in America. I've escaped by being Irish. OK, I've lived in America for most of my adult life, but I'm Irish and more easygoing about such matters.

"The Penns live in Ireland now," she went on.

Charlie rustled his paper sleepily. "They bought a place in Dalkey. Movie stars are buying there – pushing up prices."

Are they? First I knew of it, but it's true, house prices are still going through the roof – all to do with the wretched Celtic Tiger, which won't lie down and die. Cars choke the roads, there's no air and no houses for people to live in. And now Hollywood movie stars are adding to the problem. We thought it was bad when we bought here, but what are young people to do? Soon they won't be able to afford anything.

Lisa was still making notes. "Yeah, the Penns are perfect for our characters." She looked at me. "We gotta get stars, Peggy – to hook the distributors."

I was dubious. "You think the stars'll be interested?"

She looked outraged and spoke slowly, as if to an idiot. "Yes, Peggy. Actors always wanta work."

I didn't like to say, will they wanta work for you, Lisa? After all, they're probably in demand elsewhere. Most definitely, or they wouldn't be stars, would they? Is she crazy or what? Still, I admire her confidence. Amazing the way she gets things done.

Then Charlie perked up. "How about a star for my part, Lisa?"

She beamed indulgently. "Nope, you're perfect, Charlie."

"Hmm." He frowned disappointedly and went back to his paper. He's not too happy about acting with real Hollywood types, and can't say I blame him. He'd do anything to sign off.

But Lisa says the camera loves Charlie.

He's to play the irascible priest in the story. He beats lovers out of the ditches with a stick and yells at the parishioners for *céilí* dancing. But I can't see Charlie in a dog collar. And with stars as possible leads, he's naturally nervous – very. Don't blame him.

He's never acted in a movie before. He's only had small parts in long-ago college theatricals. But this doesn't deter Lisa. She says he's well able to act with movie stars, who despite their reputations aren't always much competition. And all the other actors are to be Irish. As well as making the documentary on this trip, she's scouting for actors, production people, locations, etc. She wants to create employment here.

I'm to be locations director.

At first I was all puffed up about my new title, but it just means recommending places to film in. I know Wicklow pretty well, and we're driving down there today or tomorrow.

Lisa's energy rubs off. It's a tonic. Told Charlie I was looking forward to a new career. No more computer hackwork. He'd have a new career, too, as an actor. But he said it'll never happen.

"But what about her talk?" I said.

"What about it?" he replied.

What a party-poop!

Friday 11th:
This morning Lisa met a top-notch stockbroker about funds. She came home a bit deflated, I thought, as he made her no promises. I was cooking liver, bacon and chips for supper. Thought a mixed grill would be a change. But ran out of potatoes, so Lisa insisted on

buying some for me. Told her to go around the corner to Mrs Murphy. In a few minutes, she returned empty-handed.

I asked what happened?

Lisa held up her credit card, the wide-eyed puzzled look on her face. "She wouldn't take this."

"Ah, no," I said, "she wouldn't."

Sent Charlie for them.

Lisa forgets she's not in America. But even there you wouldn't buy a bag of potatoes with a credit card, would you? At least I wouldn't. But Lisa seems to have no cash. How does she intend to fund a movie?

Later:

Charlie's nerves have cracked.

It happened like this: we went into town tonight – the three of us – to see a preview of the film *Dancing at Lughnasa*. It was good but a bit depressing and stage Irish. Afterwards, on the way home, Lisa was full of chat, thought it wonderful, blah, blah, blah. I said Meryl Streep was a bit too American for the part, but Lisa said no – she was an ensemble actor and did a great job. Charlie agreed with me, that she wasn't Donegal at all, and this might've irked Lisa a bit – that we disagreed with her. Something did.

We continued walking home, up Grafton Street and into Stephen's Green. When we got to the Shelbourne, Lisa wanted to go in for chocolate dessert. She has this obsession with chocolate. She has to have chocolate dessert nightly – a cake, or brownie, or chocolate ice cream or both. Every dinner so far, I've made her chocolate sauce for Combridge's vanilla ice cream – which is the best in Ireland.

Well, Charlie wouldn't go into the Shelbourne.

I think he thought he wasn't dressed up enough. He was wearing

blue Levis, which nearly everyone wears now. But he's a bit con-
ventional in the dress line, so he suggested another café on
Stephen's Green.

This irked Lisa. I mean – really. But she's pretty good-natured,
so kept her cool. "Are you comin', Peggy?"

Charlie wouldn't budge, and I didn't want to desert him.

"I'm going in, Peggy!" She made for the hotel's swing door
which almost knocked her out.

I asked was she OK? Then looked pleadingly at Charlie.

"I'm tired, Peggy," he said.

Lisa turned on him, obviously in pain from the door. "Now I
remember why we divorced – Charlie's a cheapskate!"

He went red in the face. I thought he was going to explode, but
he didn't. What did Lisa mean? Charlie's no cheapskate. He's generous to a fault. If anyone's penny-pinching, it's me. Have to be,
married to a Rockefeller like Charlie. But honestly, I'm the one
who grumbles at his generous tips. I just worry about money all the
time. It comes from having endured such an impoverished youth.

I made light of it. "Lisa, we're all a little tired."

Why wouldn't we be, with all her talking? But couldn't say that.
"Charlie?" I begged.

But he stood his ground. "I'll wait for you here!"

"No, go on home," I said. "We'll be OK."

Charlie had his stubborn face on. I knew because he folded his
arms – he always folds his arms. "No, I'll wait for you girls."

Lisa was still holding her face where the door had hit it. I stood
between man and ex-wife.

Then Charlie shrugged. "OK, I'll go on home. But you two take
a taxi!"

I promised, following Lisa into the hotel. Charlie has an
obsession about women walking home alone after dark – we'll be

mugged, raped, murdered, etc. He says house robberies are on the way out and muggings are in. I always tell him that I wouldn't stay home all the time if I hadn't married him, but resisted now. My appetite had deserted me, but I had a cup of tea under the hotel's luxurious chandeliers, as Lisa cut bites off a sinful wedge of double chocolate brownie cake. She ate slowly, with deep, savouring concentration. In the background, a pianist played "As Time Goes By".

"Life is short," Lisa sighed. "You gotta eat desert first."

I smiled – it's a good philosophy. But how come she never puts on an ounce of weight? She's about three stone underweight, whereas if I eat anything extra, I puff up. It takes half an hour's jogging to work off two hundred calories, which is about a slice of bread and butter.

In the taxi home, she explained the chocolate obsession. "My shrink says I didn't get enough love as a child."

I said I'd heard this theory and apologised for Charlie's stubbornness.

"Oh, it was all my fault. I should've gone to a café." She laughed good-naturedly. "Is it a strain having me?"

"No, Lisa," I lied.

"But the house's so damn small."

"We're used to it. Charlie's just nervous about the part."

She patted my knee. "He's perfect for the part, Peggy. You're married to a tired man."

I don't think so. But when we got home, Charlie was in bed and, when I joined him, muttered dozily, "You got home OK?"

"Of course!" I wanted a hug.

But he rolled over and went back to sleep. I lay awake for hours, hoping the tiff with Lisa wouldn't be repeated. Charlie forgets Lisa's an *ex*-wife. He can't be impatient with an ex, that's only for present wives. Actually, Charlie and Lisa met in the first week in high school, when they were both freshmen. Charlie says they got married in their last year because she was pregnant – Molly, then Jake, are the results, so it wasn't a bad thing. Charlie says the reason the whole family get on so well now is because they don't see each other much. I used to think this was typically pessimistic of him; because Molly and Jake spend holidays with Lisa and her new family and Lisa always phones at Christmas. And we spent that time in New Hampshire with Lisa. But now I think it's probably true that they irritate each other.

Charlie says Lisa's obsessive. She is a bit, the chocolate desserts prove that. But she's also a shot in the arm, an injection of hope and cheerful get-up-and-go. I love her energy.

Monday 14th:
As well as being locations director, I'm to help Lisa find actors – which makes me a casting director as well. Never had so many titles in my life. Our whole street's to be the supporting cast. Lisa goes into ecstasies over the "wonderful faces" of our neighbours – they remind her of Fellini's characters. I know what she means, but don't think they'd be too happy at the description. Firstly, hardly any of them would have heard of Fellini, and secondly our neighbours don't consider themselves "characters" at all, just ordinary Dubliners. A dying breed to be sure.

This morning we ran into Poopdeck Pappy – already drunk at ten o'clock. He had his usual old belt tied around his overcoat. His white hair was wild, but, as always, he beamed cherubically, held out his hand and burst into a cracked tuneless rendition of "When it's springtime in the Rockies, I'll be comin' back home to you!"

"Stop right there!" Lisa yelled, pointing her camera. "Gotta get him."

"When it's springtime in the Rockies, yer bonnie eyes are blue."

Lisa filmed him singing, then chatting to Mrs Roche next door. She and her son are to be recruited, too – for a crowd scene. They were surprised, but mildly interested in the idea. It's a bit of a novelty.

Introduced Lisa to Philomena – thinking it might cheer my neighbour up. I worry about her bearing up, since this damn wedding's been called off. But she seems OK since her episode in St Vincent's and was intrigued by the prospect of being in a film.

Lisa's cameras are worth about forty thousand dollars, so we have to be careful to keep our eye on them at all times. Even though Packy's robbing somewhere else now, I asked her not to leave them in the hired car.

We went into the film centre in Eustace Street this morning. As always, it was buzzing with new young-Ireland talent. There's wonderful energy in Dublin and more cinematic interest than any other city in the EU. I didn't know it, but we hire more videos than anywhere else – you know why, when you go to the film centre. There's so much more opportunity than when I was young – in TV, film and everything. But, thanks to Lisa, I'm learning about making movies, as she talks about it non-stop – better late than never to branch out is what I say. We got some information about hiring grips, etc. – all technical stuff – for next year. Also we met a costumes designer who's done some work on the latest Michael Collins movie. She introduced Lisa to more contacts.

One was Con Quirke – a small, wiry young man with a blond crew-cut and a wispy little rat's tail of hair hanging down his neck. He speaks in an American accent, although he's never been there. He's "gonna" be our assistant director.

Lisa sipped her herb tea. "I need a wake scene."

"Sure, Lisa, sure," Con parrotted – he's like some lapdog.

He was on herb tea, too – I had a sinful coffee.

I didn't remember a wake in the story and said so tactfully.

"Then we'll put one in, Peggy! We can't have an Irish movie without a wake." She bit her lip. "Can you suggest someone to play the corpse, Con?"

Con didn't know anyone old, naturally, as he was so young, so I suggested Bill Hickey, an elderly American movie actor, who's retired into a nursing home. He started out on the New York stage and went to Hollywood where he got idiots' parts and sometimes eccentrics'. I knew of the actor from old westerns. In his day, he was a Spencer Tracy lookalike.

Lisa was "enthused", so I made an appointment for us to meet him tomorrow at 4p.m. at his nursing home on the outskirts of Dún Laoghaire.

Thursday 17th:
Lisa had appointments in RTÉ this afternoon, so we arranged to meet at Bill Hickey's nursing home, *Saoirse*. An odd name?

Well, I got there and no sign of Lisa's car in the drive, so went on in as we were already late. It wouldn't do to keep an old man waiting. It's a big Victorian redbrick with a spacious garden. Rang the bell on the locked door. At first no one came, so I nervously studied the potted plants in the porch. The place looked well tended, but I couldn't help shivering inwardly at the thought that I'll most probably end up in such a place. It's unavoidable; you grow old or die. You certainly can't stay young. Things change all the time – daily. I'm literally not the same person as when young. Or even the same as the last eight years. Not muscles, bones or blood. Consoling in a way.

No one came.

Rang again.

Finally a white-coated male nurse appeared. He opened the door from inside with a huge key and locked it again after us, laughing, "We hafta lock in our visitors."

Slightly apprehensively, explained I had an appointment with Mr Hickey.

"Ah, yes, Bill's in his room." He showed me the way. "When you want to leave, ring." He pointed to a big ship's bell which hung in the hall, then led me past a TV room full of old people staring vacantly at an afternoon quiz show. Then along drab, airless, disinfected-smelling corridors to Bill's room.

There were two beds in it. In one a half-naked old man played babyishly with the blankets. Bill Hickey sat in an armchair at the end of the other, reading a book. He's distinguished, with thick white hair and brilliant blue eyes which lit up as I came in.

He held out a hand. "Delighted to meet you, Miss – eh?"

"Mrs – Peggy O'Hara-McCarthy."

As we shook hands, I glanced nervously at the other bed. The bony occupant looked deranged, absolutely mad.

"My friend, Lisa, seems to be late," I said nervously. "She wants to talk to you about a part."

He seemed amazed. "An . . . acting part?"

I nodded.

He sighed sadly. "As you can see, Mrs O'Hara-McCarthy, I'm retired."

"You couldn't be persuaded?"

He coughed chestily, perusing me anxiously. "Well, now. The memory, my dear. It goes."

"Oh . . ."

An awkward silence.

Then, "What sort of part is it?"

I didn't want to say it was a dead man. "Lisa'll explain. Uh –
there isn't much memorising."

He looked relieved, then sighed sadly again. "I'd do anything to
get out of here."

Felt sorry for him. For all the old. Philomena's fiancé couldn't be
that much younger, yet he was thinking of getting married again.
Why had the children stopped him? There are so many lonely
people in the world who can't find each other. Philomena needs
someone to love, that's all. She needs to be married. Everyone
should be married.

He didn't speak for a minute. "You and Lisa are related?"

"In a way. I'm married to her first husband."

"Well, what d'ya know." He chuckled. "That's thoroughly
modern."

I smiled nervously. The old man in the other bed was now completely entangled in the bedclothes. Why was Lisa so late?

"Did Lisa phone?" I asked.

He put his hand to his ear. "Phone? I don't think so." He nodded to the other bed, where the old man had the blanket wrapped
around his head. "Now don't mind him."

"Should we call the nurse?"

"Ah, yes, perhaps." He staggered up then reached for a bell over
his bed. "Come on, we can wait in the hall."

We left the old man to his blanket. I followed Bill as he hobbled
slowly to the hall where we sat down and waited for Lisa. She was half
an hour late by now. I stopped myself getting annoyed and chatted
amiably. Bill told me he'd started life as a child actor in the teens of
the century and had been in silent movies. Amazingly, he knew Charlie Chaplin and Katharine Hepburn. He said it was difficult to live
with so many old people. Again thought of Philomena. She needs
someone to take care of. Would she be interested in Bill Hickey?

Lisa finally came – red in the face and flustered. "That goddam Dublin traffic! Peggy, why didn't you warn me!"

But before I could answer, she turned to the old man. "Now, Mr Hickey, can you play a corpse?"

Bill was delighted. "That I can."

"Fine!"

He looked worried. "There's just one problem. When're you shooting?"

"Next June."

He seemed disappointed again. "But I'm not a young man, I may be dead by then."

Lisa waved a hand dismissively. "You won't be. It's being shot in Mayo. We're going out west to film Moore Hall tomorrow, for a documentary."

He grabbed her hand, his blue eyes lit up. "You're going west? Take me with you."

Lisa taken aback. "I don't think we can, Mr Hickey. We're doing it in a day. It'll be pretty tiring."

He held on to her. "Please, take me out of this place."

Lisa hesitated for a second. Then she nodded. "Sure, Mr Hickey. Why not? You can ride in back. Do we need clearance?"

"Would you mind saying you're my niece from the States?"

Lisa winked. "Gotcha."

So we rang the ship's bell in the hall. When the male nurse came running, we said Lisa, Mr Hickey's favourite niece, wanted to take him west on Sunday to meet another long-lost cousin. She'd get him back by nightfall. Amazingly, they didn't make difficulties. After what Bill intimated about his health, I was nervous, but said nothing. Couldn't spoil the party.

Later:

Slipped in the bath tonight – it was all oily. Lisa must've put something in it and forgotten to wash it off. Thought I'd broken my back. I was on it, my toe amazingly stuck in the tap.

"Charlie!" I screamed.

He came running. "You OK?"

I gripped the bath. "No, I'm stuck."

"Hang on!" He pulled at my toe, but it wouldn't come.

"Maybe some oil?" I suggested.

He huffed and puffed. "Don't want to hurt you."

"Thanks, I need a big toe!"

"I'm doing my best, Peggy!"

Finally it came out. Thank God, he was there. Thank God for husbands. I can't imagine asking anyone else to de-tap my toe.

Friday 18th:

Lisa saw someone else about funding yesterday.

Also she introduced me to Gabriel Byrne last night – lovely man. They seemed to know each other. We were having tea in the Shelbourne again when he walked over. I offered to buy him a drink, but he was in a hurry. I'm so impressed with Lisa's get-up-and-go and said this to Charlie later. He still said he doubted the movie would ever be made.

Lisa definitely wants a graveyard scene, so we drove all around Wicklow today. We went down as far as Glendalough, for heaven's sake, but ended up back in Powerscourt House, Enniskerry, where they said we could use the gothic family graveyard.

"Great!" Lisa yelled, picking her way among the tumbling tombstones.

It was like something out of a Victorian poetry book – choking weeds, ivy, depressing cypress trees – all overgrown.

Then I froze – a rat.

It was paying no attention to us, nibbling on some grass on a grave.

Lisa stared into my face. "What is it, Peggy?"

I didn't want to frighten her. "Nothing."

She stretched her arms upward. "Isn't this beautiful?"

Is she totally mad?

We're going west tomorrow to film Moore Hall, the ruined mansion that was George Moore's family home. I'm to give a little speech on Moore, as Charlie won't. With all his knowledgeable reading, his Ph.D. etc., he's much better qualified than me, but claims he's too busy. I'm sure it's something else. Is he sneaking off to be with Erin?

Anyway, to look my best, I went into the Shelbourne and used up Billy Boy's gift of a facial. I had to take off my clothes down to my bra – thank God it was clean. The beauty therapist said I had a good skin and shaped my eyebrows. She also dyed my eyelashes, so I won't have to wear mascara. Never do, but it's nice not to have to. Also, she showed me the proper way to put on lipstick. Look better, I think.

While waiting my turn in the beauty salon, I read an article in a magazine about a dying marriage. It said the way to rejuvenate things was:

1) Be totally honest with each other. (Charlie won't.)
2) Talk things out. (Won't do that either.)
3) Remember the good times when we first met. (Do, all the time.)
4) Even if you don't feel any love – pretend you do. (I don't have to pretend.)
5) Persevere – the good times will come back. (Can't count on that.)

Later:

I've been working on a little speech to make before the camera, with the Moore mansion in the background. I think it'll be OK.

Sunday 20th:

Something terrible's happened. Remember, remember the twentieth of September. I'll never be able to forget that date.

I'll begin at the beginning: Lisa and I picked up Bill Hickey, as arranged, at about seven this morning from his nursing home and drove west, all the way to Mayo. He was like a little kid out from boarding school. He sat in the back with a knee rug, looking eagerly out the window. But for all his enthusiasm, he was soon asleep and slept most of the way. At Galway we all got out and had lunch.

"What'll you have, Mr Hickey?" Lisa nudged him awake.

He ordered a pint of stout.

"You're allowed *alcohol?*" It was like a dirty word.

He took off his old hat and opened his heavy overcoat. "I might as well."

"I'll have one, too," I said for solidarity.

Lisa looked at me aghast. "If you crave alcohol, you might need professional help, Peggy."

I was taken aback. "I don't crave it."

She sighed primly but got two pints and water for herself.

Mr Hickey drank his, a yellow foam forming a moustache. "A pint of plain is your only man!"

I said it must be bleak in that nursing home.

"It is," he said simply. "But what can you do? Life's a blessing. At my age every day's a wonderful gift."

A great character. As soon as we were mobile, he fell asleep again. Then a long, confusing drive from Galway to Moore Hall. I had to get out and ask all the directions. We stopped beside one old man who said, "Aye, Moore Hall. Go up a hill and down a hill, pass the hedges on the right and then turn left and keep going for a good bit until the road rises into another hill."

"You got that?" Lisa barked.

"Yes . . .!" I repeated the directions to myself in an effort to remember them.

Were we in modern Ireland or not? Is James Stephens still alive? Are there Little People, too, maybe behind the hedges? Anyway we got there finally. But by then it was raining and Lisa refused to get out of the car.

I was put out. We'd spent the day driving there. Why was she acting like this? "You're not going to film the house, Lisa?"

She looked at the dreary rain. "Rain's bad for the camera."

"But we've come all this way! Can't we put a coat over it?"

In the end she got out reluctantly and hauled the camera up the wooded path. The last time I was at the house, it could be seen from the road. This time it seemed to have disappeared into the woods. We walked on and on.

"Are we nearly there?" Lisa grumbled, staggering under the weight of the camera.

"Yes, it's here some place," I placated. "It's a spectacular ruin."

We walked on.

Nothing – only damp feathery branches in our faces. God, had the house completely disappeared? Maybe they'd knocked it down and I missed it it the papers? Lisa puffed beside me. Even the small walk seemed to be too much for her. She kept saying, "Peggy! How much further?"

"Just a little way," I coaxed. When you come from California, the Irish weather is difficult. There's so much rain.

Then the house appeared through the mist.

"There it is!" I was relieved.

It was like a ship suddenly appearing through a foggy seascape. A great ruin, a magnificent granite spectre of better days. We stood on a gravelled front and discovered there was a long avenue leading to it, which we could've taken – I hadn't seen it. I don't know what style the house is in. Maybe Georgian – actually it looked more like the ruins of an ancient castle. It was disgraceful vandalism to burn it down. No wonder George Moore never wanted to come back to Ireland. I wouldn't either if the IRA had done that to my family home.

It had stopped raining. Lisa set up the camera and took some long, then close shots. I glanced at my notes and mentally prepared myself to say my piece about George Moore's life.

"Should I stand in front of the house? It could be background," I asked nervously.

Lisa sighed wearily. "No, Peggy."

"Where then?"

"Nowhere. You look like a drowned rat."

"Oh. . .!"

"We can't film you today."

"I see. . ." After all the trouble I'd taken, getting a makeover to look my best for the camera. "It's all off then?"

"Yes, it's a bad hair day, Peggy."

"Oh. . .!"

But it was to be more than that.

Of course, it didn't matter at all whether or not I made my debut as a documentary star. Now I'm getting to the really bad bit. When we got back to the car, Mr Hickey seemed to be still sleeping. But I looked a little closer. He was pale. Too pale. Then it occurred to me – he wasn't breathing. Felt his pulse. God.

"Lisa," I said. "I'm afraid. . ."

"What?"

"He's d-dead."

She shook him. "He's drunk!"

"Dead."

Her eyebrows shot up. "I don't believe this!"

But he was definitely gone.

"Alcohol!" she gasped.

"He must've had a weak heart."

Lisa bit her lip. "They think I'm his niece. I'll have to pay for the funeral. What'll we do with the body?"

I suggested we ring 999.

As we waited for an ambulance, I held back tears. The old man's death was an omen. Nothing lasts: not our galaxy, our world, us. Why worry about a marriage? Suddenly, I felt awfully lonely for Charlie. If he was here, he'd cope. He'd know what to do.

The ambulance came and took the body to the nearest hospital morgue. We followed and spoke to the doctor, who declared him dead. On the way home we stopped at a country pub which incidentally doubled as an undertaker's, and went in for a drink. Lisa was still hysterical that she'd have to pay for the funeral, so I said I had my credit card. Then I rang the nursing home, but they said there were funds for such an event. There may be an autopsy first, so they'll give us some notice about the funeral arrangements.

In the bar, I ordered a pint of Smithwicks.

Lisa looked at me worriedly. "You're craving alcohol again!"

I sure was. I needed a stiff drink, preferably a double brandy.

But in the end we both had tea and a sandwich and drove back to Dublin, feeling terribly sad. Poor Mr Hickey. He got out of the horrible nursing home but had suffered a worse fate than that. He was hired to play a corpse, but became one. It's a case of life imitating art.

When we got home, Charlie was giving Erin a cup of coffee in the kitchen. So she was back. And looking lovely, tanned and rested. Her hair was cut and looked thicker, and she was dressed in the same slinky denim. Hell!

"Hi," I dumped my handbag, looking irately at Charlie. Now I'd caught him red-handed.

He had the decency to look embarrassed, then hurriedly introduced Lisa to Fuckoffey.

"Gee, hi! Charlie's told me about you," the strumpet cooed.

Lisa chatted to her matter-of-factly. We told them what had happened to poor Bill Hickey. It didn't seem to occur to Lisa *who* Fuckoffey was – Charlie's *bit on the side*. Why was she being so friendly?

"Tired, Peggy?" he asked me at last.

"We covered quite a bit of ground," I said, glaring at Fuckoffey.

"Well, travelling's hard on older people," she blurted.

Jesus, I hate her.

Something flipped. "What're you doing here?"

She lisped sexily that she'd come to show Charlie another poem. This time I didn't hide my irritation and didn't answer when she spoke to me again. Am I supposed to be a saint?

"I guess Peggy's tired." Charlie looked embarrassed.

"Yes, you run out of energy in middle age!" the brat declared.

It was too much. "*Stop* talking about age! And why can't you leave my husband alone?"

Erin flabbergasted. Lisa pretended not to hear. Charlie fumbled for a cigarette.

I went straight up to bed. I was so sick of her stupid ageist insults that I cried myself to sleep.

Charlie came up later. "I'm getting tired of this, Peggy."

He's tired. What about me? Pretended to be asleep. That

child-woman's been haunting my life for nine months, almost a year. Slept terribly. Then got up in the night to pee.

Lisa was on the phone again and saw my red eyes. "What's wrong, Peggy?"

"Oh, everything. Bill Hickey – I liked the old man."

She sighed. "I know."

"And that girl, the one who was here when we came back. She has a crush on Charlie."

Lisa widened her eyes. "So what?"

I wiped mine with a hanky. "So, he doesn't love me any more, that's what!"

"Oh, don't be silly! Charlie adores you!"

How's that for loyalty between women?

"If you're sexually frustrated use a vibrator, Peggy."

"What?"

"A vibrator. Have you got one?"

"No."

"I'll send you one. I have two."

Then she asked me if I needed HRT?

Told her I was already on it and drank three whiskeys in the kitchen.

Monday 21st:
Hangover today.

At breakfast Lisa stared accusingly as I sipped strong coffee. "You're dehydrated already, Peggy – coffee'll make you worse."

"I couldn't feel worse," I muttered, grabbing a packet of pills. "Coffee and Solpadeine go well together. Like gin and tonic – you should try them."

"I don't take chemicals. You're poisoning yourself! Blend a banana and two tablespoons of aloe vera juice into fresh vegetable or fruit juice to raise your blood sugar levels. Then eat beetroot, broccoli, cabbage or cauliflower – artichokes are good, too. They cleanse the system."

I blinked. I didn't have all those vegetables in the house. I hadn't any.

"And have a glass of water before every drink, Peggy – that's if you must drink. Also eat a protein snack first. If you crave alcohol, you may need professional help."

I shook my head. "But I don't crave alcohol."

I never want to see it again.

Later:

This afternoon, Lisa and I drove back down to Wicklow and took some more shots of graveyards. I'm quite sick of the sight of them. Why does she need a graveyard in her movie? There's absolutely no mention of them in the George Moore short story. I read it again and told her so.

"You can't have an Irish movie without a graveyard!" she insisted.

I said nothing. It was another exhausting day, during which we must've circled the whole county. At one stage we found ourselves in Carlow. If this is the work of a locations director, I dread to think what next year will entail. Ended up in a pub. I had some strong drink, while Lisa sipped herb tea – which amazingly they had. Didn't feel guilty about not rushing home to Charlie. He was probably entertaining Erin anyway.

Tuesday 22nd:

Hung over again.

Another lecture from Lisa, telling me how much Charlie loves me. That she was sending me a vibrator as soon as she got back.

Asked me what size. I said medium?? She wrote this down, matter-of-factly. Then had to go off to some French festival, which I'd never heard of. So she left in a hurry, giving me a tube of proges-terone cream to rub on and a packet of tofu — it contains natural oestrogen which she says I'm lacking.

Poured myself a strong whiskey.

Charlie and I had a long talk — rational, calm, sane. He says he can't help Erin having a crush on him. He has to let her down gen-tly. I said he doesn't. He can tell her to piss off — politely. He only encouraged her by publishing her crap. Well, that did it.

He blew his top. Said it wasn't crap, but very promising poetry. I had no soul, I'm a philistine. Me? Now that's really unfair. Feel-ing pretty awful — miserable in fact. If we split up — I'll miss Char-lie so much. Worse — I won't be Jake's stepgrandmother any more. I was a hopeless stepmother, but better at the stepgrandmothering.

Coincidentally — we got a charming letter from him.

> *dear grandad and peggy,*
> *mom says i gotta thank you guys for the holiday. thanks.*
> *jake.*

Friday 25th:
Feeling a bit more relaxed now that Lisa's gone. I love her, but she exhausts me as well. Attended a mass for Bill Hickey in Glenageary. Very few people there.

Loud knocking in the middle of the night.

Mona, the fanatical street sweeper and Sweetie's mammy, was outside crying. She begged Charlie to come to her house and revive her husband, who'd fallen out of bed and was now lying uncon-scious on the bedroom floor. Charlie went and immediately diag-nosed a heart attack. He tried to pump his chest. Mona frantic. Wanted Charlie to change her husband's underwear, so that the ambulance men wouldn't see he was wearing grubby underpants. Charlie wanted to continue pumping, but she wouldn't hear of it – wanted the underwear changed. So Charlie changed it. Then pounded his chest, but no use. Poor man was gone.

Ambulance came and took him away.

Charlie's very kind – I have to say it, although I'm still furious with him about Erin.

That's two fatalities in one week.

Who's next? Anyway, death's a ill omen – an omen for the end of things. Charlie doesn't love me any more. He couldn't be attracted to me. He wouldn't notice if I wasn't here. Feeling very miserable. And definitely not looking forward to my future with a vibrator.

OCTOBER

Sunday 11th:

Fuckoffey failed her Trinity exams and has to repeat them. Ha, ha, ha! Always knew she was thick. She actually rang Charlie again today, trying to disguise her voice. I got the phone and recognised her immediately. "Oh, Peggy," she drawled nauseatingly. "You've become my role model."

Before I could ask why, she volunteered the reason. "You work so hard."

She said it like I'm a drone or something, while she's the queen bee. A bit sick of this. Don't know how I'll cope. Now it's all going to start up again. I know there's a difference between love and sex. A wife is an old shoe. I have a cupboard full of them – too comfortable to be a challenge, yet not easy to throw away. Charlie and I know each other too well. There's no excitement any more, and that's the awful truth. Maybe marriage is an unnatural bond, but it's been such a happy state for me. I can't let it go easily.

Thursday 15th:

Uncle Tommie's in Dublin for the weekend.

He arrived this morning and phoned from the airport. I invited him again to stay with us. But no, he wanted to stay at the B & B I'd found for him in Rathmines. Then he goes down the country on Monday to visit some extended family on my mother's side. I remember meeting them once, when a child. Wouldn't know them now. My mother was one of those thousands of young country girls who came to Dublin in the forties to work as a domestic. There was no choice – it was either that or emigration to England. She was lucky and landed a job with a a wealthy doctor in Merrion Square. Then she worked for other doctors. She brought me up alone on her few pounds a week after Daddy died. Then, as soon as I was grown, got cancer herself. Then death, after a life of toil. She wasn't old at all. Uncle Tommie's her eldest brother, and he's still alive.

"Don't wanta cause ye any trouble, girl," he wheezed down the line, breaking into a racking cough.

When it stopped, I told him to take a taxi from the airport to Khyber Place and we'd have breakfast here.

But after an hour, no sign of him.

Beginning to worry when he phoned again. This time he was in the phone booth at the end of Palmerston Road. He'd taken a bus and gotten hopelessly lost.

Told him to stay put and ran to meet him.

Worried in case I wouldn't recognise him. Although we've always sent each other Christmas cards, I haven't seen him for years. He's still a bachelor, and emigrated to New York from Kerry in his teens. He's worked at many jobs – a waiter, a roadsweeper, finally he trained as a carpenter and joined the union. So he was making a bit of money when I first went to the States. He was very kind to me then – met me at the plane, took me under his wing. I was never gladder to see anyone, as, armed with my X-ray and travel documents, I dragged my case through the barricades at Kennedy – although he didn't call it that. What did he call it? Forget. God, am I going senile?

Whatever he called it, I can still see him waiting patiently among the airport crowds. A small, dapper leprechaun of a man in a cloth cap, with a lift in one boot from some serious childhood illness. TB,

I think, then the scourge of the Irish. I remember we took a long bus ride from the airport into Manhattan. Then another bus ride to Brooklyn where he was living in a poor walk-up apartment. The apartment was bare and clean. I slept on the sofa in the small living room for weeks. I tried to cook for him, but he preferred his own sparse diet. When I got a secretarial job, I moved out and saw him regularly for a few years. He came to our wedding, but then we lost touch – because he was always so diffident about coming to dinner. Then he moved apartments and I lost his address for about a year. Anyway, he's always been on my conscience.

Yesterday he was by the phone booth on the other side of the square where the trees were beginning to turn into their lovely colours. I always think fall's sad, although it was one of those brilliant days. And Uncle Tommie looked sad, too, his thin figure leaning obediently against the wall by the booth. At his feet was a small black old-fashioned suitcase.

"Peggy!" His navy blue eyes lit up.

I hugged him, noticing the reek of strong cigarettes. "Uncle Tommie."

He seemed even frailer and shorter, but was still dapperly dressed – this time in a loose white London Fog raincoat and soft Irish tweed cap. He had the same lift in one black boot. My mother told me this disability had kept Uncle Tommie from participating in sport in his youth, to his great regret. So he became a passionate follower of Gaelic football and hurling. He's always been passionate about everything Irish – politics, history, music, even literature. He was a member of the Ancient Order of Hibernians and marched in the St Patrick's Day parade when I knew him all those years ago. He's just a typical Irish-American immigrant – New York's full of them.

As we made our way slowly back to Khyber Place, Uncle Tommie offered me a Marlborough.

I laughed, declining. "You're still smoking the same brand, Uncle Tommie. They haven't got you yet!"

"Haven't long left now, girl," he wheezed.

"Bet you'll bury us all!"

"Naw, girl. I've come home to buy a grave."

"A grave?"

"Yeah, and I wanna do somethin' for my country before I go."

Thought this an odd thing to say: although he's in his eighties, he looks healthy. "You're not dying?"

"At my age ye think of it, girl."

What did he want to do for his country? Increase the Celtic Tiger's revenue by spending his Social Security dollars here? Like so many immigrant Irish in New York, he spent his weekends drinking and longing for home in dark seedy Irish pubs. He disgraced me years ago with his knowledge of Irish fiddlers. I'm not musical and actually dislike most of our native airs. They're just too sad and haunting for me. And the latest craze for Riverdance puzzles me. It isn't Irish dancing at all, more like flamenco.

I suggested again he stay with us.

He still said no.

"But you put me up? Remember in '65?"

"Ah, ye were a lovely *cailín*, Peggy." He smiled so sweetly, it took my breath away.

Felt awful – why hadn't I seen more of him down the years? You drift from people. I could've had him over at Christmas or Thanksgiving. But I moved in different circles after I married. And even though Charlie liked him, Uncle Tommie was so diffident. He always made an excuse not to come. Still, I should've made more of an effort.

When we got home, Uncle Tommie took out a bottle of whiskey for Charlie, and a big box of chocolates with a rose on the lid for me. Uncle Tommie's not wealthy. He's lived a life of toil, so these expensive presents took me aback.

Charlie came home for lunch in a hearty mood. The two men struck up an instant rapport and had several whiskeys. Then several more. Uncle Tommie ended up singing. At one stage he broke into "The Road to Athea":

> *We arrived in Athea at a quarter to one*
> *And up to the clergy we quickly did run;*
> *'Twas there we were married without much delay;*
> *And we broke a bed spring, that night in Athea.*

Despite his hilarious singing, Uncle Tommie hadn't ever broken bed springs – I'm pretty sure of that. I never remember any woman in his life. He didn't ever get drunk either – despite his habits. Unlike Charlie, who was the worse for wear after a few drinks. Finally I drove Uncle Tommie round to his B & B. Charlie too drunk to drive. V. irked with him. Why does he do this? Lately he's doing it more. Can't help thinking he's unhappy about Erin. And unhappy with me for exploding at her when Lisa and I came back from the west. But I couldn't help it. I can't lose Charlie. I suppose now, we've established a sort of détente. We don't talk about it.

Friday 16th:

7a.m. Uncle Tommie on the doorstep.

We weren't up yet, but staggered down the stairs in our dressing-gowns, both still sleepy and overtired. Charlie badly hung over, although not admitting it. But I didn't say anything.

I offered breakfast.

Uncle Tommie'd already had it. But he had coffee with us, laced with whiskey, of course – he carries a hip flask everywhere. And, as usual, he chain-smoked.

Charlie joined him, fogging up the kitchen.

I opened the window.

"Peggy was born in a field," Charlie said.

"Well, her mother was a country girl," Uncle Tommie mused affectionately.

Over breakfast, which developed into another drinking session for Uncle Tommie, we talked at length of my mother and her childhood. He told me things I didn't know about her. How poor everyone was back then. How she was only fourteen when she came to Dublin to work. How she hadn't any secondary education. No one did then. People were dressed up as adults and turned out to work at fourteen.

Uncle Tommie stayed dead sober.

Charlie didn't. I'm beginning to think my diagnosis is right: he's upset.

After breakfast, I was trying to change the toilet seat (I'd bought a nice new wooden one, which is so much better than plastic) when Uncle Tommie said to leave it to him, that he'd put it on in a jiffey. It's a simple job, so I did, as after all he's a carpenter by trade. I can't leave anything complicated to Charlie – that's the truth. He's OK on bookshelves and tiling, but electrical work or plumbing's beyond him.

As Uncle Tommie criticised the construction of the outdoor bathroom, I went upstairs and immediately heard hammering. It was loud hammering, but at first it didn't bother me.

Then a loud clattering smash.

Then silence.

What had happened? I ran downstairs, as Uncle Tommie called me from the hall. "Peggy!"

His voice said something was wrong.

Uncle Tommie kept a straight face, but his blue eyes were wide. He held up his bony hands. "Now, don't be upset, girl!"

I looked into the bathroom.

Charlie was standing over the toilet.

I stared in horror.

The white enamel bowl was in bits all over the floor. There was water everywhere. What had gone wrong?

Charlie was laughing. Laughing!

I got my breath. "What happened?"

"I'm afraid the hammer slipped," he gasped.

"It broke up?"

He nodded.

"Well, fix it!" I yelled – couldn't help it. Maybe I'm losing my sense of humour. But sometimes Charlie's too much. He's like an elephant in a china shop. Give him a hammer and he'll wreck the house. I should have done it myself. Went back upstairs and did some deep breathing exercises to calm myself down.

Later:

Feel calmer. Can't let myself get upset. The men have installed a new toilet bowl from Lenihan's of Rathmines – luckily they had one in stock. And I'm phoning the insurance company on Monday, hoping they'll compensate us for accidental damage. Won't tell them it was my idiot husband's fault.

Now Uncle Tommie wants to connect up our outdoor bathroom to the house. Apparently he knows exactly what to do. He'll save us hundreds of pounds.

"This's a God-awful job of work," he sighed again, inspecting the rickety bathroom roof and tapping the walls.

I said no. Uncle Tommie's too old.

Charlie said yes – firmly.

Hate it when he lays down the law like this. But he'd already rented a sledgehammer for the job, and was waving it dangerously in a few practice aims.

"Charlie, please!" I begged.

But no use.

Charlie went out to the atrium – Rose christened the yard this and the name stuck. He expertly thumped the wall with Uncle Tommie instructing him, patting the wall higher up with his veinier hands. "Ye need ta knock down this. Then we put a door there. Brick up this section."

I pleaded with Charlie. What was he doing?

But he pushed me firmly away. "Peggy, go back upstairs and lie down. It'll be OK, I promise."

Then he took up the sledgehammer again.

"Stop!" I yelled.

He held it poised in mid air.

"Put that down!"

He hit the wall.

It's a badly built extension and collapsed immediately. Plaster and bricks everywhere. Me in tears. Why couldn't Charlie stick to writing about idiots? Or publishing them? He should know all about them, being one himself. The biggest idiot I've ever met.

"It'll be OK, girl," Uncle Tommie soothed, pushing me out of the kitchen into the hall.

I'm going to kill Charlie. I'll be up for murder. Went upstairs, flinching at every noise.

Saturday 17th:

Well, they finally cleared up all the plaster. Then Charlie had bricks delivered today and they filled up one hole with them and put a door, opening out to the atrium, in the other. I suppose we now have a proper indoor bathroom. Things were going OK until they installed a wash-hand basin and left the waste pipe exposed un-hygenically in the small yard.

I insisted they sink it in the drain – very firmly.

Uncle Tommie was patient with me. "I ain't goin' to leave it like that, girl!"

"You were!"

"It'll be OK, girl. Trust yer uncle."

"I don't want it left like that."

"No, girl."

"Stop calling me that!"

"What?"

"Girl! I'm not a girl! I'm fifty!"

He looked at me with such piercing blue eyes that I felt terrible. "Oh, call me girl. I should be glad. I'm sorry, Uncle Tommie." I hugged him tearfully.

"Now, now. Go upstairs and rest, like a good girl."

Before I could, Charlie axed into the ground – hitting a pipe. A hot spring sprayed him, the yard, the house, as he tried to hold it. He cleared mud from his face and grimaced like Oliver Hardy. I frantically tried to turn off the mains but couldn't. Uncle Tommie couldn't either. In the end I called an emergency plumber, which cost fifty pounds.

There was an awful lot of water to clear up.

Finally drove Uncle Tommie back to his B & B. "I'm sorry for yelling at you. It gets me down when Charlie starts hammering."

He patted my knee. "Yer a good woman, Peggy. Like your mother."

This brought tears. You never get over anything in life. I'm still a girl, weeping for my mother's death. It wasn't fair that she died. But there's no point, life goes on. Uncle Tommie's the only person I have left in the world. Kissed the old man goodnight at his lodgings. "I love you, Uncle Tommie. And thank you so much for helping with the house."

Charlie irritated with me when I got home. We didn't speak all night. At least, that way, we can't row.

Sunday 18th:
Bathroom finished. Have to admit it's less drafty. They've done a good job. It's a bit unusual that a guest should be a DIY expert as well. And I was so ungrateful. Have I become a terrible grump? A middle-aged harridan?

Had the brilliant idea of inviting Philomena for Sunday lunch – she might like Uncle Tommie. He's about the same age as Ollie. But she wasn't there. Ships pass each other in the night. Now I wonder where she is. Told Charlie I was worried about her.

"That little cow has caused you enough grief," he said.

Told him cow's no word to describe a woman.

He said I'd called Sweetie a bitch. Told him that was different; she/he might be a bitch. He said he/she was male. He's still irked with me for being so grumpy with Erin. Now Uncle Tommie. Gave up arguing and saw to lunch. Charlie has never liked Philomena, but no need to call her names. I have to befriend her, as no one else seems to be around.

Uncle Tommie came then and, after lunch, asked Charlie to go to Croke Park with him. Charlie went cheerfully, although he has no interest in Gaelic football. I'm too critical of him. He has many good points. Even if he's fed up with Philomena, he's kind to other vulnerable people like Uncle Tommie.

V. cold, so told Charlie to take his coat.

He ignored me.

Later:
Charlie came home chilled to the marrow. It was freezing in the Hogan Stand. Didn't say I told you so. Of course, he coughed all night and we both slept badly.

Monday 19th:

Uncle Tommie on the doorstep at about 7a.m. Bright as a button with no sign of 'flu on him. I'm right – he'll bury us all. He's catching the evening train to Tralee. As usual, he wouldn't eat any breakfast, but took out the whiskey flask, smiling his beautiful smile.

He offered it round. "A bit of the hard stuff, Peggy?"

I waved the bottle away. "It's too early, Uncle Tommie."

"Charlie?"

"No!" I said.

Charlie blew his nose loudly.

"It'll do 'im good, Peggy," the old man insisted.

Of course, Charlie took it, despite my objections.

After a while, they started singing again. This time, "My Four Green Fields". It was very lugubrious.

About 10a.m. Uncle Tommie asked where the Sinn Féin offices were. I wondered why he wanted them. Is he going to offer his services? Then I remembered what he said yesterday. And his sad singing today. Is this what he means by doing something for his country? He's surely not going to offer to fight for Irish freedom again?

Charlie looked in the phone book. "I don't know what you want with that crowd. But they're in Parnell Square – number 44, on the west side," he said nasally.

Uncle Tommie wrote down the number. "I'm goin' over there."

"You've an appointment?" asked Charlie.

Uncle Tommie looked dreamy – he has this habit of looking past you into space. He patted his pocket. "Naw, but I gotta little somethin' for em."

Charlie advised ringing first.

But Uncle Tommie shook his head no. He was staring at the floor now in the same solemn dreamy way. I couldn't help wondering what was on his mind. One thing, I didn't want him getting into a discussion of politics with Charlie. I can't stand when Charlie gets worked up about the IRA the way he did with Jake. Uncle Tommie's probably a supporter of Irish unity. He was probably in the IRA and still thinks we're fighting Britain like in the days of his youth. I remember my mother telling me about some republican gang he belonged to. He'd gotten into trouble . . . and it was beginning to occur to me that she always hinted that was one of the reasons he emigrated. In the old days, people never talked about things. They were too traumatised by the Civil War.

Later:
Thought of Uncle Tommie's name for Kennedy Airport: Idlewilde. It was called that originally. Maybe I'm not going senile, but I'll have to train my memory by doing crossword puzzles. I read that's good for it.

We were expecting Uncle Tommie back for lunch. I prepared a nice one: salads and cold meat from Tesco, things I thought he'd like. Had everything ready by 1p.m.

But 2p.m. came. No sign of him. What had happened?

Waited till 5p.m.: still no sign.

He'd obviously gotten lost again. Or had been mugged. He's a frail, elderly man, and we should never have let him out alone. We didn't know what to do. Finally ate the cold lunch for dinner – both v. fed up and nervous about Uncle T.

8p.m. Phone rang. I answered it.

It was Sinn Féin's Dublin office.

"There's a man standing outside our office all day – he says he's related to you," a strong Dublin accent said. "Is he?"

"Yes, he's my uncle – Thomas Flaherty."

What had happened?

Charlie grabbed the receiver. "What's the matter?"

I grabbed it back, and pushed Charlie away.

"He's my uncle," I said calmly. "Could you tell me what's happened?"

"Please come and get him!" the voice said. "He's been standing outside, staring up at the house all day."

I whispered this to Charlie.

He grabbed the receiver again. "Anything wrong with that?"

"Yes, he's acting in a suspicious manner," the voice insisted.

"A cat can look at a king!" Charlie snapped.

I took the phone back. "Listen, we'll be right in."

In the end Charlie went into town alone. He said the old man would be embarrassed in front of me, if he wasn't even allowed in by Sinn Féin, having come all the way from New York to see them. I suppose it made sense. But Sinn Féin were acting very unfriendly. Why couldn't they be nice to an old man? I waited at home with a miserable *déjà vu* feeling. I'd been there before with Billy Boy's amorous adventures and wondered how things were going to turn out this time.

Charlie got delayed on the way to Parnell Square – the damn traffic again. Believe it or not, a guard was questioning Uncle Tommie by then, but Charlie persuaded him the old man was harmless. Uncle Charlie had a cheque in his pocket written out to Sinn Féin – for a thousand dollars. That's all he was doing. Giving them bloody money. His life's savings, probably. And this was not welcome. Odd. Sinn Féin were quick enough to go to America and raise funds for their cause.

When they got home, Charlie was irate, saying he expected nothing better from such an organisation. Uncle Tommie looked dead beat.

I tried to persuade him to eat something. "A nice egg salad sandwich?"

But he shook his head sadly. He drank whiskey and chain-smoked again, and seemed badly shaken by his experiences.

He sighed. "I was trying to help, Peggy."

I touched his arm. "I know."

His blue eyes clouded. "I wanna see a united Ireland before I die."

I hugged him. "Oh, Uncle Tommie . . ."

Wanted to say, stop living in the past. No one cares about a united Ireland any more. The notion's obsolete. But couldn't. Finally Charlie brought him back to his B & B. We're putting him on a train to the south-west in the morning. The country air will do him good. And he wants to pick out a nice grave. Anyway, he'll be safer there, out of temptation, and maybe he'll realise that his country's managing fine without his help. It's a different Ireland from the one he left all those years ago, when so many young men of twenty said goodbye. One good thing – now he has more money for his grave.

Feeling sad and lonely for my mother.

Later:

Erin called this evening, asking us both to go out for a drink. I refused to go. Charlie irked. What does he expect? Do I have to like someone who threatens my happiness? Heard a priest on the radio saying the God of the Old Testament was a jealous god. It makes him more understandable than the other one, the all-loving god. And I understand Othello strangling Desdemona, too. And *La Bohème.* And all those other guys and dolls.

NOVEMBER

Sunday 1st:

Things no better with Charlie. Lately, he's clammed up completely about Erin. What's wrong with communication? I tackled him last night and he suggested we separate for a while, if I'm that "unhappy". He seemed outraged that I should be "unhappy". Does he think he can cavort with an infatuated idiot and not make me "unhappy"? But I can't stand the thought of separation. And why should I leave the field to Fuckoffey? Disappear without a fight? Dreamt last night we were back in New York and out shopping in Macy's. We took the lift to the top floor, and I lost Charlie in the crowds. Looked and looked, but couldn't find him. Then phoned home and discovered he'd gone ahead of me. Does this mean I'm to lose him?

Monday 2nd:

Went to the doctor today – she says I've got palpitations. She said it like some sort of accusation. Like it was all my fault. "*Why* is your heart racing?" How do I know? Maybe I'm upset. Well, no wonder. But my blood pressure's OK, and there's no side effects from the patches. So far, so good.

Called in to see Philomena on way home. She's recently got two cuddly little pups – Mutt and Jeff. Could be the answer to her loneliness problems. The whole street was invited in to admire them. Hope they do their business in the park and not on our doorstep. Last night they yapped all night, keeping us awake. But Philomena's such a proud parent, I didn't complain.

"It'll be a job to rear them, Peggy." She blinked worriedly behind her glasses. "I had to get up twice in the night."

She said this like getting up was a badge of respectability – the way people boast about their children to you. They pretend to complain when really it's a labour of love. People need something to care about more than anything. Now Philomena has the pups. She's bought them all sorts of expensive dog bones and dog toys, a basket and two little tartan waistcoats. I bought her a guide to training dogs – written by a vet. After all, had intended to give her a wedding present, but now it's a dog present instead.

Pity she didn't marry and have kids. So many lonely people in the world. Told her Charlie and I were thinking of selling up and going back to the States. Couldn't bear to tell her the truth – our marriage collapsing and all that. But she was too engrossed in the dogs to care. It shows you – everyone can be done without. No one is indispensable. If Charlie and I leave here, we'll soon be forgotten. We'll be remembered as the eccentric Americans.

Tuesday 3rd:

Pups kept us awake again last night – hysterical yapping. Feel terrible today. Don't begrudge Philomena her pets, which have made such an enormous difference to her happiness, but cannot do without sleep.

Wednesday 4th:

Alice Amethyst here.

I opened the door at dawn this morning, and there she was, standing in the rainy dark, surrounded by two huge bags. I hugged her. Her taxi headlights eerily pierced the primeval gloom, throwing her into bold, Zorro-like relief. A black Amish shawl covered her sleek black suit, and she wore a big black leather hat – quite *distinguée*. The effect was sort of Mexican, although Amish actually. Alice is seventy, but acts much younger – only her seasoned, sun-wrinkled skin betrays her age.

Whatever about our other visitors, this one will be perfect.

Alice held me warmly, smelling of expensive scent. "I love ya, Peggy."

"Me, too."

A lump came in my throat as her soft skin touched mine. I can't think of anyone in the world I'm more happy to see. She's been promising to come for the whole year, so I was delighted when she rang a few days back to say she could make it. Charlie, too – she's our oldest friend. We badly need her to pour balm on our wounds.

"Come on in." Grabbed her bags, as she paid the driver in the artisan pokiness of the hall.

He offered change, but she waved him away.

Alice's like that – terribly generous.

He shuffled off, then backed noisily down the sleeping cul-de-sac.

I dumped her bags at the bottom of the stairs and showed Alice the downstairs of the house, while hearing Charlie still moving about upstairs.

Her baby-blue eyes widened with curiosity. "So this is the famous house!"

I nodded nervously.

Alice is a wealthy realtor and used to a lot – I mean it: A LOT. She'd have to think the house small. Maybe the smallest she's ever seen. But I couldn't stand her saying it. I can't stand any more criticism – after all, Charlie's worked so hard to make it nice. His soul is in it. All our happiness and hope for happiness resides in these walls.

"Like it?" I asked hopefully.

"Love it, Peggy!"

I hugged her again, controlling tears.

"What is it?" Alice held me at arm's length, perusing my face. She misses nothing.

I didn't want to get into my woes. "Nothing."

Just couldn't tell her how miserable I am about Charlie's mid-life crisis. Seeing her brought back a happier past, a past there now seemed no way of getting back to. Over the years we've had such good times together.

"I'm just so – glad to see you," I stammered stupidly.

She laughed. "I've always wanted to come to Ireland. Now where's Charlie?"

I called upstairs.

"Let's all go out for breakfast!" she said. "I want to see some of Dublin."

I said, sure, why not?

Although she'd been flying all night, Alice didn't look tired at all. She's always been like that. Indefatigable. She's years older than us, but has the energy of someone half her age. And now that she's here things will be different – I know it. She's aptly named, Amethyst – a jewel of a friend. Maybe tomorrow or the next day, she'll talk to Charlie, make him see sense. Anyway, that's my hope.

I showed her the kitchen.

She looked at everything carefully. "Why, it's a cute house, Peggy! How many bathrooms?"

"Uh – one!" I showed it to her.

She raised her eyebrows. "Compact."

Being in real estate, it was natural for Alice to question the number of bathrooms. But how could she possibly think there was room for more than one in our tiny house? At least that was attached now, thanks to Uncle Tommie's efforts. We sat at the kitchen table, and she took off the Amish hat to reveal softly permed pepper-and-salt curls, which softly framed her face. The hat was a present for Charlie, she said.

I said she ought to keep it, as it looked so right on her, but she said no. Everything about Alice is stylish. She's just one of those people – she could put on a sack and still look good. Even her luggage is real leather – at the edges; the middle is good canvas. She's a classy lady in every way, with gracious, old-world manners. She's from New England, originally, and once told me her family came over with the *Mayflower*. So she has no Irish connections.

"The hat'll get Charlie out of his baseball cap. This shawl's for you, Peggy." She took it off, too. "Wore it to save packing. It'll be good for this climate."

"Thanks, Alice." I stroked the soft, warm wool. "I'll wear it working. I get cold sitting."

Alice is wonderful to all her friends. When she called two nights ago, enquiring if we needed anything from the States, I asked her to bring some sausage for Charlie and a packet of Bisquik – he says Irish flour's heavier, so pancakes aren't as good here. She took them out of her suitcase now. Also a bottle of champagne for me.

"Charlie'll be delighted with the Bisquik. He'll be down in a minute." He seemed to be still dressing, so I offered coffee.

But she wanted champagne. "Let's celebrate."

I got the bottle open and poured some out. We touched glasses.

"To Ireland!" she toasted, downing hers.

"To your holiday," I said – it was a first for me, champagne before breakfast.

"Let's go!" she said impatiently. "Where's Charlie?"

I yelled up the stairs again, and he ran down at last, tripping over the suitcases and looking somewhat dishevelled. "Alice! Welcome!"

They hugged like old friends.

"How's the book coming?" she asked.

He looked sheepish. "It's . . . ah – coming."

The truth is, the book's a forbidden topic, because he's getting *nowhere* with it. He's too busy mooning over that stupid Erin. Also he's taken on a lot of freelance editing work – which eats into his time.

"Get your coat on," Alice ordered. "I'm taking you both out for breakfast."

Charlie frowned – he hates eating out. "But we can have it here. Can't we, Peggy?"

I nodded. "Of course! Alice brought you sausage and Bisquik."

Charlie licked his lips. "Let's have pancakes here."

But Alice insisted, "No. I want to buy you breakfast!"

She wouldn't be dissuaded, so we walked down to Bewley's of Grafton Street, where we had to wait to be seated. They've made it so posh now that it's awful, but Alice didn't notice – she was too delighted to see Charlie. Charlie was always her darling. It's a mother/son thing, and they've always been very close. So Alice, more than anyone, will be able to advise me about his infatuation, because she knows him better than anyone and she's a woman of the world. They were buddies years before we met, yet she's become a mother to me as well. She was the first of his friends I met all those years ago in New York. At the time she was recently divorced from her own first husband. That rat ran away with a teenaged friend of her daughter's – a great blow to Alice at the time, according to Charlie.

But Alice isn't a moaner.

And she's never tired. After breakfast in Bewley's she wanted to look around the shops, so we trailed after her – Charlie reluctantly, as he hates shopping; but, because it was Alice, he didn't complain. She bought some Irish linen for her daughter who's getting married. She has four children. I'm in awe of the way she brought them up alone, without help from their father. She sent them all to Ivy League colleges. If there's another life, like the Buddhists say, I'm coming back as one of her kids.

They're dear to me, too. I mean – we've gone over to the Amethysts' apartment for a New Year's Eve party with Alice and her kids for as long as I've known Charlie. You leave one family and find another – that's what I've always thought about the Amethysts. It was lovely to be part of a family for holidays such as Thanksgiving, or her birthday, or her children's birthdays. She absolutely always included us. There was always great food and the best champagne.

Originally she worked in the sales department of Charlie's publishing company, but she went on to bigger things and is now in commercial retail. She sells skyscrapers now instead of books. She drives a Cadillac and has an apartment in John Lennon's old building overlooking Central Park – I forget the name. But wealth hasn't gone to her head.

Alice is a rarity in many ways. Her courage, for one thing, is remarkable. I remember the morning about twenty years ago that she found a lump the size of a golf ball in her right breast. It was cancer. But did she moan about that either? No. She got on with life and is still here. She's passed the five year test, but has had a few scares over the years. We went over once when her liver scan was abnormal.

I remember Charlie joked her, saying she was to will him all her valuable paintings. But, instead of laughing, Alice burst into tears and said she had her eye on Charlie, but he ratted on her by marrying me. I was so sad about her health that I suggested the three of us could get married. It was a joke, of course, but I was that fond of Alice. Luckily, the scan was a false alarm. And she remarried soon after that. Her second husband's a genial man called Sam. On the bus home, I asked about him.

"We're divorcing," she said matter-of-factly.

A bombshell.

"I'm sorry." I was puzzled.

But she shrugged. "Life, dear."

God, the whole world's divorcing. Are we next?

Now I'm upstaged – I can't very well bother Alice with my troubles when she's divorcing her husband. But I don't understand. I thought Alice was happy. When she and Sam first married, we felt bereaved. Honestly, we missed her so much, it was like our only child had left home. For years, we'd done things together – eaten out or gone to movies. Alice is FUN. She'd call up and say, "Whatja doin'?" And we'd be off. Just like that.

Or we'd go out for brunch – on a whim, like today.

But, although we missed her, we consoled ourselves that she was living her own life and happy. Love is the art of letting go. I tell myself this, yet I'll never be able to let go of Charlie.

As the bus roared up the Rathmines Road, we fell into an awkward silence. Her divorce was the last thing I expected. Sam's rather bland, but sociable, a man who'd do anything for you. He's a retired New York lawyer of means, who likes golf. After they married, Alice rented her wonderful apartment and moved in with him on the Upper East Side. They were comfortable and lived a smart, privileged, upper-middle-class New York life. How could they be divorcing? He was such a kind man. Any time we went over, he went to great trouble to fix everyone's drink exactly as they wanted.

That's what I remember – him always remembering how I liked my drink. Vodka and tonic with a squeeze of lime and no ice. Charlie's is bourbon with ice and a little water.

Walking up Khyber Place, I asked Alice what had gone wrong? But she shrugged again in reply. Then, as we got home, she sighed sadly, "You two get the prize for the most romantic marriage."

I said nothing.

And neither did Charlie.

It shows how wrong you can be. How you can misread a situation.

Thursday 5th:

Weather not too good. After all, it's November. Yesterday horrible – rain. Today cold, but dry. But lovely to have Alice here, although I must say she keeps us moving. It's hectic – non-stop. She's impossible to tire out. Brought her to the Royal Hospital to see some modern art yesterday – she seemed to like it. Showed her the Georgian Squares today.

She seemed impressed – houses are her thing. Yet I detected a boredom or slight tiredness, or depression. Maybe I'm wrong? I hope so. I don't want this visit to go badly. After Bobbye Anne, I'm probably too sensitive.

In the afternoon, I went grocery shopping in Tesco. Asked Alice if she needed anything?

She came with me. "I like to see how other people live, Peggy."

I got some nice lamb and a chicken for tomorrow.

Alice bought some toilet paper of all things – a packet of Kitten Soft tissue.

Drat – she mustn't like ours.

I could kill Charlie. He got about a ton of Bronco tissues last month in a cut-price shop – they were selling it off. It was one of

his stupid economy drives. Quite honestly, it's enough toilet paper
for the rest of our lives. And maybe our descendants' lives. But I
stored it in the coal shed, although there's barely enough room for
it there. So I thought it best to use it up and put a stack in the bathroom, too. But I'm glad Alice is assertive and expresses herself. I
can't think of anything worse than a guest being unhappy.

On the way home introduced her to Mrs Murphy.

They got on well – knew they would.

They chit-chatted for about an hour – while I cooked dinner.

Friday 6th:
Alice in better form.

This visit's going well – thank God.

I knew Alice wouldn't be like Rose or Bobbye Ann. She
wouldn't complain about the weather or not having her own bathroom. Or having to sleep on the futon. Or the smallness of the
house, the poverty of the area. Or the filth of the wildlife – pigeons
and Sweetie. Penitential toilet paper is understandable. Told Charlie to dump the lot, but he wouldn't. Told me I was too fussy. I said
we had to think of our guest.

I brought Alice into town for lunch in a restaurant where they
have wonderful salads, but she wanted to buy an egg sandwich in
a small shop and sit in the park.

"They look delicious, Peggy." She peered in the newsagent's
window like Oliver Twist, asking for more.

How could she want to sit there?

I hate eggs, and it's cold in the park in November. But perhaps
I should've given in. After all, she's the guest. But you blow it sometimes. I know this because she was a little grumpy with me when I
insisted on the salad bar. Then she was quite taciturn all through
lunch. And later she didn't seem at all interested in the National

Gallery. So afterwards we went shopping for sweaters in the Powerscourt Centre which cheered her up considerably. We found a craft centre there, and this was great, as she likes to know what different cultures produce. Unlike most rich people, Alice has a social conscience and is interested in third world development – she'd especially like to import African crafts into America. But she's saving that for her retirement. Lucky Africa – she's such a good business woman, she'll probably improve things considerably there.

Saturday 7th:
Today Charlie took Alice on his grand tour – the usual sights. Then they went on a literary pub crawl together, as I was working at home.

But he said she was bored.

I suppose it's to be expected – she's not into Irish writers and has probably no interest in the pubs where Brendan Behan drank. Why should she? And she doesn't know anything about Swift or his cathedral. I don't blame her for that either. Although she wanted to see some old Catholic churches when I met them later for a drink.

"We don't have any," I said. "The Protestants took them all."

But I showed her the Pro-Cathedral.

"Ireland isn't Italy," she reflected sadly.

"No," I said. "We had the Reformation. Then the Penal Laws. They said mass on a rock in a field. Our culture's oral. Everything went into the literature. That's why we're such great talkers."

Sunday 8th:
I detected some disenchantment at this lack of interesting Catholic churches, but I never knew Alice was even remotely interested in religion.

It was my day to entertain Alice, so brought her out on the

DART to the Sandycove Martello tower where Joyce lived with
Gogarty, had the famous nightmare and fled in the middle of the
night. It doesn't only have a literary interest. It's of historical sig-
nificance in its own right – regardless of Joyce's stay. It defended us
against Napoleon. But Alice wouldn't even go in. Charlie's right;
she seems to be bored. Odd, but then perhaps I'm too demanding
a guide. Why should she be interested in Joyce? Or the Napoleonic
Wars? I'm not particularly. The tower was just somewhere to go on
the DART, as the traffic's too terrible to drive. And Alice isn't one
to stay home. She's a party gal. In New York this was a bonus, but
now we're having trouble amusing her.

After dinner tonight, she announced, "Dublin's a mess. I'm
gonna hire a car and have some FUN!"

There was accusation in the word: FUN.

Charlie and I looked nervously at each other. But her baby-blue
eyes blinked innocently. "I want to see the country! You guys
coming?"

Charlie was hesitant. "W-well, I don't know. Whatcha think,
Peggy?"

A holiday isn't on the schedule right now. I've got work to finish – it's the story of my life, I know. But maybe I can take a few
days off. A trip with Alice won't be anything like travelling with
Henry and Rose. It'll be relaxing to go with her – she's our best
friend after all.

Monday 9th:
Weather's still terrible – all to do with global warming, I've read.

And something awful's happened.

I'd better begin at the beginning.

Well, our old banger of a car was voted too decrepit for a long
trip to the country, so this morning Alice and Charlie went into

town to hire one – she insisted on paying for this. While they were out, I packed a picnic lunch (French bread, baked ham and wine), and we set out on our adventures as soon as they got back.

We headed south en route to Waterford, as Alice wanted to see the Waterford Crystal factory. And, as we wanted Alice to see rural Ireland rather than the impersonal motorway, took the Military Road to Glendalough in Wicklow. The bleak beauty of that lonely road over the mountains never fails to touch me. It touched Alice, too; I knew by the happy look on her face. We were all so happy and carefree, driving over that mountain. It was like old times.

"This road was built during the Famine," I explained, trying to make the drive interesting. "And rebels hid out in the mountains while on the run."

Charlie did his sheep routine. "You think those sheep are sitting down in the grass, Alice?"

She peered through the window. "Well, aren't they?"

"No, they don't have any legs. They've been amputated. Agricultural policy here."

Pause.

Then Alice laughed heartily – she's no fool. "Oh, yeah?"

Our first stop was Glendalough. Alice was delighted with the beautiful peaceful lakes and the surrounding mountains. We visited the ancient cemetery with its crowded and crooked tombstones. And the round tower, where she was puzzled by the slit halfway up. "That a door?"

"It kept the Vikings out," I said. "They got in and pulled up the ladder. Then poured things down on the invaders."

Alice was intrigued.

"You can make a wish here!" I walked over to the famous Celtic Cross and showed her. "You touch your fingers like this and wish."

I wanted Charlie back.

Alice hugged it, too, closing her eyes. Did she want Sam?

Had our lunch in the picnic area – Charlie was driving, so only had a glass of wine. He's very good about not drinking when driving. He only overdoes it at home, so maybe I'm generally too critical of him. Anyway, Alice and I finished the bottle off. Then, as we got into the car, Alice wanted to drive.

Glancing nervously at me, Charlie handed her the keys.

She'd had a few drinks, so I was nervous, too. "You're OK with the left-hand drive?"

Alice was irritated. "Peggy, I've driven all over the world!"

"But on the left?"

She reddened. "Sure, on the left! But if you're nervous, I won't!"

"No, I'm not nervous!"

Could've kicked myself. I trusted Alice. She's sensible, and it's true she has travelled widely. For heaven's sake, she's gone across the Sahara in a jeep. But now I'd offended her – somewhat. Dammit, she hadn't had that much wine. What had I said? Looked mean-ingfully at Charlie, and he raised his eyebrows back in reply. As if to say, was this our old friend? I'd never seen her irritated before.

The N11 could be any American interstate, so we kept to our initial plan of using less-travelled roads. The one to Rathdrum was sleepy and tree lined, so I relaxed in the back and went with the flow. Or tried to. But Alice was driving too fast – about sixty – and didn't brake for the corners.

"Maybe slow down a bit," Charlie said. "There are sheep – and potholes."

"Oh, yeah!" Alice accelerated.

"About thirty-five would be safer," he added worriedly.

We hit a pothole.

Bang!

Screech of brakes.

I hit the car roof. Charlie yelled, "Christ!"

All shaken, not stirred.

"Damn!" Alice put her foot down again.

But she had to stop immediately, as a front wheel wobbled horribly.

"That's done it!" Charlie groaned.

We all got out to investigate – tyre ripped badly.

"Shit!" Charlie pushed back his baseball cap. He fumbled with the boot lock. "Should be a spare."

There was.

He tried to change the wheel, but couldn't.

All this time Alice sulked silently in the background. She didn't say anything, but stood with her arms folded disapprovingly, breathing heavily. Her anger was palpable. Maybe she thought Charlie should be more efficient. I don't know. A man should be able to do these necessary things, but that's Charlie. He's not mechanical. He can't help it. Finally he hitched a ride into Rathdrum to find a garage, while Alice and I waited by the car.

Her anger seemed to sizzle in the damp quiet of the Wicklow afternoon. "These roads are a disgrace!" she fumed, through a fog of cigarette smoke.

I agreed. But why was she overreacting like this?

"What kind of country is this, Peggy?"

I shrugged. "Potholes are a problem OK."

"It's like some third world republic!"

"They're getting money from Europe to repair them," I placated.

Honestly, she acted like it was all OUR fault – like we'd done something wrong. Were personally responsible for the Wicklow potholes or something. I didn't say it was all HER fault. That she should've driven more slowly. She didn't need to act like Michael

Schumacher on a winding Irish country road. Why didn't she listen to Charlie?

At last a boy cycled toward us. His blond hair blew in the wind, reminiscent of an angel of mercy. In a few deft minutes he took off the tyre and replaced it with the spare. He was wonderful; he didn't even want to take any money, but we paid him anyway. Then, after picking up Charlie at the Rathdrum garage, were on our way again.

This time Charlie took the wheel – Alice insisted.

Then she sat in the back, although I offered her the front. She was terribly, ominously silent, so, on the Wexford road, I made efforts at cheerful chit-chat. "See those bungalows. There's a big row going on about bungalow blitz in Ireland."

No answer.

"We don't have a visual sense." I turned back, apologetically. "Some people say it's ruining the countryside."

Still no answer.

Vibes terrible. You could cut the atmosphere. And Alice's face was frightening. Her eyes were dangerously dark and her lips were clamped tightly, as if she were damming a terrible Vesuvius-like rage. It would erupt any minute and drown us all in angry lava.

"You OK, Alice?" I asked nervously.

She nodded grimly, staring straight ahead – blinking on the verge of tears. God, I'd never seen anyone look so miserable. What was wrong? Was she mad with me? Charlie? He'd been mildly irritated with her. But his reaction was nothing, NOTHING, to what it would've been if I were driving. Then there would've been an explosion – Mount Etna at least. It's always easier to blame a wife. What else are we for?

I tried again. "There's another bungalow with an arch. The conservationists hate those arches. They're horrible."

No answer.

"But this country was once populated. Before the Famine there were eight million . . ." I gave up talking and silently contemplated the bungalows. People have to live somewhere, but they could be designed better.

Raining in Wexford.

Luckily we had the cover of an umbrella as we searched the narrow streets for a restaurant. Alice seemed to take the weather personally, too, and still wouldn't talk. What the hell had we done? Were we responsible for the rain? The ozone hole? Global warming? I was fed up. It was no way to behave. She was the one who wouldn't slow down. She could've wrecked the rented car badly. We were lucky to get out of the mess so easily, in one piece, all alive and unhurt. But Alice didn't seem to think that. She wanted to make us pay for something we hadn't done.

We had a meal in White's Hotel. Food fine, heaps of salmon and salads and wonderful value all round, I thought. Yet Alice griped about everything there. Nothing right – fish frozen, fruit tinned, ice cream God-awful; even the coffee, a single filtered cup, was inadequate.

Alice pursed her lips. "What a country! No decent coffee."

"It's not America," I agreed, "but the coffee's OK – Rombouts."

"I've never seen coffee sold like this." She peered at the filter.

Charlie looked at me, puzzled. He didn't know what to do or say. He was thinking the same thing as me, I know. Was this our dearest friend? What had happened to her? She seemed like a different person from the one we knew in New York. Was it the Irish air? The rain? Was she well? Had her cancer come back? Or was she upset about her impending divorce? That was probably it, I decided, as she looked so healthy. Was this my future, too? A sad and griping old age? A personality change?

Next we couldn't find a B & B.

It was the middle of winter, and naturally some were closed. One offered us a room for three, but Alice wouldn't hear of it. I was relieved that she'd taken this stand – saved us from being cooped up with her all night. Finally we drove out to Rosslare Strand and booked into a large vulgar bungalow. But inside everything was clean and new, and the owners were lovely.

As we said goodnight at Alice's door, she grabbed Charlie's whiskey bottle and shakily filled her tooth-mug, spilling some on the carpet. "I need this to get to sleep."

"I'll get a cloth," I said.

"It's OK." She frantically wiped the doused carpet with a tissue, then slammed her bedroom door in our faces.

Charlie and I went into ours. I poured two stiff nightcaps.

Miserably he threw his Amish hat across the room. "I hate this!"

I didn't like the hat either. It looked OK on Alice, but it seemed to big for Charlie, sort of shortened him.

"What's wrong with her?" I kept my voice low, fearing the walls had ears.

Charlie lay on the bed, a bewildered look on his face. "I criti-cised her driving," he whispered back.

"You didn't. You were upset, but understanding. Did you see the size of the drink she poured?"

He nodded.

"You think she's an alcoholic?"

"No more than I am." He sipped his whiskey in silence.

I finished mine and poured another small one. Had to have something to soothe me. Then I lay awake, remembering better times and endlessly going over the day's events in my mind. Alice was always a heavy social drinker, but never an alcoholic. I mean, her personality didn't ever change before. But an alcoholic changes when drunk, I've read. So perhaps that was it. She was drunk from the wine at lunch. Yet she hadn't had that much. The whole day was so desperately upsetting. We're like kids being punished for something we don't understand. Now I'm writing this in the middle of the night, unable to sleep. I've ended up praying, asking God why we're so unlucky. Imagine, me? No answer, naturally.

Tuesday 10th:

Lousy night's sleep. This morning Charlie and me red-eyed. When I got to the breakfast table, Alice was already seated and primly sipping orange juice. Neat curls framing her round, wrinkled face.

"Morning." My tummy squeezed with nerves.

No answer.

If only she'd talk to me, tell me what's bugging her. I tried again. "Uh – you slept well?"

"Not at all!" A forced smile. Baby-blue eyes hurt.

I cleared my throat. "Was the bed too hard?"

"Too soft!"

"That's worse," I sighed. "I'm sorry."

"It's OK." She placed her paper napkin neatly on the table and announced, "Peggy, I've something to say."

My tummy turned over. Her smile was too sweet.

"I was mad yesterday."

"Uh, yes, I noticed."

"But I'm all right now."

"Oh . . . good."

Charlie came in then, hailing her heartily. "Alice!"

Her smile vanished.

He looked nervously at me, pulled out a chair and sat down. Then we ate our way in silence through corn flakes, eggs, bacon, sausage, fried tomato and mounds and mounds of toast, while Alice nibbled monastically on a slice of brown soda bread.

I broke the silence. "The bread's good."

She nodded sulkily.

"You should eat!" Charlie joked.

He was forgiving, considering how bruised we both felt after yesterday. But Charlie's like that, bounces back, doesn't bear grudges.

"You'll be hungry later," he said again.

"Don't boss me!" she barked.

He nearly choked on a rasher.

She threw down her napkin and stood up. "I'm not your wife!"

We looked at each other. God, she was still mad with Charlie. Were we in for another day of this?

After we'd packed up, we checked out of the B & B in silence and hit the Waterford road. As the countryside flashed past, I sat there miserably. None of us talked on the way. Alice is/was our best friend. What's happened? How can things change so fast? Everything in life is so ephemeral. You can't count on anything. A relationship can crack like an egg.

All day I've been thinking of last year in New York when Charlie was sick. Alice was such a support then. One night in bed, I noticed his breathing was odd but thought he was having a nightmare. Then, in the middle of the night, I awoke to find him writhing in agony on the bathroom floor. He was in such terrible pain, I didn't know what to do. Was it his cancer? I rang our own doctor and was told by an answering service to get to an emergency centre. I didn't know of any. Thank God, we'd never been sick in the middle of the night before. Finally, I rang Alice and she took us to a medical centre on the Upper West Side, near Broadway. While Charlie was being attended to, the two of us waited anxiously for the all-clear. Charlie's pain had eased on the way to the centre, but the doctor there made all sorts of suggestions – his cancer had spread, it could be a kidney stone, an ulcer.

It was none of the above. But I realised how lucky we are to sleep in bed at night. It's something you never even think about. Later our own doctor diagnosed a gall stone the surgeon had left in from an old operation. But Alice was the one person in the world I could call in the middle of the night. What's happened? Why has everything changed?

When we arrived in Waterford today, Alice looked around the glass factory while we hovered in her wake. She loved it and went on the tour with great enthusiasm. Much to our relief, she was UP again – but still chatting only to me. We were a bit bored by cut glass, but trailed dutifully after her. Honestly, I'm not keen on cut crystal. It's a lot of money for something that might break, and I don't care what things are made of. But in the States crystal's a status symbol, so I understood Alice's enthusiasm.

After the factory we looked around the town and then headed for Cork. The afternoon turned out wet, so this didn't help things, as Charlie tried to manage the bottleneck of jammed traffic through the city. We're now in Acton's in Kinsale. We've stayed here in happier times with Jake and found it great. I'm wondering how my boy is and promise myself to send him an e-mail as soon as I go home.

Later:

A rock band played all last night.

"Jesus," Charlie said at dawn. "I can't stand this."

He got up and went for a walk. I dozed, wondering what Alice would say.

But at breakfast, she ate in martyred, red-eyed silence.

I made several efforts to talk, asking if she'd also been kept awake, but she answered me in monosyllables. I've sworn never to have another visitor. She is the last – definitely. But why won't she talk to me? What have I done? Talked to Charlie after breakfast and we've decided Alice is drinking heavily and this accounts for her mood swings.

Wednesday 11th:

Alice in jollier mood. But things are getting worse. I'll begin at the beginning. She insisted on driving again. Almost grabbed the wheel from Charlie this morning. We headed west after Kinsale in the direction of Bantry. There's a huge anchor outside that town, commemorating a famous shipwreck, and, of course, we stopped to read the inscription to the glorious dead. And almost joined them.

I mean it – Alice pulled out, without looking in her rear mirror.

Blaring horn.

Terrible screech of breaks.

Skidding tyres, as a Mercedes-Benz swerved to avoid us.

"Jesus!" Charlie yelled.

Head in my hands.

The Mercedes ended up across the road, facing in the opposite direction. Charlie and me shaken and stirred – definitely.

"SHIT!" Alice screamed. "The Irish are rotten drivers!" Alice glared at the man in the Merc.

He looked back in shocked disbelief – I never saw such a blank, horrified expression. He didn't say anything. He just sat there, staring numbly. Then turned the car and drove slowly on.

Charlie whistled. "We should be grateful for our lives."

"Left-hand driving takes getting used to, Alice," I mumbled – don't know why we were consoling her.

"Let me drive, Alice," Charlie said gently.

"Oh, you sonuvabitch!" Alice screamed again. "I've paid for this damn car! And I've driven all over the damn world!" She shook with rage. "Here, drive then!"

She threw the keys at Charlie – right in his face.

He blinked and caught them. Afterwards he said the keys hurt, but it was nothing. That we're lucky to be alive. It's true. But both our nerves are wrecked. Found a B & B and went to bed early.

Friday 13th:
We're in Killarney. Today's date ominous. Is it to be unlucky for us? Perhaps our last day on earth if Alice drives again? No, things are a bit better; although Alice still barely talks to us, she seems happy with the Irish countryside. We drove through the most beautiful mountain valley this afternoon. At least, it would be beautiful in summer. In November you can't see anything, but there's still a starkness and windswept majesty about the place. But right in the middle of a valley we found a craft shop, where Alice bought some more Irish sweaters. Shopping seems to be her elixir. An instant mood enhancer. A shot of Prozac.

She chatted happily to the owner, while we hovered nervously in the background. She still has few words for us. What's wrong with us? Are we horrible people? Charlie says people change, but I can't accept this. We looked at a few B & B's around Killarney, but Alice didn't like any. Finally we checked into a nice one outside the town. It's run by a Dutch woman and is extensively extended with all sorts of bathrooms, showers and toilets stuck in every possible nook and cranny.

Alice sniffed approvingly. "I like lots of bathrooms! The Irish seem to forget them when building their houses."

A dig at us?

Perhaps the Irish are less anal, or poorer than Americans. Whispered this to Charlie later, but he shrugged resignedly at me. We're both pretty fed up. Why's Alice behaving like this? We've driven with her now and again in America, but she was never, ever like this. Not once. Is it insecurity about being abroad? Is she another person out of her environment? Or is she an alcoholic? Perhaps this is the answer. She's bought her own whiskey now, so we don't know how much she's drinking. But alcoholics are notoriously different and grumpy in personality when NOT drinking. She's drinking, so what's the answer?

Saturday 14th:
Things no better.

We're in another B & B in Kilorglin. Naturally, it isn't up to scratch in the bathroom dept. But after breakfast, Alice found another Irish sweater shop and bought more for her children's Christmas presents. She has bought at least a dozen sweaters so far. She must be giving them to all her friends as well – or else the kids are getting three each. She had them all mailed directly.

At least she's talking to us – well, to me. Polite, meaningless chitter-chatter. She still snubs Charlie – it's the silent treatment.

Sunday 15th:
Drove around the Ring of Kerry today. Beautiful scenery, again, if you could only see it. Covered in winter fog. Ended up back in Killarney in the same B & B with all the bathrooms. Went to Muckross House this afternoon. Then took a hackney cab back to town. It poured raining, but we found a nice warm pub. Looked like drowned rats, but dried off over hot whiskeys by the open wood fire. Then Alice deigned to play darts with us. Amazing. Had a meal. Went to bed. Thank God, we're home tomorrow.

Monday 16th:
Alice announced first thing she wanted to drive home via Waterford to see the glass factory again.

Charlie resisted. "It'll take double the time."

I nudged him to give in, but he wouldn't.

"But I want to see the factory again," Alice groaned.

"And I want to go home," Charlie insisted.

But Alice pouted so much, he gave in.

Drove home the long way via Limerick where we did the Hunt Museum in fifteen minutes flat. I heard a guide there say that the amethyst was the stone which protected against drunkenness – which made me wonder again if Alice is alcoholic? Certainly she's had some severe personality change. I'm going to watch my own drinking. I don't want to end up like her, old and lonely and divorced. Then we crossed the Blackwater Valley towards Waterford. Beautiful, and there were more things to see, I'm sure, but we charged through it without stopping. Lismore Castle interesting from the outside. An ill-wind blows good sometimes. Might never have seen it, but for Alice. Must go back some day.

At the Waterford factory, she bought more cut glass. I went in, while Charlie waited in the car.

Then home via Kilkenny. Dark, so saw nothing.

Alice drove – too speedily.

Almost killed us again by the canal at Portobello Bridge. That's two near misses. Will it be third time lucky? I'm a nervous wreck. Dublin's traffic is worse than New York's, but Alice isn't as good a driver as other New Yorkers. How come I never noticed this? Or her moods? Her silence tyrannises us. Passive aggression on a big scale. Both very tired and dispirited.

Tuesday 17th:

It's good to be home, but we're both feeling rather confined with Alice in such a small house. The only relief is that she regularly goes into Mrs Murphy's for a chat. I wonder what she's saying about us? She's picked up a bad cold somewhere and wasn't well

enough for the Gate Theatre tonight. We'd paid for the three tickets, so went without her. They were doing a Chekov, translated by
Friel – *Uncle Vanya*. Charlie loved the bit where Vanya shot the
professor. Laughed hysterically. It was such a relief to be alone with
Charlie. To be away from Alice. Charlie and I seem to have shelved
our differences for the moment. The stress has driven us into each
others arms. We had a really happy time. The peace of being
together, just us two? An ill-wind blowing some good?

Wednesday 18th:
Alice here for thirteen days now – the longest thirteen days of my
life. She's mellowed a bit, but taken to teasing Charlie. Maybe my
mother's theory about being nice to people at the beginning and
end of their visit will work. Maybe Alice will forget what happened
in between if we give her a great send-off. Planned a duck dinner
last night. While I was cooking it, our one-armed coal man
appeared at the door, asking if we needed a bag of coal. He's a
blond-haired traveller with an angelic face, who comes round regularly in a little pony and cart with bales of turf as well as coal. He
sells vegetables, too, and Christmas trees in season.

I got a bag of coal.

As he hauled it awkwardly in, Alice peered out the sitting room
window to the street where the traveller's fat little pony waited
patiently. It has a ragged red mane, but is healthy looking and not
neglected in the way urban horses often are in poorer areas of
Dublin.

Alice dropped the white net curtain suddenly. She turned to me
– talking normally at last. "Peggy, ring the police at once!"

I was puzzled. "But why?"

"That poor little horse!"

Charlie was in the hall. He was preoccupied with the

one-armed man staggering in under the weight of the coal. "Let me help you."

"You should be sorry for the animal!" Alice railed from the sitting room door.

Charlie ignored her and went to the traveller's aid. This startled the poor man. He lost his balance and dropped the coal. The bag split and it went everywhere – on the tiles and all over our clean white-washed wall.

Charlie stared in horror.

"Sorry, sir, ma'am." The coal man was flustered and frantically tried to make things right by refilling the sack and then sweeping up the coal dust, all with his one arm. But he only made things worse. I went for a dustpan and brush.

"Is *no one* doing anything about this pony?" Alice fumed, frightening the traveller.

As he gaped, open-mouthed, she took a notebook from her pocketbook. "I'm reporting you for ill-treatment. Could I have your name, sir?"

"What, ma'am?"

"Your name, sir?" she rasped.

He fled into the street, jumped on his cart and flicked the reins, shouting giddy-up. The stout little pony trotted happily off.

Charlie ran after him with money, while I swept up the mess.

Over pre-dinner drinks, I explained to Alice that horses are still used for hauling coal in Ireland. It's the custom of the country, and the man wasn't cruel, I was sure – the little horse looked too happy. The traveller probably lived in worse conditions than the horse.

She wasn't convinced – looked at me accusingly. "Don't you know his name, Peggy?"

I shook my head. "We call him the one-armed man."

When she didn't get anywhere with me, she turned to Charlie.

Thought they'd have another row, so fled to the kitchen to see to the dinner. Alice followed. I was checking the duck in the oven, when Alice tackled me. "How can you tolerate such cruelty, Peggy?"

I was afraid to say anything, so changed the subject. "I'm doing crispy Chinese duck for dinner. Charlie loves it." A mistake.

She peered at the half-cooked bird.

"It's my famous Julia Child recipe."

Her chest heaved. "You're not cooking the breasts separately in the oven with an orange sauce?"

"No, I've filled the inside with soy sauce, onions and celery. Oh, and Chinese five spices. You'll like it, I promise."

She pursed her lips primly. "No soy sauce for me."

"Oh . . ." At least we were off the horse. "It's fermented, I suppose?" I remembered Bobbye Ann's food fads. And Rose's snobbery about vinegar. But I'd never noticed this in Alice.

"Soy contains salt!" she snapped.

"Salt?"

"I have HIGH blood pressure!"

The first I'd heard of her high blood pressure, but to keep the peace, I did the duck her way. I took it out of the oven, half cooked, emptied out the soy sauce mixture and chopped it up into bits and poured orange juice and honey over it and cooked it for a little longer in a slow oven. Anything for peace.

Charlie was disappointed it wasn't crispy.

"Give him the wings!" Alice teased.

He was miffed, but didn't fuss. "The wings?"

She picked one off the platter and put it on his plate. "Is that crispy enough?"

Charlie gnawed the bones, quite hungrily for such a faddy eater. All I needed now was for him to have a tantrum and blow up at Alice. Luckily he didn't.

Later:

Today Alice was feeling better, so, as she wanted to use the rented car by driving somewhere, anywhere, I told her about Castletown House in Celbridge. It was one of Ireland's finest Georgian mansions and open to the public.

We went out on to the terrible M50 – a tangle of spaghetti highways. Managed to miss the turn for Lucan and the west. Drove on and had to pay a toll fee to exit, and another fee coming back. £1.60 won't break the bank, but it vastly irritated Alice.

She seemed to think it was my fault.

Dammit – I'd never been on this motorway before. Honestly, I can't believe the change in Ireland from my youth. It could be the New Jersey Turnpike. I know I'm always saying this, but things are so very, very different.

Well, we finally got to Castletown House and were shown around the house. Alice admired the banquet hall particularly – the ceilings were restored impressively. Afterwards, she gave her business card to the pretty young guide with whom she seemed to be getting on famously, inviting her to visit New York. The girl was naturally delighted and will probably take her up on it.

I joked about this to Alice.

She gave me a funny look. "It was a pleasant change to meet one nice person in Ireland."

Are we that bad?

Had intended to try and talk to Alice, ask her what's wrong. Explain Charlie sometimes is too blunt, but doesn't mean it. But couldn't. Honestly I just want her to go home. Rue the day I pressed her to visit. I invited her, so I've no one to blame but myself.

Unfortunately, it was still early in the afternoon. So the Castletown guide advised us to go on to the Japanese Gardens, beside the

National Stud. I vaguely remember the gardens were somewhere near Kildare. We found the highway and drove.

And drove.

"How much further?" Alice kept asking, putting her foot down hard.

"A bit," I kept saying, tensing at the sight of the articulated trucks we were passing out. You never saw those in Ireland in my youth either. Now they're everywhere, and terrifying.

Finally found the famous gardens outside Kildare town. I'd visited them in my childhood and was looking forward to seeing them again. We paid a fiver each and walked in through the Gate of Oblivion. I didn't remember the gardens being so small. Either they've shrunk or I've got bigger. Of course, it was raining and Alice slipped in some mud. She was grim-faced and wouldn't come into the café for a cup of tea. With umbrella up, we hurried on through the Tunnel of Ignorance, over a few bridges and through the different life stages until we came to the Gateway to Eternity.

Jesus.

It was ominous – eternity?

A prophecy of something worse to come? I believe in symbols and was convinced I'd never see home again – the thought obsessed me. Charlie would be a widower, which would solve all our problems. I was worn out by the tension of Alice's driving and absolutely dreading the journey back on that killing motorway. Was it to be my last hour?

But got home OK.

Nerves in tatters though.

Thursday 19th:
Alice's last day.

She sulked over breakfast because I had to work today and couldn't go into town with her. Dammit, I have a deadline. We're not all wealthy realtors. If I don't get a job finished, they'll never use me again. We'll be on the breadline.

"You could go into Trinity and see the Book of Kells," I suggested. "Just be careful. There are a lot of professional pick-pockets."

Alice was irritated. "Peggy, please!"

I flinched under her belligerent baby-blue gaze. "It's a fact."

"I'm a New Yorker, Peggy," she snapped, "not a mid-western hick! I'm used to coping with pickpockets."

"I know," I insisted; "just be careful."

Angry red blotches appeared on her cheeks. "Peggy! I've lived all over the world!"

"OK, OK." I fled upstairs to work.

Got some badly needed e-mails off and finished up an instruction manual. So feeling pretty good about myself. I was out shopping for dinner in Rathmines when Alice returned at about five. As I carted in the groceries, Charlie grimaced, implying something was wrong.

"What is it?" I asked.

"Alice was pickpocketed."

I still can't believe it. I let her out of my sight for one afternoon, and she's pickpocketed. Her wallet was stolen in Trinity. It contained all her credit cards, but luckily she knew the numbers to ring the bank and stop them. At that moment she was in the police station, making a formal complaint.

Put my head in my hands. "I can't stand any more visitors."

"I know." Charlie touched me gently. "She's going tomorrow."

Alice definitely driving us into each other's arms – but is it too late? Charlie's still sore with me for being so jealous of Erin. We haven't talked about it since. But don't know what the future holds. Just know I'm not having any more visitors.

They come to Ireland, looking for something. Some expect a *Tír na nÓg* populated by the little people. They want wrinkled, toothless peasants on donkeys and freckled, well-behaved children. Or interesting Catholic churches. But instead they get mugged. Or it rains. Or they want their own bathroom. Or Danish pastry and coffee-to-go, instead of tea and Irish Pride toast.

You can't please everyone. The country is too backward for Alice, yet too advanced for Henry and Rose – they wanted castles and thatched cottages. Shevawn wanted it to be a small island. Billy Boy wanted a red-headed countrywoman like Maureen O'Hara. Jake wanted to walk in Shelley's footsteps and buy *An Phoblacht*. Uncle Tommie wanted to help Sinn Féin. Don't know what the Grosses wanted – maybe good weather like in a Canaries brochure. Alice wanted some kind of happiness, some high at the end of the rainbow with plenty of bathrooms. But instead she's had a terrible time – and so have we. Where does friendship go? Why couldn't ours survive a bit of Irish rain?

Poor old Ireland. We're at the edge of Europe, so maybe people think they can step off. But you can't get off the world. There's only one way, and that's to die, and nobody wants that. Unless you go up into space. But that's in the future. They say space suits will be in the supermarkets in our lifetime, but I'm not interested. It's hard enough to cope with this planet. One world is enough.

Friday 20th:
Alice flew home this morning.

She left a small present of lace mats for Mrs Murphy, but nothing for us. I drove her to the airport – usual traffic on motorway and no space at airport car park. I eventually found a space and

followed Alice in. She had already checked in, so we had coffee in
silence, while she waited to board.

"I'm sorry you didn't enjoy yourself," I said finally.

She stared into her coffee, stirring it slowly.

Tried again. "I'm sorry about your divorce then. That must be
upsetting."

Tears brimmed up and fell over her face.

I was shocked.

"Oh, Peggy." She patted her eyes with a hanky. "It ain't fair —
you two have it all. You always did. A happy marriage was the one
thing I wanted in life."

I couldn't speak.

"I'm dying," she said flatly.

"What?"

"Dying."

"Oh, Alice . . . The cancer's back? But you look OK."

She looked right at me. Her blue eyes desperately sad. "The doctors say I'm not going to make it, Peggy."

I took her hand. "But you look OK."

She shook her head. "Charlie was lucky."

"I know." Didn't want to get into that.

At least, it explained things. Her anger with Charlie. How did
the poem go? "Rage, rage, against the dying of the light." Alice
told me she'd been given a few months to live. The new drugs
weren't working any more. That's why she wanted to come to Ireland while she still had time. Suddenly I was crying, too. It was,
oh, everything. Life. Alice's last holiday being such a disaster.
Charlie not loving me any more, when we were meant to be the
perfect couple.

I wiped my eyes. "Sorry."

"You weep for others, Peggy."

"I should be supporting you."

"You are."

"The doctors could be wrong," I blurted. "You can't count on anything."

She laughed bitterly. "Except dying."

We sat there until it was time to board. Then she hugged me goodbye at the departure gate. It was like old times. My friend was back. I wanted to ask her if there was any hope for a reconciliation with her husband, but didn't dare. What had happened? He was a rat to desert her now.

"Sorry about –" I broke off. "I know Charlie sometimes rubs people the wrong way."

"You have a happy marriage, Peggy, and that's a great achievement." She smiled her old smile, put a finger to my lips, then turned and walked through the departure gate. As the official checked her boarding pass, she waved, still smiling. Then walked gaily on. Oh, Alice . . .

I went home, stunned.

Told Charlie.

Both feel awful. We did our best, yet made a dying woman miserable. You can't win. The same thing had happened with Bobbye Ann. Is there something wrong with us? Or is it the visitors? Why did we invite them? Maybe we need other people around. You see married couples like that in Scandinavian plays, people bored with each other who always have a hanger-on. Charlie seems to need people. He's the one who usually extends the invitations, and I've mainly agreed to keep the peace – except for Alice. I invited her.

Later:

Very sad about Alice – we've had so many good times together. I can't believe she's dying. She's too full of life. But something else has died, too – a friendship. It's like the Yeats poem – "Murmer a little sadly, how love fled." Can't remember the rest. Something about hiding its face among a thousand stars.

That sums up Alice and us.

Charlie and me, too.

Gave Mrs Murphy Alice's gift. She kept me chatting for an hour, about how nice Alice was. I agreed. It's true, she is nice. V. nice. Just not nice to us. Also, there's a rumour Gay Byrne's retiring, which upsets Mrs Murphy.

Later the same evening:
Big row tonight. Doing some laundry and found a letter from Erin Fuckoffey in Charlie's jeans' pocket.

> *Dear Charlie,*
> *You say I should date men my own age, but I can't. You are the most important person in my life. You have believed in me and published my poetry. Who else would do that? No one on earth. I walk in the sun now, in the knowledge that somewhere in your soul you love me. I live in hope of the day that you might return my love. I miss you so much and live for the Irish class . . .*

I freaked.

So that's what he's doing at Irish class! When Charlie came in, handed him the letter silently.

He was naturally outraged. "You've been reading my letters!"

I didn't care. "I was doing the laundry. You shouldn't leave them around."

He scratched his head. "Listen, Peggy, you're misjudging this."

Then the whole thing flared up terribly. I lost patience. He said if I didn't trust him what was the point? I said, men are all

the same – if he thought that I trusted him, he must be crazy. I
didn't have student boyfriends writing me brazen love letters
daily.

"There's nothing wrong with letters!" he yelled.

"Well, an affair then!"

"It's not an affair, Peggy!"

"What then?"

"I didn't sleep with her!"

Don't believe him. Why has he deceived me? Why didn't he tell
me she was in the Irish class? That's the unkindest cut – me thinking what an idealistic husband I have. Pretending to be interested
in the Irish language, while all the time he's been groping Erin
under the class desk. It's revolting.

Charlie slept in sitting room. Told him he was free to leave, but
he didn't go.

Saturday 21st:

Fuckoffey called around again tonight – bold as brass. Freaked
again when I saw her stupid sexy face at the front door. She had
the nerve to ask me if Charlie was in? I said no, he couldn't go out
to play.

"Peggy, you're being unreasonable," the child lisped.

"So, it's unreasonable to object to my husband's affair?"

She batted the lashes. "Listen – Peggy!"

I slammed the door in her face.

"Who was that?" Charlie asked, coming out of the bathroom.
He was wrapped in a towel and on his way upstairs to put on his
dressing gown. I was planning a quiet evening, watching TV by
the fire.

"Your girlfriend!"

"Erin? Ask her in."

"I will not! It's my house!"

"It's my house too!"

"See your girlfriends somewhere else."

Erin still outside in the street. She leaned against the glass of the hall door, cooing, "I called to collect my typescript, Charlie."

I wouldn't open the door.

"This is your age, Peggy," she said patronisingly.

"What's age got to do with it?"

"It's hormonal. You're menopausal."

That finished me. Ran into the sitting room, grabbed the typescript from the coffee table and threw it out the front door. The pages were caught by the wind and flew everywhere, landing flutteringly in the mud of Khyber Place.

Charlie very mad.

He pulled on trousers and ran out the front door.

Later the same evening:

We're finally packing it in, putting the house on the market. A rational decision. We've had a good marriage, but it's over. Maybe we can be friends again sometime like those modern, post-divorce couples you read about in novels. Maybe go on holidays with each other, the way we went with Lisa? But don't think I could. Feel too murderous. I couldn't be forgiving like Lisa.

Other news – Republicans want to impeach Clinton.

Hope they do. That's one thing I feel differently about.

Charlie's gone west to see about buying a cottage – a love nest for him and Erin. Good riddance. But feel so miserable. How'll I manage on my own?

Even later the same evening:

Charlie back.

He sat in Heuston Station for an hour, then came home, full of injured innocence. He's sleeping downstairs on couch. Too unhappy to write anything here. Everything over. A lonely, vibrator-ridden old age awaits me.

December

Charlie's sleeping downstairs.

I stumble blindly through the days. In Tesco's there's a photo machine which says, "Keep taking your picture until you are happy." But it's like some weird joke, because I'll never be happy again. We're talking, but just about. Don't ask him about Erin. I assume she's waiting somewhere in the wings, ready to grab her man as soon as we wind things up with the house. Charlie says we must approach the break-up in a rational manner, like civilised friends. But don't feel at all rational or civilised. I don't know what I'll do. Maybe go back to New York? He's still looking for a cottage in the west, but they're expensive. He can't buy it without cash. And I don't want to go on living here without him. Couldn't bear the humiliation.

The house is on the market.

We went to an estate agent last week, and it's advertised in today's *Irish Times*. It's been valued at one hundred and fifty thousand pounds. We can't believe it, or the glowing terms of the ad.

> Khyber Pass Place – Quaint takes on real meaning in this delightful little backwater between Ranelagh and Rathmines. Mid tce 2 up 2 down in excellent decorative order, surrounded by original cottages. Interior rich and warm in fired earth shades with terracotta tiled floor,

painted wood floor upstairs, loads of Provençal atmosphere. Acc: Ent hall, living, Kit/b'fast, 1 dbl bed, 1
single bed, bath. Elec heating, yard. Price Region
£150,000

There's even a photograph, showing up the mark where we had
the gutter moved. Sad to be saying goodbye, after all our work.
Our joint soul's in this house. Our karma.

"The ad doesn't mention the book shelves," Charlie grumped.

"And 'yard's' stretching it," I said. "And why Provence? We've
never even been there."

"The quarry tiles, I suppose," he sighed.

Didn't say I was right about them.

We both stared sadly at the photo.

"We'll make fifty thousand pounds in a year," I said.

He rustled the paper. "You can't lose 'em all. What're you doing
with your half of the loot?"

"I'm going back to New York."

He frowned. "I – I don't know if I'm ready for this, Peggy."

Felt like pinching myself. What was he saying? "But – it's what
you wanted."

"I just hope we see each other sometime," he said.

I want a clean break. I still can't see myself as a resident ex-wife.
It's all or nothing. And it looks as if it'll be nothing.

Later:

Went next door to tell Philomena we were definitely splitting.
Didn't get a chance as she was very upset about her pups. She
showed me a posed studio photograph she had taken of them with
herself. Why not? People show you photos of their children all the
time. But like children, the pups are giving her great trouble. They
refuse to be house trained. She brings them to the park, but they

won't do it there. They wait till they come home to do it, and then rub it all over her sofa. Now they're biting each other. She rang a vet who told her she's another dog to them. They're trying to put her in her place. It was a mistake to take two from one litter. Now they're having a war about who is to be top dog.

It was the same with Sweetie. He/she wanted to show Charlie who was top dog. Or bitch. Still haven't found out his/her gender. And still can't stop him/her doing him/her job outside our house. Soon it'll be someone else's problem.

Later:
Got an e-mail from Alice.

> *Dear Peggy,*
> *I want to thank you for your hospitality when I was in Ireland. I had a pretty ghastly time as you seem to have noticed. I could have done with seeing a few more churches. I expected Ireland to be like Italy – an ancient Catholic culture. But I did like the countryside – especially the south-west and Waterford.*
>
> *Have to admit I hated Dublin. I think those armies of kids in black are the key. A combination of free money (but not enough of it) and free time might explain why everyone from the American embassy to the tour books do indeed warn tourists about the rampant thievery in Dublin; that, in turn, explains why Dublin looked more like an armed camp – on the weekends especially. Too much time, too little money and the thefts might also indicate that Dublin's young have a massive drug problem, or are about to.*
>
> *Take care of yourself,*
> *Alice.*

It was a bit much after her Sidney Carton exit. She didn't mention dying once. Or Charlie. I hid it from him. Despite everything, I don't want his feelings hurt. We're both too shattered and, whatever about anything else, he did his best for Alice. It's grim breaking up. And coming up to Christmas it's particularly bad. As soon as the holidays are over and the house sold, we'll both feel better. Won't we? We'll make a clean break. We'll axe our orchards as in Chekov's famous play.

Monday 7th:

I was in the off-licence today, buying a bottle of wine, when Poopdeck Pappy came in. As usual he had the old rope tied around his overcoat. He came up beside he, grinning toothlessly and whispering, "Weird."

"What?" I said.

"Absolutely weird."

"Yes, but what?"

"Life," he said.

I agreed.

"It's all these computers," he said. "In 2003 they'll have taken over the world. And we won't be here."

"We might be," I said.

He shook his head. "Weird."

Then the assistant gave him his baby Power.

Otherwise, nothing much happening. People just trek through the house. No offers yet. Not surprised. Asked agent if he wasn't asking too much. He said no.

Philomena rang the dogs' home and asked them to take her pups. She's worn out completely and gone to a psychiatric hospital for a rest.

Tuesday 8th:
Today someone offered £140,000 for the house. I wanted to take it, but Charlie wouldn't.

Said I never knew he was a capitalist.

He slammed out of the room. "I'm not a capitalist!"

What else is it when you make such a profit of £20,000 each in a year?

Wednesday 9th:
Bid increased to £145,000.

Charlie still won't budge.

Thursday 10th:
American Congress impeaching Clinton – can't say I'm sorry.

We got our asking price.

House sold – closing date is the week after Christmas. It'll be a very quiet one. Mostly we'll be packing. I'm going to miss Charlie. After all, it's been over fifteen years. Ironic, Erin's gone to America for Christmas and left him in the lurch. Oddly enough, we're getting on well these days, but it's too late now. You can't go back in life. That's for sure.

Mrs Murphy told me Poopdeck Pappy has gone to a home for alcoholics in the country. She misses him and was sad that we're going, too. She said we both looked tired and she's tired looking at us, looking so tired. Confided in her that Charlie doesn't love me any more.

She shook her chins indignantly. "Your husband loves you."

She's a nice woman – very. And seems to be angry with both of us about the split.

Thursday 24th:
Something happened today.

I'll begin at the beginning.

We were at the door of our Grafton Street bank when a stocking-faced man shouted, "Get down on the floor!"

He was in our face.

It was about 10a.m., a snowy Christmas Eve morning, and almost exactly a year since we came home to live here. Dublin still asleep and not yet crowded with last-minute shoppers. Us sleepy, too, bundled up against the cold. We were on our way into the solicitors to sign the contract to sell the house. We'd taken all our cash out and were on our way out of the bank and down the street to Bewley's for coffee.

I'd just handed Charlie his half – I'm strict about sharing everything. I was fumbling in my untidy handbag to deposit the rest.

"Get down on the floor!" Stocking-face shouted again. He barred our way with a funny gun.

A crazy joke.

The man was dressed up as a bank robber.

But Charlie wasn't laughing. He wore his fat down jacket and a black stocking cap pulled over his ears. The gun was in Charlie's chest and the witty man was repeating his joke:

"GET DOWN ON THE FLOOR!"

I clutched my half of the money. It wasn't Hallowe'en, but we'd surely got caught in some sort of street theatre. It was all the thing now, unlike the drabber days of my youth. "Oh, come on –"

But the man waved his gun belligerently. "Get down on the floor, stupid! This is a bank robbery!"

A what?

I couldn't believe it – how thick can you get? The gun was only a toy. These things don't happen in real life. Certainly not in dear old dirty Dublin on a bleak mid-winter's morning. No, we'd accidentally wandered on to a movie set. They're all the thing in Dublin now.

"Ha-ha-ha!" I was about to laugh, but Charlie brusquely pulled me down on the floor.

There were panicky screams.

More shouting.

We were about to be shot.

Taken hostage at least.

Dammit, I'd lived in New York for thirty years and never seen a gun, except on a policeman's hip. Never had one waved in my face. This was Ireland of the Welcomes. There was always trouble in the north, but not down here in the south. We'd come here for peace and quiet. We were walking the city for one of our last times. Next month I'd be back in New York. Charlie'd be in the west of Ireland.

But now we were in a Chicago-style bank robbery.

Ireland had really taken its place among the nations of the earth. It wasn't fair – a minute earlier and we'd have been safe in the slushy street. Surely we could still make a dash for it?

But no, we were trapped.

And, oddly, the only customers in the bank.

Then everything went into slow motion. Other younger bala-clavaed men appeared from nowhere and vaulted over the bank's beautiful old mahogany counters. There were stifled screams from the girl tellers.

Another stocky fedora-hatted raider waved a handgun, shouting, "Hand over the money, I'm telling yez! Or I'll shoot!"

A gangster movie.

"Don't look at them, Peggy!" Charlie hissed, spreadeagled on the floor.

I was on my haunches, staring curiously around. "Are you serious?"

"Peggy! Get down!" He hugged the ground like a character in a B movie.

Only last night we saw Dustin Hoffman in a film about a bank robbery on late-night TV. "Hand it over," Dustin had pleaded, shaking terribly.

Our robbers were shaking, too.

Behind the counter the younger men scooped money into bags while the older men stood guard. I looked back at the bank door. Stocking-face listened to a radio in a plastic bag. Oh, God, how professional, and just like the Dustin Hoffman movie.

It still couldn't be happening.

But it was.

This was *fin de siècle* Dublin. My life didn't flash before me, but I swore to send £100 to African famine relief if we survived. And I regretted all the mean things I'd ever said to Charlie. He couldn't help falling in love with Erin. He wasn't a bad person. Just a man with a mid-life crisis.

The raiders were still stuffing bags behind the mahogany counters. The fedora-hatted one waved a handgun at one of the girls. He wore a raincoat like Humphrey Bogart.

"Get your head down!" Charlie hissed again.

I was still on my haunches. "What?"

He pulled me to the floor in a rugby tackle.

"Stoppit!" I yelled.

"You're a stubborn woman! You never listen to me."

"You're the one who never listens!"

We wrestled.

I pulled free.

"Peggy!"

"Just leave me alone!"

This disturbed Stocking-face. He came over and aimed the gun unsteadily at us. "Don't move, I'm tellin' yez!"

Charlie held up his hands. "OK! OK!"

"We're married!" I didn't say this is what married people do. It's called floor play.

Stocking-face stepped back, shouting at the robbers, "Come on! Come on! Hurry!"

He glanced furtively out at the street and slammed the bank door shut.

Just then a small elderly woman came down the stairs from the Foreign Exchange. She was dressed in a camel coat and wore a brown felt hat with the brim pulled down over her ears. Wisps of white hair escaped from beneath it, giving her an innocent baby-doll expression.

Stocking-face waved the gun at her. "Down on the floor, lady!"

"Oh . . . Can't I sit here?" She spoke teacherishly in an Anglo-Irish accent. "I'm too old to get down on the floor." She pointed to a hard mahogany chair. "Can I sit here?"

"Sit down there, love," he said kindly. "You won't get hurt."

She did, primly clutching her handbag and looking around disapprovingly.

I breathed more easily. He'd called her "love". Maybe that meant he wouldn't shoot us. Then it occurred to me that the robbers had made no effort to take my money. They were decent bank robbers. Robin Hoods. We'd be OK.

We lay there, suspended in time. It seemed to have stopped. It was weird. My heart drummed loudly in my chest. I was surely having a heart attack?

Promised God £75 for Africa.

All sorts of things ran through my head. How mad I was at Charlie. How we'd been warned about coming back to Ireland. We'd be killed in the Troubles, our friends said. Well, it was happening. Now we wouldn't live long enough to get divorced. This was some sort of IRA raid.

Obviously not our day.

Stocking-face turned from the shut door. "Christ, the guards are here! No one move!"

We looked at each other. Now there'd be a gunfight. I'd never get back to New York. Charlie wouldn't get to the west. Erin would be jilted.

"We've made a big mistake," I whispered to Charlie.

"What mistake?"

"Coming back to this country!"

Charlie looked up from the floor. "Peggy, maybe we should re-think things?"

"It's a bit late now."

Stocking-face pointed his gun at us again. "Stay down! I'm warning yez!"

The arrival of the guards outside had really panicked the robbers, but nothing happened immediately. I started praying seriously. I always pray in crisis, although I don't believe in God. Not really.

"Stay away, or I'll shoot!" Stocking-face shouted through the big wooden door.

They said something inaudible back.

"There's people here could be hurt!" the robber yelled.

Another muffled answer.

We were petrified – definitely £100 for Africa.

Then the younger two robbers fled up the bank stairs with a bag of money each. And the stocky fedora-hatted one followed them, his gun drawn. I thought they must be escaping through the roof. Whew! The whole thing probably lasted about three minutes. The longest three minutes of my life.

Stocking-face backed after them toward the stairs, warning us not to move. But the old woman stood up, scolding him, "Give back the money."

"Sit down!" he shouted, tripping backwards and waving his gun dangerously.

"Give it back now and everything will be all right," she scolded nannyishly.

There were noises outside.

"Sit down!" Stocking-face was shaking terribly.

The old woman hobbled over, her arm lifted to take the gun. "This is disgraceful behaviour! Now give me that gun!"

"Sit down! Sit down!"

She wouldn't. "Just give back the money! And –"

He shot her – CRACK!

It was horrible. She fell back on to the chair with a startled look on her white babyish face. ". . . everything, everything. . ."

Terrible screaming and confusion.

Stocking-face ran up the stairs after his pals, waving the gun and cursing the old woman, "Yeh wouldn't sit down, yeh fuckin' stupid cow."

We went to her aid.

She sat moaning and bewildered on the hard chair. Her arm hung limply under the camel coat and was pumping blood. She stared at it, as if it didn't belong to her. Me shaking. I'd never witnessed violence and know nothing about first aid. But Charlie sprang into action – his army training had come in useful at last. He took out his handkerchief and, opening the woman's coat, tied it tightly around her arm just below the shoulder. "That'll stop the bleeding, ma'am."

It did.

She muttered in bafflement, looking sadly at her blood-stained and bullet-ridden coat. "They've absolutely ruined my best coat."

"Don't worry," I said stupidly. "You can send it to the cleaners."

"But it's a *Jaeger* . . . blood stains terribly."

It sure did. It was all over the floor, the walls, Charlie, every-where.

"Don't fret, it'll come out," I said.

There were no alarms or screeching police cars. The guards came in soon after the raiders left, looking like skiers dressed for the snow. They took over the old woman. An ambulance screamed up almost immediately, and paramedics carried her away on a stretcher.

They asked if we were OK.

We were – just shaken and stirred.

After the police had taken our statements, a bank official told us to have a drink in the pub across the road – on the bank.

Charlie washed blood off in the bank's bathroom. Then we trudged over to Neary's pub through the grey drizzle. It had begun to rain lightly.

We found a seat in the downstairs bar. Charlie took off his jacket and hat and numbly ordered a double bourbon. "Might as well, if they're paying," he said apologetically.

I ordered Irish coffee.

We sat there dumbly, as the Christmas lunch crowd came in.

While drinking, Charlie pulled on a small cigar – his gesture to quitting smoking and the worst thing for him. But Irish coffee was the worst thing for me, because it gave me palpitations. But needed something strong, so drank it quickly and ordered another. After all, it was on the bank.

Ironically, that very bank had refused us a mortgage. They owned banks in Maryland, but as "Americans" we were considered a bad bet. We'd finally begged one from a building society, and used Charlie's copper handshake from his New York publishing company for the house deposit. But that was all in the past now. We were losing the house, and each other.

Charlie looked at me irritably. "Why didn't you lie down?"

Hysteria bubbled up inside me. "I WAS down."

"You weren't. He might've shot you."

"But he didn't."

He pulled on his cigar. "You took an unnecessary risk."

Cigars are worse, but I didn't say so. It'd only cause a row. Life itself is a risk. Every damn thing in the world.

"You never listen to me," he grumped.

I was patient. "Oh, I do. Now and again."

He frowned. "It's my job to look after you."

"Not any more." Then I noticed tears in his eyes – probably from the shock. "Anyway, I always thought it was the other way around."

"I'm serious, Peggy."

What was he saying?

"Can you forgive me, Peggy? I've done nothing, but forgive me, anyway."

I was irked. "An affair's NOTHING?"

He gritted his teeth, speaking slowly. "I didn't have an affair. I liked her poetry. Then I was trying to help her. Her boyfriend was diagnosed with leukemia. He was in Vincent's. She wanted me to encourage him." He shrugged. "Then . . . she got fond of me. And when we decided to split – I couldn't stand the thought of being alone."

I sat there, stunned. I'd seen Charlie walking near the hospital after Philomena's suicide attempts. Then he had all those books around, about cancer and diet. "How is he now?"

"He should make it."

I couldn't believe it. "But why didn't you tell me?"

"Any mention of Erin made you see red. So I made up the story about someone at the library. I – was afraid of upsetting you."

I couldn't say anything. It was all so stupid.

"Can we give it another try, Peggy?" he pleaded.

I couldn't believe it. "What about Erin?"

"I love you, Peggy. When that gun was pointed at me, that's all I thought of. You . . . our happy life." He put his head in his hands. God, he was crying. I'd never seen that before. Not in all our years together.

I touched him gently. "Oh, Charlie – I've been so stupid. I just worry about being . . . older than you." At last I got it out.

He looked amazed. "Older? You're not that old! But that's why I love you."

"Really?"

He took my hand. "Really."

We didn't say anything more for a while. We just sat, heedless of time. It occurred to me that I'd never find someone else I could sit in silence with. I'm always giving out about Charlie not talking to me, but marriage allows you to be silent. There's absolutely no one else in the world I can be silent with. Then I remembered Charlie once saying, "I married Peggy because she didn't talk all the time." At the time I thought he meant I was different from Lisa. But maybe talking isn't everything. Analysts go on about it so much, but there are different ways of communicating. Having a gun to your head helps.

We finally got ourselves out of the pub and back home. Dammit, we'd left New York to get away from violence. Now it's happened here in Dublin. But this time an old woman was almost murdered. Why did that robber have to shoot her?

Friday 25th:

Very quiet Christmas. Charlie gave me Delia Smith's cookery book, *How to Cook*. I gave him a book of comic poetry. Things happen after a bank robbery – it's like a Badedas bath. We made love last night and it worked. So we're having another go at marriage. Can't believe it.

Charlie rang Erin in New Jersey and he said she understood. Nice of her. I think she was probably relieved. Now she doesn't have any big decision to make. Our fate just happened. You only value something you're about to lose. Charlie even offered to go back to New York with me.

But I want to stay here – "My country is Kiltartan Cross," etc.

"But we'll always have visitors here," he warned.

I think he's probably right.

So we've taken the house off the market. Another thing – we've talked and decided to be more honest with each other. He's given up Erin, so I have to change, too. Nervously asked him how I could improve.

He laughed. "Don't cook any more quail tarts."

I was taken aback – after all my gourmet efforts. But I promised to cook hamburgers and scrambled eggs. Nothing but plain cooking from now on. It's just the ordinary, trivial, everyday things that hold life together, things like mashed potatoes. Not the big things.

Then Charlie said nice things about me being more perfect than he is. I didn't argue. But I'm the same as everyone else. Imperfect and jealous and full of all those horrible insecurities you need to keep down. As the Queen Mother said, "I'm not as nice as people think."

Thursday 31st:

They say certain events are fixed in memory – like everyone remembers what they were doing when Kennedy or Princess Diana

died. The reason for this is synapses connecting, I've read. Whatever it is, I'll always remember that stocking-faced man and the
way he held the gun, sort of cradled like a baby against his chest.

For days after the robbery, I couldn't stop smiling – a fixed, eerie
grin. And when I told people about it, I giggled idiotically. God,
what's so funny? An old woman was shot, almost fatally. We
could've been killed. But I felt hysterical. After the high wore off, I
felt exhausted and depressed and was unable to work all week. I
scoured newspapers and kept my ear to the radio for news of the
raid or the old woman, but I didn't even see it reported anywhere.
Is violence so common in Dublin? Obviously, yes. Syringe attacks
are a daily event now. Men are knifed all the time, women murdered walking home in the dark.

Told Charlie I was never going into another bank.

"With our account," he grunted, "you'll have very little reason
to."

That's true – now that we're not going to be capitalists. But I
can't help wondering about the old woman. I heard nothing more
about her. Is she OK?

Later:

Life's like falling off a horse. After a bad experience, you have to get
back in the saddle immediately. I can't go on being afraid of town.
So I bought a book, *Feel the Fear and Do It, Anyway*. It says you can
get rid of fear by facing it. Well – I went into town today but still
felt the fear. But I had to get money for the weekend – Charlie,
naturally, still has an aversion to anything modern like ATM cards.

At the bank, I got money from the wall, then went nervously
inside to ask about the old woman.

This time the bank was crowded, but with people around, it was
safer. I learnt from an official that the old woman had lost her arm.

It was severed too badly to be reconnected. But she was out of danger and was alive, thanks to Charlie. The raiders got £10,000. One made a getaway on a motorbike. How the others got away, I didn't find out. Apparently they just disappeared through the bank roof, then escaped over other rooftops.

And robbed a bank in Camden Street the next day.

That wasn't reported either.

But Charlie's quick action in helping the old woman has somehow redeemed his regret about the old man back in New York. A life was saved thanks to his white handkerchief, which I always said was unhygienic. He's quirky about not using Kleenex. But these days you never know when you might need a tourniquet, so I've sworn never to pester him about that again. Also to learn first aid. Why didn't we learn essential things in school? What use is algebra to the average person? You need things to help you get through life, make it more enjoyable. Latin grammar blighted my youth.

I'm still afraid of town.

I'm even afraid of the local supermarket. Agoraphobia? Weird, as Poopdeck Pappy would say. Ireland's meant to be a safe country, but the cosy Dublin of my youth's gone for ever. It's no longer "heaven, with coffee at eleven", like the old song says. But we're back a year now and no ghosts have grabbed me. I'm a different person, come back to a different place. Things change all the time – despite Mrs Murphy's fondness for delinquent bishops.

Amazing – out of bad comes good.

Our marriage was saved thanks to a bank robbery. And Charlie, thanks to modern medicine. Things have to get better. A cure for all cancers is just around the corner. After all, they once thought the sun healed most things, even melanoma.

I suppose Charlie's right about visitors coming. Several friends have sent Christmas cards, booking in for next year – lovely card from Jake. And Shevawn sent us presents – a scarf for Charlie and table mats for me. Charlie won't be able to refuse anyone. Anyway, we're all visitors in life. We all have to adapt. It just takes some longer than others. I suppose, we'll always have a crowded marriage. Maybe we should sell up and open a real bed and breakfast? But then we'd miss Khyber Place. I haven't the energy to do up another house. Instead, Charlie's converting the coal shed to an office. He says he wants to work at home more.

At midnight tonight the bells of Christ Church rang out the old year again, just like last year. The neighbours opened their doors and came out to the street. We all shook hands like old friends. Mrs Murphy said Packy had gone back to prison. I'm sorry about that. But Poopdeck Pappy has escaped from the home for alcoholics in the country. They failed to rehabilitate him, so she's back looking after him.

Charlie opened a bottle of champagne and invited her to join us. The three of us toasted in the New Year. Then Mrs Murphy left and we went to bed. Things are working again, thanks to the bank robbery. I mean, Charlie loves me again. He says he never stopped. Sometimes you lose your life to find it. "In my end is my beginning." Maybe T. S. isn't such an idiot after all.

Sent £20 to African famine relief.

Friday, January 1st:
Poopdeck Pappy found dead in the lane this morning. Fell down drunk and died of exposure, sometime during the early hours. Sweetie was guarding him. Weird. Feel terribly sad. The whole street is. They're bringing him to the church tonight. But this afternoon Mrs Murphy arrived in with a black and white kitten. It's a sweet, playful little thing, and Charlie took to it immediately. Mrs Murphy again spent the whole time talking about how awful the

media attacks on the Catholic Church are. So things are back to normal. With a kitten, we're a proper family again. Don't know the future, but hoping for the best. You're dealt a hand in life, and you don't know all the cards until it's over.

SOME OTHER READING
from
BRANDON

Elizabeth Wassell
The Thing He Loves

"A very fine novel: intriguing, dynamic and heartfelt." Colum McCann

Tormented by a cruel family background, an aspiring artist leaves New York to start a new life in Ireland where, amidst the beautiful scenery of West Cork, an international community of artists flourishes. A sensitive, compelling story of love and violence, of the impulses to create or destroy, this haunting novel explores extremes and contradictions. Erotically charged, it maintains a carefully modulated pulse of threat as the novel builds to its climax.

ISBN 0 86322 290 0; Paperback

Marie McGann
The Drawbridge

"Marie McGann is a real find. She writes with the exhilaration and defiance of youth and the wisdom of age. A moving and triumphant novel." *Fay Weldon*

"An assured debut... At its heart [it] is about love in its many forms, and the struggle to throw off the shackles of defensiveness and self preservation and at last attain the freedom to love without fear." *Sunday Tribune*

"This is a first novel with the kind of story established writers would die to produce... A page-turner, a delight, a revelation... I loved this one." *IT*

ISBN 0 86322 271 4; Paperback

Jennifer Chapman
Jeremy's Baby

"A page-turning tale of contemporary mores." *Rosemary Friedman*

"Set against a backdrop of Aga cookery, weekend lunches in the country, arts review programmes on television, it's also a novel about birth and death, love and jealousy, friendship and betrayal... But it's in the development of the characters, and in the author's near-scientific fascination with the workings of their minds, that the book's strength lies." *Sunday Tribune*

"Anything Jennifer Chapman writes must be taken seriously." *The Times*

ISBN 0 86322 277 3; Paperback

KEN BRUEN
THE GUARDS

"Edgy, pitch-black humour... With few, if any, antecedents *The Guards* is one of the curiously rare Irish crime novels, and the first set in Bruen's home town of Galway." *Guardian*

"A masterful black novel, full of unforgettable characters and a never dissipating cloud of menace that mirrors the persistent Galway rain, coming down hard on all concerned." *Bizarre*

"Bleak, amoral and disturbing, *The Guards* breaks new ground in the Irish thriller genre, replacing furious fantasy action with acute observation of human frailty." *Irish Independent*

"Both a tautly written contemporary *noir* with vividly drawn characters and a cracking story, *The Guards* is an acute and compassionate study of rage and loneliness... a true original." *Sunday Tribune*

ISBN 0 86322 281 1; Paperback

KITTY FITZGERALD
SNAPDRAGONS

"A unique and extremely engaging story of two sisters, each of whom is looking for love and salvation in their different ways." *Irish Post*

"An original, daring book." *Books Ireland*

ISBN 0 86322 258 7; Paperback

BARBARA REES
OSCAR'S TALE

A Latin-American dictatorship; an emigré in London; echoes of Pinochet in a family's hidden history of complicity in torture.

"Barbara Rees writes with clarity and momentum. Her characters are sharply defined, and the end is secured by the logic of providential revenge. Her sense of dialogue is crisp and the novel tightly bound within the plot of unwanted discovery so that all its elements cohere... *Oscar's Tale* is a stimulating return to prose fiction." *The Brown Book*

ISBN 0 86322 268 4; Paperback

www.brandonbooks.com